FULL HOUSE

House of Jewels, Volume V

Amber Jakeman

Lorikeet Press

This is a work of fiction. Similarities to real people, places, or events are entirely coincidental.

FULL HOUSE
First edition. July 19, 2022

978-0-6458483-0-4

Written by Amber Jakeman.

Also by Amber Jakeman
House of Jewels series
House of Diamonds
House of Hearts
House of Spades
House of Clubs
Full House

www.amberjakeman.com
www.lorikeetpress.com

For my readers, who spur me on, and for my family.
Let us treasure each other, as well as our dreams.

FULL HOUSE

Foreword

Dread sparked somewhere deep inside Nicole as her brother James Huntley the Third, CEO of Huntleys House of Jewels, began to speak.

"I've called this meeting not only because of the rapid growth of our company to include Mum's House of Clubs in France and Will's House of Hearts in the US, but for another key reason I'll go into shortly."

Nobody moved. James cleared his throat. Forcing herself to breathe normally, Nicole took a swig of coffee. It burned her tongue.

"I know this is not an ideal way to conduct a meeting, with some of you videoing in and others here in person, but there isn't time or spare operating cash to fly you all in," James said. "I'll do my best to ensure that those of you joining remotely will have equal input. Most importantly, this meeting will give you equal time to contemplate our options in the short timeframe we've been given."

Chapter 1

Four months earlier

Beside the old sink, in the tearoom on the second floor of the iconic Huntleys House of Diamonds jewelry store in the heart of Sydney's Bondi Junction, Nicole Huntley frowned, rinsed out her coffee cup and tipped it upside down.

She adjusted the bow of her yellow blouse as she glanced out the window at the plaza's smattering of shoppers and business people, their takeaway coffee cups in one hand like talismans. Bows were in and the color was cheerful, but the material of the blouse was scratchy, the bow still wouldn't sit right and the tone wasn't a great match with her gray skirt. Today, though, her choice of clothing was the least of her troubles.

"What's up?" said Stella as she rushed in, reached for her own mug, threw a teabag inside and switched on the kettle.

Nicole admired Stella. She worked hard, never ran out of ideas and was kind enough to ask about her life now and then without interfering.

"How are things downstairs?" Nicole asked.

"Okay," said Stella. "We've got a couple of minutes to ourselves. There's just that woman who comes in every week and browses for an hour but never buys anything, and Lorna's keeping an eye out for her. Something on your mind?"

"My flatmate's left," said Nicole.

James strode in with his own coffee mug and placed a caring hand on Stella's shoulder as they waited for the water to boil. Nicole smiled at the two of them, so glad her brother's fiancée was no longer a business rival but a colleague, and soon to be family, if they'd ever set that wedding date.

"Was that the Italian one, Nic?" said James.

"Lucia, yes. Frankly, I'm relieved. Bit of a drama queen. She kept life interesting alright. Too interesting. Every moment was either a joy or a tragedy. It's peaceful now, but I'll really miss her rent! I need a new flatmate to help pay the mortgage and bills. Know anyone?"

Stella shook her head, poured the steaming water into her and James's mugs, and reached across to the fridge to grab the milk.

"Lucia was perfect in her online application, but she never let up about my lack of style and the blandness of my cooking," said Nicole. "She wasn't wrong, and she did share a few useful cooking tips, but I could have done without all those temper tantrums about the bus home roaring past without her, or how she missed out on the last pair of Jimmy Choos in her size. And the parade of strangers she insisted on inviting home was the worst. If I never have to clean up another cigarette butt in my life I will never complain again."

"Never complain again, Nicole?" said James, not too unkindly. Brothers.

"Nice," said Stella.

"And she used every kitchen utensil every time and never cleaned them up!"

"She's gone, Nicole," said James, taking a sip of tea and striding back towards the office.

"Yes, well, the point is, I need a new flatmate. I'm not willing to risk putting up an ad again."

James paused in the doorway. "Scottie's on the move," he said. "You know he and Beck broke up? He just needs somewhere short term. He's heading off on some overseas trip; finally taking a holiday."

"Oh!" said Nicole. "Did you say Scottie and Beck separated?" Why hadn't James mentioned this sooner?

"Want me to let him know about your place?"

"Ah …" A thousand memories flickered. "Sure. Okay. You can tell Scottie. Sorry to hear about him and Beck."

With James gone, Nicole turned to Stella. "Well," she said. "I'm not sorry, really. To be honest, I never liked Beck. Scottie's such a gentleman, and Beck was never his type."

Stella smiled and nodded and rinsed her own cup.

"Sorry, Nicole. Gotta go help Lorna on the ground floor. Hope it all works out for you."

"See you!"

Nicole headed down the stairs and out into the sunny plaza towards the printers to pick up the Huntleys' sale catalogs. The idea of sharing with Scottie appealed to her, especially since it would only be for a few weeks. She'd sworn off living with men after both her previous male flatmates put the hard word on her after too many beers. She didn't blame them, but it sure complicated daily life, and she could have done without their claims she had "issues" with men just because she wasn't attracted to them.

But she'd known Scottie all her life. Scottie was practically part of Huntleys. Scott & Sons accountants and Huntleys went way back. James's best friend since childhood, as well as the Huntleys' financial consultant, Scottie knew how to take turns, how to lose with a sense of humor, and how to win with grace. At least she could be sure he'd clean up after himself.

The pedestrian lights turned red as she approached, and she paused. On the other hand … There'd been that brief period in high school when Scottie annoyed her, staring at her with puppy dog eyes every time she came near—but those days were well and truly gone. He'd behaved perfectly normally since they'd both grown up. Then he'd fallen head over heels with Beck, the fake blonde with puffy lips and an enhanced cleavage. If men went for types, then plain Nicole would be safe from any unexpected propositions from Scottie.

That evening, Nicole's apartment was quieter than ever. She considered phoning her Mum, Cynthia, who'd turned her back on a quiet retirement in the Southern Highlands an hour and a half out of Sydney, flown to France on a one-way ticket and ended up staying.

But they'd only spoken a couple of days ago, and all was well in Provence. Besides, it wasn't her mother Nicole needed to call right now.

She picked up the phone, then put it down. What did you say to someone whose marriage had ended? If she told Scottie she was glad, that she'd never thought Beck worthy of him, he might take offense— think she was accusing him of poor taste—but everyone made mistakes. Look at the long parade of no-hopers she'd dated.

Though Scottie often dropped in to talk to James about the company's finances, the last time Nicole spent any time with him was last Christmas. Run off her feet, she'd sold Scottie something for his mother. He'd chosen a simple gold bangle with an elegant twist. Classy. It was a generous gift, even without the hefty discount she'd given him as a supplier.

She'd brought out tissue paper, finely watermarked with the classy Huntley's H insignia, as she'd done a million times, then placed the boxed bangle in a paper gift bag, shiny black, with the gold H on two sides.

As she handed it across to him, he complimented her on the branding. It was a rare acknowledgement of her work, not just marketing all the stock, but building brand recognition and brand value—all that invisible weaving of meaning her father had understood; that their business was so much more than the sum of its parts. Before he died, Jim told her that "brand" consisted of every encounter with anyone who had anything to do with the place, and she'd grown up knowing you had to put the business before yourself, and do your best and be polite, even if customers were abusive.

Not that Scottie was ever a difficult customer. Anything but. He'd given her a warm, braces-free smile as he'd left that lifted her heart. It jumped straight over the awkward years and landed her back in the middle of their good times—how as children they'd splashed together in the shallows at the beach and made sand castles, ever more elaborate, with moats and tunnels and seaweed flags and sea glass decorations. They'd laughed as the summer sun seared their shoulders and groaned together as the waves washed away their handiwork.

They'd scramble along the rocks and throw themselves into the harbor pool at Watson's Bay, or race along the beach. On wet days, they built card houses, or played ping pong or Monopoly. They'd push tiny red hotels onto their properties and haul in each other's money with glee. Once, Scottie built a card house three storeys high, and she bumped it with her heel. For one silent moment she feared his reaction, but Scottie just shrugged, then laughed, and built it up again. Scottie was the best of company.

But then, after a family holiday at Pearl Beach, something changed. He'd stare at her, dumbstruck, tongue tied and useless. It made her uncomfortable.

Her old pal grew taller and increasingly awkward with her. They both wore braces on their teeth and sported a few too many spots, so it wasn't that. It was just ... She couldn't explain it.

So she'd avoided him and spent her free time wandering around shopping malls with school friends instead. They teased her about him.

"Can't you see the way he looks at you?" Thalia said.

"Don't! I hate it."

"Nic's got a boyfriend; Nic's got a boyfriend."

"Stop it."

Her friends eventually switched topics—dissecting the latest movie or boy band, or weighing in on whether cucumber face masks really worked, and she'd stop blushing.

Back then, Nicole avoided Scottie. He gave up on her, went on to university, and married Beck.

Nicole stared at her phone. Might as well get on with it.

"Nicole?" His voice was pleasantly deep, but she knew him well. He hadn't hidden his surprise.

"Hey, Scottie." Awkward silence. "Ah, James said you need somewhere to stay for a few weeks."

"Yes. Five weeks."

"Well, I've got a great spare room. It even has a bit of a view. It's good to hear you're taking a holiday," said Nicole. She wouldn't mention Beck at all. No big deal. She needed a flatmate and he needed a bed. Easy. She rushed on to fill the silence. "Europe. Lucky you! Want to come over tomorrow night and take a look, just to be sure? Seven o'clock? You can eat dinner with me and I'll show you where you can leave your stuff while you're away."

"Okay. Thanks."

Perfect. Now she could think ahead to the next sales catalog and social media marketing schedule.

Next evening, back at her apartment Nicole tidied up and threw together a quick spaghetti with basil and tomato, added a simple salad and laid it on the veranda table. Lucia hadn't been all bad. She'd certainly taught her a few Italian cooking tricks, especially the one about adding pitted savory olives to the sauce to give the pasta extra bite.

It was a mild evening. Candle? No candle? It wasn't like this was a date, when she'd have to angst over what music to play, and do the whole thing with champagne and five kinds of beer on offer. Scottie was just an old friend. Last time they'd eaten together, green cordial had been their drink of choice. She laughed in anticipation, just as the doorbell rang.

Not surprisingly for someone who'd just been through a rough breakup, Scottie looked a little older, but strangely, those new shadows under his eyes suited him, and his glance was full of warmth and light, as if he were genuinely pleased to see her.

She loved it that there was no other agenda here, no expectations that this was anything but a meal between friends to discuss a possible flat sharing arrangement. The dating game was exhausting, with all its pressure to get through the meal and juggle expectations about sex, when all she'd ever really wanted was good company.

Scottie had lost so much weight, Nicole commented.

"Didn't James tell you about our runs on Bondi Beach and our push-up competition?" said Scottie. "I got a bit down after Beck left. It was James who suggested we work out instead of hitting the bottle. Too much drinking wasn't helping. James is winning on the runs, but I've got the push-up record," said Scottie, flexing his muscles and smiling sheepishly.

His pecs and abs were nicely defined under his casual deep gray t-shirt. He looked healthy in his soft blue jeans. What was wrong with Beck?

"Shoes off? Shoes on?"

"Not too many rules here, Scottie," Nicole said. "You decide." She took the paper bag he offered and hummed with approval. Ice cream; salted caramel with dark and white chocolate chips.

"Such good taste! You can stay."

As he stooped to slip off his shoes she caught the slightest whiff of laundry detergent—such a comforting change from the aggressive aftershaves of the strangers of too many failed dates.

They padded through her spaces—the living area with its jumble of furniture from her grandmother's house and items previous flatmates had left behind.

A pang of hunger hit her as she waved her arm at the kitchen on the way to showing him the bathroom, the laundry in a cupboard, the long corridor, the spare bedroom with its built-in wardrobe and view of the

14

harbor, and then the kitchen. She took him out to the corner balcony with its own view across to Watsons Bay.

"Wow," said Scottie.

"James, Will and I were so lucky Mum sold Jim and Eleanor's old house on the harbor," said Nicole. "We never could have afforded our places otherwise."

"I was talking about the smell of dinner actually, but you're right. This place is beautiful, Nicole."

"I'm not much good with decorating. One of the reasons I need a flatmate is to help with the mortgage and eventually replace the furniture with something I really like, but it's not urgent. I just love the fact my place is so close to the beach and the station, and to Huntleys of course, and the city. You could catch a bus or a train, or even walk it."

Was she selling the arrangement to him? Yes. Scottie listened carefully. His comments were sensible, and a sense of humor lurked just under the surface, despite the shadows the breakup with Beck must have caused.

"It's perfect, Nicole," he said, his tone warm but not too warm. Not at all like a needy puppy dog. These days, Scottie was his own man. He kept his distance—didn't even seem particularly keen. "Are you sure you don't want to advertise it on the open market? I'd be happy to pay you for the weeks I'll be away, but you might want a longer term tenant. I'm thinking about buying a place myself, though I haven't done the homework yet, so I can probably promise you at least another two months after I get back. But with this place, you could ask a premium and know where you stand a year from now. Don't feel obliged to offer me this, Nic. Think about it and come back to me. I've got another week before I move out. Give yourself room to make a decision that's in your best interests, not just in mine."

"How can I resist a tenant with such great taste in ice cream, Scottie? And you might want to think twice about whether you want your life in the hands of this cruel and evil landlady."

As they forked up strands of spaghetti in the soft summer night, they laughed and entertained each other with tales of previous landlords and flatmates, of leaky shower recesses and nosy and noisy neighbors.

If Scottie's knee brushed against hers, she barely noticed. It wasn't as if anything beyond living arrangements was up for discussion.

15

It surprised her what good company grown-up Scottie could be. Why hadn't she thought to invite him to share with her sooner?

Oh. Because he'd been married. Oops.

"Ice cream?" said Scottie. "Here, I'll take these. Which cupboard are your bowls in?"

He helped stack the dishwasher before he left, far too soon. She would have liked him to stay and maybe watch some rubbish television, or listen to some music with her.

What was going on? Nicole shook her head. None of that. Scottie was recovering from the last woman who'd screwed him over. She wasn't about to mess him up on the rebound. She liked him far too much for that. Old friends and flatmates. That's what they would be to each other and nothing more. Besides, he was heading overseas. Anything could happen.

Chapter 2

Scottie turned up the following Sunday with a couple of suitcases, a large heavy box and then, out of his pocket, a seashell.

"Is that all, Scottie, and what's with the shell?"

"I didn't like anything Beck and I bought together. She had expensive taste, and I was happy to pay up, but it only ever made her happy for a little while. No amount of showy furniture was ever enough," he said, and swallowed. "You don't want to hear about my failed marriage."

"You can talk about it if you want, Scottie."

"It made me think about the things I really treasure. I gave away all the big stuff. So, you remember this?"

Nicole took the shell and turned it around in her hand as she stepped back to let him inside.

"Pearl Beach?"

He nodded.

"I was going to leave it behind, but then I thought you might like it in the bathroom, to hold the soap."

"That'd be great."

How amazing he'd kept that shell all these years! Was Scottie sentimental? Maybe, but maybe not. He'd also kept every coffee mug with an accountancy theme he'd ever been given.

"Can I make you a coffee?" he said, later in the day.

The hissing of steam and aroma of freshly brewed coffee filled the apartment, and he brought one out to her on the veranda.

"*Sum caffeine*," said her mug.

"*I depreciate a beverage*," said his.

"Cheers," said Nicole.

Scottie smiled as they touched their mugs together. Funny. She'd forgotten that dimple on Scottie's left cheek when he smiled. She jolted when he met her eyes, so she stared at the steaming mugs.

"Very funny," she said.

"In an accountant kind of way," he said.

Scottie and Nicole settled into life together like the old friends they were. Nicole loved Scottie's dinner choices, and she adored his feedback on her clothes.

With her stylish mother, Nicole always found selecting the right outfit to be a battleground. Cynthia had taste, and Nicole's ensembles never quite worked. Though it didn't stop her experimenting, she had no confidence in her fashion sense. An awkward child of an elegant mother, she knew she was no beauty. The middle child, she'd always felt slightly neglected. She missed her grandmother, Eleanor, who would take her aside for "our days" and let her play with an old hat box full of ribbons and sort a jar of spare buttons. They'd been her own toys, when her parents owned the haberdashery and department store that Jim transformed into the House of Diamonds.

She'd even taken her to *Swan Lake* when she'd recovered from Chickenpox.

"Am I an ugly duckling, Grandma?"

"No one is ugly; Nic. Beauty and ugliness are inside you. They're the way you behave."

"That's not true. You and Grandpa sell jewels to make people beautiful."

"Oh no! Jewels are gifts. They're beautiful, and they carry beautiful messages between people, like 'I love you' and 'marry me' and 'thank you' and 'I care about you'."

"But don't people wear them to be beautiful, to look beautiful?"

"A greedy or cruel or selfish person wearing a beautiful jewel is still ugly inside."

Sometimes Nicole suspected she was ugly inside as well. At school, Nicole always felt different. Other girls had fathers who were vital. Some were absent and some divorced, or too busy to show up on Speech Night, but her own father was unwell and getting worse, and despite his brave smiles, the whole family knew deep down they were going to lose him, their beloved Jimmy Huntley the Second. It was hard.

It made her friends awkward to mention their fathers, and also made Nicole's Emo phase utterly convincing, and for a while the company of other Emos was what she craved. Emo guys, slouched, vacant or miserable. She and Zach were an item for a while, but then he slouched off to Melbourne, never to return.

Cynthia banned her from working in the front of the shop.

"Our customers don't understand black nail polish, darling," her mother said.

It was only while trying to prove her wrong that Nicole discovered "market segments" and had to concede her mother was right about the kinds of people who came into Huntleys. They had money and wanted to spend it, to impress, to express their love or to meet the expectations of those who loved them.

The more she looked, the more she found. Birds of a feather flocked together. She and her friends experimented with dress codes throughout high school and she lurched from one fashion extreme to another.

Her new flatmate proved himself useful, unlike Lucia who made her feel ugly with one sleek glance.

She'd parade in three or four jackets every morning, and Scottie always had an opinion.

"That one," he said, as he ate his cereal. "That works. You look great."

For a middle child who'd spent her life trying to get a word in edgeways or gain the attention of her parents who were forever praising James, the eldest, always so adept, or laughing at the outrageous antics of Will, the youngest, Nicole relished Scottie's presence.

Her new flatmate's wise counsel and ever attentive ear was pure joy. She loved it—cherished it. In Scottie's orbit, she loved her work and everything and everyone around her. It was miraculous. She was the first to admit it.

She calmed. She settled. She thrived. Her new flatmate was a godsend, his company a salve. He was the one person in life who gave her their full attention.

Scottie even cared about her marketing ideas, and he became her sounding board.

Nicole never managed to pinpoint the exact moment she changed her mind about Scottie. How was it that everything that made him so repellent in high school suddenly made him so desirable now?

Scottie, solid as a tree trunk beside her, unyielding in his loyalty, dependable and helpful, was exactly who she needed in her life.

His warm gaze told her he supported her no matter what she wore, and no matter what crazy hair style she experimented with, and he praised her every idea. No. That wasn't true. Not all her ideas. Instead, he considered each one deeply, scrutinized it and gave serious responses, but only after saying "hmm. Yes. I see how that could work."

One evening he turned up and said "*Ya sas.*"

"What's that?"

"'Hello' in Greek."

"Oh. '*Ya sas,*' Scottie. Is that where you're going? Greece?" She'd managed to push the reality of his departure from her mind, and now it was imminent.

He nodded.

Next day, Nicole left work early so as to serve moussaka for dinner. Dashing out at lunch time to collect the ingredients kept her smiling all day, and Scottie's surprise warmed her, not that she was trying to impress him.

"*Efharisto,*" he said.

"How do I say 'I don't understand'?"

He pulled out his phone.

"*Den katalaveno.*"

"Well, '*den katalaveno*' then, Scottie."

"I thanked you. The moussaka was great."

A vision of him eating at some Greek restaurant on the Mediterranean with a bunch of tourists or local women twisted in her gut, and she rose from the table to hide her face. This was ridiculous. He was just a flatmate, an old friend.

That was the problem.

How did you say "I think I'm falling in love with you" in English, let alone in Greek?

"Where else are you going?"

"Italy, the Dalmatian Coast, France of course ..."

"Oh, you must drop in on Mum. You know she's living in the south of France now, not far from Nice."

"Nice idea, but I'm not sure I'll have time. It's a bit of a whirlwind. Spain, Germany and Austria, too. And Switzerland."

"Oh. Is it one of those tours for singles?" She hated her question, with the emphasis on singles.

"I did end up booking one of those. The reviews were great, and I'll see so much more in a short time."

"Of course."

Chapter 3

The date of Scottie's departure raced towards them.

If Nicole found herself whipping out at lunch time to purchase ingredients for European dishes to make and share with Scottie, she considered the new habit merely courteous. She'd do the same for any old friend heading overseas, especially if they were staying together.

Besides, Scottie volunteered to cook for their French evening.

"Coq au Vin," he said. "Can't see what all the fuss is about. Leftover wine and a few mushrooms, and *voilà*."

It turned out so moist and delicious she gave him an involuntary hug. Another evening, he made Salad Niçoise —"tin of tuna, what could go wrong?"—followed by a cheese and fruit platter that lasted two nights in a row.

"You really must drop in on my mum and share your French dishes, Scottie. She's no great chef. And I'm sure she'd love to see you."

"Not so sure about that, Nic."

"Why's that?"

"Never forget I'm Huntleys' financial controller. Besides, I think James is planning a trip."

"Oh?"

"Look, let's not talk business. It's after hours. And I need to finalize my packing. How cold do you reckon Europe will be? I looked it up and their autumn doesn't look much different to our winter."

"But you're going all over the place, Scottie." Nicole grabbed his itinerary from the fridge door. "Look. Santorini."

They flicked through the destinations and read out temperatures from their phones. Nicole wished she was going with him. The vistas were stunning, especially in Greece, with all those ancient white walls and blue domes.

"Layers; that's what you'll need," she said. "Add a t-shirt under your shirt and a coat up north, and you can peel them all off when you travel south."

Scottie smiled at her, the warmth in his eyes making her want to peel off a layer or two right here in her kitchen. She busied herself stacking the dishwasher.

"Go on. Do that packing." She'd miss him. She really would. Should she get him a present? Something fun? A passport holder? Unnecessary. A suitcase label with an Australian flag? Were Australians popular in Europe or would it be a red rag to a bull somewhere? Would Scottie be safe?

She chastised herself. Scottie knew how to look after himself, and what could possibly go wrong on a group tour for under thirty fives? She bit her lip. Scottie was still vulnerable. The tour could be full of people like Beck, just waiting to latch onto a good looking Australian male. For the first time, a stab of protectiveness came over her.

She sidled down the corridor. From his room came the glide and thump of drawers being opened and closed. She put a hand on his door. Knocked.

"Yes?"

"Need a hand?"

"Sure. Welcome to my chaos."

An empty wheelie bag lay open on the floor. Scottie's hair was pushed up on one side, possibly due to the hasty change of t-shirts, now piled up inside out on the bed. Nicole had to fight the urge to smooth it. She had a déjà vu of Lucia in the same space and similar disarray, though Lucia's clothes had been bright crimsons and emeralds, slinky numbers and the highest heels she'd ever seen.

Scottie's clothes were blokey—jeans, t-shirts, sweatshirts and a few collared shirts and casual trousers. Nicole was hopeless at coordinating her own clothes, she knew. She could spend a small fortune on a new top or skirt, only to discover it went with nothing else she owned.

"Come to give me a hand, eh, Nic?"

"That would be the blind leading the sighted," said Nic. "You know I struggle with this kind of thing every morning, so I don't see what I can offer you."

"Doesn't matter to me a bit. That was Beck's thing. She drove me crazy, dressing me up in this and that."

"Well, she certainly knew how to put her own best foot forward." Should she even be going here? Who was she to judge Scottie's ex-wife?

"That she did. Tell you what. Let's just throw in a few things then get out of here. Fancy a walk or a run? Who cares about clothes. I can buy something over there if what I've packed is totally unsuitable. Come on. I've been indoors all week setting up my clients for while I'm away. Need to clear my head."

"Sure!" Nicole ducked back to her room, pulled out a tangle of black and fluorescent gym clothes, and then shoved them back in the cupboard. If Scottie didn't care, nor should she. She threw on a t-shirt, shorts and some old runners and met him at the front door.

The smile he gave her was straight out of her childhood. It was like old times, heading out on a beach adventure.

They shared a glance in the lifts. What was that smile? Was he comparing her faded t-shirt with Beck's glamor? Maybe Scottie really did care that she hadn't paired the hot pink bike pants with the lime green fitness halter … and Nic cursed her insecurities.

"Too bad," she tried to tell herself. "It's a jog to the beach, not a fashion parade."

When Scottie set off up Bondi Road at a pace, Nicole put on a burst of speed, but after several blocks she struggled to keep up. Saved by some red lights, she dropped her hands to her knees and tried to catch her breath.

Scottie's hand on her arm startled her. "Stitch?" he said. She shook her head, and wished she'd brought a bottle of water.

"I'm so unfit, Scottie. I forgot you were a cross country champ back in school and have been giving James a run for his money. I've got no hope."

"My bad," he said. "Let's walk. It's not a competition."

Past pizzerias, shoe shops, sushi, nail bars, a tattoo parlor and a coaching college they walked, then past the council chambers and the darkness of Waverley Oval. The familiar jumble of shops blurred into the background as the smell of the sea began to overtake the fuel fumes and Nicole's spirits kept on rising. It was wonderful to walk in pace with

Scottie. She fought the urge to touch him, to tuck her hand into the corner of his arm. He was such a great guy, such a kind companion. Why didn't they do this every evening? She'd miss his company, that was for sure.

Scottie was silent. Was he thinking the same thing or was he still longing for Beck?

They took the path through Hunter Park to the Bondi to Bronte coast walk, then turned left past the bright lights of the Icebergs. The bars and baths were bright against the darkness of the sea as keen octogenarians thrashed through their laps before seven o'clock closing time. Away from the shops, a cold southerly wind batted her hair and whooshed in her ears.

"What are you thinking, Scottie?" she shouted.

"That'd be us, Nic, swimming all winter."

She must have misheard him, but a vision of walking and swimming beside Scottie for decades wouldn't go away and she laughed with the joy of it. So simple.

"What's so funny?" he said.

"I thought you were implying we'd still be together for the next fifty years," she said.

"Good joke, eh?" he said. Was he testing her? That same light in his eyes she'd glimpsed in the elevator lifted her heart again, just before he glanced away. Was he saying they'd still be pals, or exploring something more serious? Surely this wasn't Scottie's way of proposing. They'd only been living together just over a month, and marriage was about far more than companionship, wasn't it?

Now Nic was the silent one, and Scottie solid beside her, head up, about to go and explore Europe with a coach full of young women.

The famous beach was a pale crescent under a half moon. At this hour, the golden sand was almost empty of the usual crowds.

"Mind if I stretch out a bit?" he said. "The prospect of 24 hours in an airplane never excites me like a beach run."

"Of course I don't mind. Go be the race horse, man."

"Thoroughbred, off the leash."

"Go for it, Scottie. I'll just sit here and admire you."

"You do that."

So she did. She gripped her knees, her back to the cold wind, and watched Scottie dash up the beach in the darkness, all long legs and masculine profile, wide at the shoulders and slim at the hips. There was something sleek and wild about Scottie as he ran, something alien, so different to the mild-mannered accountant he presented to the world by day. Was this the real Scottie, the one Beck had entrapped?

For the first time, she allowed herself to wonder how it might be to kiss Scottie, to truly hold him in her arms, beyond friendship, beyond quick snatches of fun touches between friends, to hold him as she'd hoped to hold the string of dating partners who'd shown such promise by their profiles, but who'd let her down in person, one after another. She could barely remember their names. Scottie would never do that to her—use her and then ignore her. But did he even see her that way?

What could you do when you'd "friend zoned" the one man you truly loved?

As Scottie pounded back to her along the beach and up to the headland, he drew one hand through his wild hair and panted.

"Thanks for that," he said, still catching his breath.

"For what?"

"Everything, actually," said Scottie. "For waiting here for me while I ran; for taking me in; for all the fancy meals and language lessons. It's been great."

He sat down beside her, the warmth of him an aura. In the cold wind, she leaned a little closer.

"Though I'll be in trouble in Greece if I use the wrong word." He turned his head to her and she caught his joy, even though she was puzzled.

"What do you mean 'the wrong word'? Surely you're an expert now under my tuition."

He squinted his eyes, blew through his lips and shook his head.

"No offense, Nic. Did you know the Greeks have eight words for 'love'? How hard would it be to stuff it up? Like, what if I say 'I'd love an ice cream' and I get it wrong?"

"Oh, so you'd like to sleep with an ice cream? Kinky!"

They threw back their heads and laughed. She waited for him to speak, but he was silent.

"Well, I'm excited for you, Scottie," she said. "It'll be a fair bit more interesting for you over there than Bondi Beach, that's for sure."

"I don't know," he said. "There's nothing much wrong with being right here. It's a world-class destination, and we've got it to ourselves tonight."

Was he going to put his arm around her shoulders? She leaned further into him in the buffeting wind. Now was the time she could have passed him a special present if she'd bought one. Just casually slipped it into his hand, maybe.

Nicole wasn't sure what made her do it, but she caught his fingers in her own chilled ones anyway, and their warmth was better than a radiator. He glanced down at her and away again, and while he didn't exactly hold her hand properly, he didn't remove hers. She nestled even closer.

"Cold?" he said. "Your fingers are freezing and I'm roasting. How selfish of me to keep all my warmth to myself." Then he did it. He placed one arm around her shoulders and she leaned into him, into the familiar Scottie smell of him. Heaven.

"Thanks," she said. Would it go further? Of course not. He was sharing his warmth like he might shelter a stray kitten. Did she want more than this?

Before she could find out, Scottie scrambled up.

"Best get back," he said. "You'll get exposure out here, and I've got a huge day tomorrow. I leave at first light the next day."

"Want a lift to the airport, Scottie?"

"No thanks. I'll just jump on the train. It's the first flight of the day. No need for you to get out of bed so early. Transport's convenient from your place. It's been absolutely wonderful, Nic. Great place to stay. I'm in your debt."

"You've been paying me rent, remember?"

"But still."

She knew she should say it; that she'd miss him, that she adored his company and hoped he'd come back to her and be her Scottie forever, but every moment that passed, the opportunity retreated. They were old friends and flatmates; nothing more, and to pretend otherwise was to risk the great friendship they enjoyed.

On her way to work the next morning, Nicole hot footed it through the arcade as usual, where the locksmith was just setting up. His display of anodised dog tags caught the light—gold, blue, green, crimson, orange— and she stopped and inspected them.

"Rufus" read one example. "Be my Valentine" read a heart shape, and she laughed. She pulled off a large titanium gray square with rounded corners and laid it on the counter.

"Could I get this engraved, please?" she said.

"Sorry, love. The engraver's been off sick all week. I can send it out and have it back for you next Tuesday."

"Oh. No, I really need it today. Look, I'll just buy it as it is."

"Suit yourself. Sorry about that. I'll throw in some leather. How big's your dog?"

"Oh, no. It's for a suitcase! Just a small length is fine. Thank you."

She hurried on to Huntleys, the disc warm in her pocket. Maybe old Jim would engrave it for her, or one of the apprentices.

Up in the tea room, Jim was making his instant coffee.

"Nicole, my girl." He tapped his teaspoon on the top of his cup, rinsed it under the cold tap and dropped it in the drainer as he'd done every day of her life.

"Jim, can I ask you about engraving?"

"Sure. Want me to engrave something for you?"

"I'd actually like to do it for myself for once, Jim."

He narrowed his eyes. Long ago when she'd still been a girl, to his great disappointment, she'd told him she would leave him to the practical side of making jewelry, while she would stick to serving, marketing, and store and office tasks.

He raised an eyebrow.

"It's just a fun thing. For a friend. She pulled the tag out of her pocket and held it in her palm."

Jim picked it up, turned it over in his tough old fingers, and nodded.

"Aluminum," he said. "Couldn't be easier. What you need is a little portable engraver. Mine's for gold and silver and would go right through that. If you're in a hurry, why not go down to the hardware store and pick one up. They're like a pen, with a battery inside. Fine for plastic and tags like that. The trick is to hold it steady, and keep it moving, or otherwise you go too deep. And don't touch the end or you'll burn yourself."

She added it to her shopping list and found just what he'd described. Back in her apartment, when she flicked the switch, it whirred into life. Scottie's bag was beside the front door, ready for his departure. She used the leather strap to attach the label to the handle, and ran her thumb over the name she'd engraved. How she'd miss him!

While the weeks had organized themselves into homemade black forest cake, crepes Suzette, and paella, for this, their final evening together, Nicole drew the line at making apple strudel to accompany their schnitzel. There was an excellent patisserie, so she'd brought the sweet and flaky treat home in a brown paper bag.

When she ducked out and bought five beers to accompany this final meal before his departure, it was like déjà vu. How many times had she brought home exactly this cold, clanking bundle, excited about a new date? About as many times as they'd disappointed her.

She sighed as she lined up the beers in the fridge door, ready for display. Then, as if on auto, she took on her habitual date night routine. She soaked in a fragrant bath, lit a candle, and set the cutlery and glasses on the outdoor table in the twilight.

Chapter 4

On his final night in Sydney, Scottie let himself in, dumped his briefcase in his room, returned to the kitchen and whistled at the display of drinks in the fridge. Nicole had gone to a lot of trouble.

"What's this VIP treatment, Nic? What's the occasion?"

"Oh. Just that my flatmate's off on a long European holiday," she said. "I thought you might like to celebrate."

"Are you that pleased to see me go?"

Light danced in his eyes as he seized a second bottle and went to open it.

"One for you, too?"

"I don't normally drink beer. But okay. Why not? Thanks, Scottie. How was your day?"

"Not as exciting as my evening and that's for sure. Mmmm. Smells so good in here. How was your day, Nic? Would you like yours in a glass?"

She shook her head as Scottie handed her a bottle and clinked his own open one against hers.

Scottie spooned on the mashed potato as she plated up the steaming schnitzel.

"If I'd known you were cooking Austrian I'd have brought home some sauerkraut," he said, adding the steamed carrots and mashed potato.

"Not my favorite, thanks anyway, Scottie."

They sat companionably on the high stools at her outdoor table as the streetlights twinkled and the white headlights and red taillights of rush hour snaked past below. It was so easy living with Nicole, nothing like the neverending emotional roller coaster of life with Beck.

"You're a great friend to take me in, Nic," said Scottie as he held up his bottle.

"To friendship," said Nicole, clinking hers against his. "This time tomorrow you'll be ..."

"36,000 feet above India," he said.

"And then?"

"*Bongiorno, Roma.*"

"Hello, Rome. Very good. Some of our phrases have actually sunk in. I'm so excited for you."

"I'll let you know if I find anywhere half as good as Bondi or Pearl Beach."

"Thanks."

He meant it.

That shell, fan shaped and rough, the color of a faded sunset. When she'd opened her door to him and taken it in her hands and turned it over and over, did she remember? One afternoon on one of their childhood holidays at Pearl Beach, when the late afternoon sun slanted through the little waves, he and Nicole stood together and pointed out fish, burnished silver in the strange light. Her ankles were pale in the water, like saplings planted in the sand.

"Why do they call it Lion Island?" Nicole asked him, pointing out to sea. "It doesn't look anything like a lion."

"Maybe not from here."

"No. And there's no way those bushes look like fur. There's no tail, no ears, no eyes. It's olive green and made of rocks. Lions are golden. Even in this light, it's not gold "

He remembered her body aglow, radiant in the dying light. He stared and stared at her, and she'd stared back.

"Well?"

She'd expected him to have an answer.

"I'll bet the Aboriginal people had a different name for it," he said.

When she'd nodded, finally satisfied, pride shot through him like a flame, and he laughed and rushed into the waves and swam out as far as he could go.

She was waiting for him on the sand when he returned, the big shell in her hands. She turned it over and over.

"Weren't you scared about sharks?"

"I'm still here, aren't I?" he'd said, and she'd nodded. Then she'd given him the shell. No wonder he'd had a crush on her. She was the only woman he'd ever met who made him feel ten feet tall—until Beck claimed him. Well, that was short lived.

Too bad Nicole had frozen him out all through their high school years. He'd finally got the message, but it didn't mean he wasn't still fond of her. They'd had great times together.

Nicole was beautiful. So familiar to him—with her ready sense of humor, her endearing awkwardness, her searing honesty, and that way of making him want to be his best self. So unlike Beck, whose preoccupation with appearances covered a complete lack of substance verging on soullessness. What a lucky escape. With that divorce he'd seized another chance at life, a better life.

Nicole. How he'd have loved her company on this trip. In these few short weeks, she'd allowed him to grow back into himself. Her quiet lack of graces and games had been exactly what he'd needed to finally get Beck completely out of his system, to remember who he was and what he wanted in life. The vacation no longer seemed necessary.

But how to tell Nicole? Here on the dark veranda, the city and harbor lights twinkling around them in the mild evening, he longed to tell her how much he enjoyed being with her. Last night, when she'd let him hold her hand and tolerated his arm around her, it was all about the cold wind. There'd been no notion of romance. Tonight there was no such excuse to hold her. There she was, just across the table from him, with all those curves he'd longed to explore since they were teenagers. She smelled divine.

Suddenly, Scottie was awkward around her. They both reached for the saltshaker at the same time, each offering it to the other. He loved the way she laughed it off. He loved everything about her, but the memories of how she'd cold shouldered him throughout high school still hurt. Those scars ran deep. He'd have to be nuts to try to convert this rediscovered friendship with her to anything more serious, particularly on the eve of his world trip.

"Let me get the dessert," he said. They bumped hands collecting each other's dinner plates. The cutlery clattered onto the tiles. They bent at the same time to pick them up, brushing against each other.

Nicole grabbed them first and slipped into the kitchen. Something twisted inside him just watching her retreating form, those curves in the tight jeans, the play of light in her hair. Suddenly he knew he wanted to cup her head in his hands and kiss her, properly, deeply, and more, to tell her he still loved her and always had, that Beck had been but a brief nightmare and that being with Nicole forever was all he'd ever wanted.

Thank goodness he hadn't felt this way for the whole five weeks. He'd never have been able to keep his hands off her.

It was hard not to stare when she returned with the sweet, sugar dusted pastry, and when she inhaled a flake of it and began to cough, he leaped across to pat her back. His resolve almost crumbled, but he was a man of discipline if nothing else. That's why his clients entrusted him with financial decisions—he knew exactly how to read a balance sheet and check that the numbers stacked up, how to keep a business safe. Scottie had warned himself repeatedly to avoid making a move on precious Nicole. That way, he'd never be banished again.

Luckily he'd be leaving first thing in the morning. The way she looked at him as she gathered up the dessert plates; it was more than grateful. Did Nicole feel it too? Was there any way she too could be sensing something new between them, something powerful that begged exploration?

He placed his hand on her forearm. "No, let me, Nicole. My turn to clean up. What a great dinner. I can't imagine my meals in the real Austria will be half as delicious."

He snatched his hand back. Something fresh pulsed between them, something electric in her skin, something he longed to investigate. So much for his resolve. It had lasted barely half an hour. He must really watch himself now.

"Oh sure, Scottie."

"And what I'm really looking forward to is good old Aussie fish and chips with you when I get back."

"It's a deal."

Chapter 5

That special night, had it just been the evening light, or was Scottie more handsome than ever, with the air of adventure about him.

Nicole's mind reeled. She couldn't help but compare him with all the dates she'd invited to her apartment for the same treatment—a drink and a meal. At the start they'd big note themselves as they ogled her view, as if they were threatened by her advantages.

There was none of that nonsense with Scottie. Their conversation flowed, with plenty of laughter. It was so easy to be with him, and then he'd offered to clean up the kitchen.

She stood in the doorway and watched him, those strong arms carefully stacking her plates and cutlery in the dishwasher, the swipe of the bench with the cloth in his capable hand, removing all the strudel crumbs. This man knew how to behave. That was the trouble. She could hardly rush him at the sink, could she? Maybe they could nestle down on the couch together and watch some junk television, but it was already past midnight. Where had the time gone? What if his plane crashed and he never came back?

Nicole wasn't vain. The good looks in the family had gone to James and Will, with their sun-bleached hair and too-blue eyes, but she'd gone to an effort tonight, with blusher and eyeliner and hair product and a push-up bra and little black dress with the low neckline and short hem, and even her most uncomfortable shoes.

If he'd found her at all attractive, he would surely have made a move by now. This was it, then. Scottie and Nicole—best friends forever, but nothing more. A wave of anguish engulfed her. Was she destined to always be alone? For all Scottie had told her that glamor meant nothing to him, she'd failed to light even a glimmer of interest throughout the whole of this romantic evening. She'd thrown everything at it; even her scented candle.

As Scottie stood in her doorway beside his suitcase, a great wave of love for him rose up inside her. Here was everything she loved about her childhood friend, her careful and kind flatmate, and something more—something new and strong and impossible to resist.

Plain Nicole, she told herself. Might as well go and be a nun. Something collapsed inside her, all hope extinguished, and she dashed away a tear. Pathetic. Imagine feeling sorry for herself like this. No wonder Scottie didn't want her.

She stepped closer to him, willing him to stay there—willing him not to turn and open the door just yet; not yet. Here was her Scottie, everything she'd loved about her childhood friend and her good-humored flatmate, so easy to be with, but she wanted so much more. Could there ever be more between them?

"You okay, Nic?" he said. His face softened with concern.

"Must be the beer," she said. "It never did agree with me."

He placed a caring hand on her shoulder, and then removed it, as if she were a hot potato. She was. She was burning up inside, burning for Scottie, burning to show him how much he meant to her, how much she'd miss him, how much she could offer him if he'd only show a glimmer of interest in her that way.

She glanced up at his face and away again and turned off the hall light, anxious to hide her blatant need for him.

He smiled at her the way he'd always done. She couldn't look away. There was that tiny dimple in one cheek, that little indent—and before she knew what she was doing, she'd reached out her hand to touch it, and he'd grabbed her fingers and cupped his own warm hand against her own cheek.

He wiped away her tear with his thumb, inclined his face towards hers, and closer still. Her eyes held his, his breath was a whisper, as his lips brushed hers and returned, inevitable, essential, with the hint of the certainty of so much more between them. Her heart pounded, her lips softened. She reached her hand behind his neck to bring him closer.

She leaned towards him, up on her toes. Yes. This flash of strength from the man beneath his kindness, and within his tenderness, his own spark of need, with an urgency that begged fulfilment, inevitable as the curve and crash of a mighty wave against the shore, a hunger that would not be denied.

Scottie moaned and pulled her closer, but then his other hand pushed against her shoulder and he pulled away. He turned around as if scalded and lurched towards the door, the back of his hand against his lips.

Behind him, she leaned against the wall, gasping, heart pounding, still hungry for so much more.

"Sorry. I'm so sorry, Nic," he said. "I shouldn't have done that. Look. I might as well head out right now, actually. It's only a few hours before my flight. Thanks for everything, kiddo. See you in five weeks."

He was out her door and gone before she registered what was happening, her body on full alert for love, not for this abandonment.

"Kiddo?" It was his old name for her, back when they played ping pong together. Is that how he still saw her? As some kind of child?"

"Addio," she said to the back of the door. "'Farewell.'"

She knew she should be happy for him as she wandered past his empty room week after week.

It still smelled vaguely of polite, clean male, of Scottie, and she inhaled deeply, her hand on the door frame.

Loneliness stabbed her deep in her chest. She missed him. And what if he met someone else on the tour. What if he never came back?

Chapter 6

In the dark tunnel, alone in the train carriage with his suitcase, Scottie could barely think. He'd nearly blown it.

Moving in with Nicole, even temporarily, had been a mistake, a slippery slope of mounting desire, of remembering every detail of her that he'd never stopped loving.

All through high school, she'd punished him for that love. She'd literally told him to "get lost."

Living with her, grabbing cereal every morning in the kitchen, he loved to watch her face, fresh from sleep, before she covered it with makeup. He loved her freckles and the soft ginger tips of her eyelashes, and her fragrance, like fresh fruit; the familiar shoulders and hands and feet he'd loved since childhood, the way she'd slant her face towards him, quizzical, then smile as he answered a question about the weather or his plans for the day. It opened up a golden stab of joy in him, every time.

His attraction to her was deeper than ever. He longed for her with every fiber of his being. But surely he hadn't suffered for nothing back when they were teenagers. That they could be friends now was worth protecting. Why risk losing it again by making a wrong move, especially after the disaster with Beck?

Back there in her apartment, as she'd kissed him goodbye, it was only with the strength of his rational mind that he'd been able to wrench his body away from hers.

He'd miss her. He missed her now—a mere ten minutes after his departure—more than he'd ever missed Beck. Beck's absence was a relief, but with Nic there was a visceral longing, as if part of him were missing.

He groaned.

Had he made a lucky escape? Or was this whole trip a big mistake? Should he get off at the next station, catch the next train back and confess to her his love that had never gone away?

As the carriage accelerated, something shiny caught his eye, swinging from the handle of his suitcase. A bag tag. Had Nicole put it there?

R Scott

71/99 Grafton St

Bondi Junction

Australia

He smoothed his thumb over it. The R was wobbly, and the Scott in a childish hand, the script becoming more confident line by line.

Nicole must have made it for him. She'd engraved his name with her address. Could he hope their living arrangements might become permanent, that she wouldn't get another flatmate? At least she expected him to return to her after his trip. He had to hang on to that hope. To go back now and profess his undying love for her might ruin their relationship forever. It wasn't a risk he was willing to take.

Scottie's flight was delayed in Dubai. He traversed acres of polished marble and gleaming glass, trying to distract himself from the certainty the tour would leave without him. He tried to interest himself in the goods on offer—a thousand watches, decorative camels and chocolates. Every time he passed a perfume vendor he remembered Nic at her doorway, their almost kiss—then he'd set off again, past handbags and briefcases, up escalators and down, past identical waiting gates and a thousand more strangers.

International travel had never bothered him in the past. He'd spent a semester of his university degree in Canada and loved it. Surely he'd settle soon and find the right frame of mind to enjoy this first true holiday in years.

By the time he finally boarded his connecting flight, his tour had left Heathrow. It would have made more sense to meet them all on the continent, but he was unable to reach anyone by phone.

When he caught up with them all in Amsterdam he'd spent more than thirty six hours in transit. The tour company contact, a curly haired American who chewed bubble gum, whisked away his suitcase before he could shave and refresh his clothes. She insisted he meet his travel companions during their tour of one of the grand canals, practically pushing him aboard an open boat reeking of fresh oranges and tequila. Just how the cruise acquired a Mexican vibe was anyone's guess, and tequila sunrise for breakfast at four o'clock in the afternoon with accumulations of jetlag didn't help Scottie feel welcome. The others stared at his rumpled travel suit and laughed, making some joke about Van Gogh, but a couple of young women from the Netherlands latched on to him and made him more welcome, juggling oranges, then making more drinks and plying him with them until he practically passed out. He skipped the dinner venue and slept for fourteen hours straight, missing their guided tour of the Rijksmuseum. Was this supposed to be fun?

He managed a walk up and down the canals by himself at five o'clock the next morning, when he admired the quaint, multi-storied houses, all jammed against each other, and wished a tourist shop was open so he could buy some salt and pepper shakers for Nicole's apartment, but they were jammed into their tourist coach before the shops opened. In San Sebastian, they all traipsed out for a smorgasbord of exotic fish preserved in salt and garlic.

By Day Three he developed a cold and gave the city a miss. His dreams were full of Australia's beaches, of lorikeets screeching in the branches of bottlebrush and gum trees. Ridiculous. It wasn't even summer back in Australia. It was summer here. Didn't the tour book say something about nightingales? He forced himself out of bed, determined to enjoy himself.

Seeing the sights was exciting, even though the actual sights were often smaller and less spectacular than the photographs showed them to be. Maybe tourists felt that way about Sydney's Harbour Bridge and Opera House.

Sharing Milan with his twenty eight forced companions was frustrating. Italy may well have provided the best fashion shopping ever. The larger than life American college graduates were a ton of fun, carting back armfuls of great buys, but their hour-late arrivals for every rendezvous began to wear thin. Why didn't the tour guide leave without them?

Because they were taking turns to sleep with him, of course. And if all everyone else seemed to want to do was sleep with each other, why hadn't they stayed at home and shagged? Was he the only one who really wanted to see inside the Pinacoteca and the Milan Cathedral?

Scottie knew he sounded like a bore. Maybe he was one. Maybe that was why Beck had left him.

Beck. She'd used him alright. In their whirlwind romance, it had only ever been about Beck. It was nearly two years since she'd zeroed in on him in that beer garden. They might never have met. He rarely went to those places, but he and James went to meet an old school friend there who now lived in London and had come back for a visit.

They'd just been about to leave when she'd pranced in, all legs and high heels. Not his type at all.

"Ooh, I love the serious ones," she'd said. She'd stopped right there at their table, leaned in to him, taken off his glasses and pushed his fringe back at a rakish angle.

"Eastern suburbs gentlemen, ladies," she'd said to her friends, as if he were a shop mannequin with neither ears nor brains. "They'll have serious money, these boys."

All the warning signs were there alright, flashing on high beam, but even more dazzling was her interest in him and the way she'd seemed to need him. Beck should have been an actor. Then again, with Scottie the sole member of her audience, she'd made quite a living. She'd worked out exactly how to pull at his heartstrings and wallet. It was only after they were married that he became aware of the way she turned her tears on and off to manipulate others. He'd kept hoping he was wrong about her. How could anyone be so calculating, faking vulnerability simply to make him jump to please her? He'd known love was about give and take. The trouble was he did all the giving and she did all the taking. He'd hoped against hope he was wrong about her, and he would have forgiven her, would probably still be with her if she hadn't simply ditched him— hitched a ride with another blind fool. It made him wary.

Here on tour, it wasn't as if he couldn't have had some action if he'd wanted. He'd rebuffed a couple of them. They reminded him too much of Beck. When he lay down at night in yet another mid-range hotel bed, alone, it wasn't the sights and scenes of arches and stone and bridges and fountains and renaissance art at the back of his eyeballs. It was Nicole's apartment, that doorway and their broken kiss that stole into his mind and disturbed his sleep. Several times he resolved to call her and tell her he missed her, but a companion would start up another inane conversation, or he'd remember the way she'd treated him in high school. To confess his everlasting love for her was to risk both losing her friendship and making their working life awkward for the next thirty years, assuming she'd keep working for the family firm, and he'd keep advising them.

But how was that going to work, hiding his attraction to Nicole for the rest of his life?

Maybe he should leave the tour, and strike out on his own on the Via Francigena. Go find himself. Maybe he was never meant to be an accountant anyway in this one life.

But Scottie was always one to follow the rules. On the coach and in the restaurants and bars, his travel companions stuck together like shipwrecked souls, and perhaps that's what they were, drinking too much in yet another iconic location as if their lives depended on it.

Scottie had no interest in one-night stands and sex that meant nothing. He'd heard talk that three of the women aimed to sleep with as many of the men as possible, but he had no interest in their complicated mating game. Maybe he was too old for this caper.

Once again he told himself to phone Nicole and break this black reverie, but there was always another distraction, especially when Melodie from Canada was motion sick on the switchback up to Santorini. He stayed with her on a bench overlooking the sea while the others headed out to join the non-stop party.

Santorini was exactly as he'd pictured it. White walls, blue domes and cobblestones, and impossibly romantic. It was the place to be with someone special, not all these strangers pretending to have fun, drinking too much in yet another bar, with the music far too loud.

When Melodie recovered and dragged on his arm, urging him to join the party, he made his excuses and wandered alone, admiring the way the arches framed so many views of the famous city and water. He longed to stay a while in each location, to do more than snap a selfie in front of one famous spot after another. The deep history of these places fascinated him. He would have loved a travel companion prepared to discuss what they were seeing, interested in the architecture, the language, the volcanic rock formations—someone like Nicole. Nicole in fact. What was he doing over here without her?

Restlessly, he picked up a brochure about a monastery on Mount Athos. Was that what he needed, to retreat from the world?

His phone buzzed. Probably Melodie. He ignored it. It buzzed again and reluctantly he pulled it out of his pocket. Nicole!

"Nicole! Great to hear from you. Everything okay?" said Scottie.

"Of course."

"Great."

"Having fun?"

"Of course. Well. No. Not really. I wish you were here, Nicole." The truth came out before he could censor himself.

"FaceTime?"

"Sure." There she was on her balcony, the lights of Sydney Harbour spread out behind her. Her smile lit up her eyes—those treasured eyes, framed by her hair that never sat quite right. It was his Nicole. He told her how he missed her.

"You're not just saying that?"

"Of course not. I don't say things I don't really mean."

There was a long silence as she stared at him and smiled. Had the call dropped out? Was her picture frozen? Scottie saw his own smile in the little square in the corner. Nicole made him happy. It was that simple. He cleared his throat again.

"Nicole? What can I do for you? Is it about the marketing account? Or the apartment? Is there someone else you want to rent it to? Is that it?"

"Oh no! I just wanted to hear your voice. I miss you, Scottie."

"As a flatmate."

"It's true you're an excellent flatmate."

"Well, you're an excellent landlady. I miss you, too, Nicole. You know I booked this trip before I moved in with you."

"Yes?"

"I would never have left if I hadn't already booked it."

"Really?"

"Nicole. I really do wish you were here with me. I'd like to bring you here."

"Yes?"

"Nicole, would you ..." Scottie swallowed. He'd considered their situation from every side. Nothing would ever change the fact he loved her. She might as well know it. It was time to find out if he had a chance with her. In those final days before he'd left on the trip, he'd almost dared to hope she might be attracted to him beyond friendship. That kiss—he couldn't get it out of his mind. Just lately he'd been wondering which of them had started it. Nicole still hadn't told him why she'd phoned. Was she waiting for him to speak? Well, he would. Why not?

"Nicole, there's no way for me to ignore this anymore. I'd like to know where I stand."

"What do you mean?"

"Nic, you made it clear when we were in high school that you didn't feel the same way about me as I felt about you, the way I've always felt about you…"

Silence. But at least she wasn't laughing at him, or so he hoped.

"I thought I could be the friend you clearly wanted." Scottie plowed on. "But since I moved in with you, I've known. Nic, I can't keep this platonic any more. I'm sorry. I don't want to just be your flatmate; just be your friend."

"What do you want to be, Scottie?"

"When my divorce comes through … Nicole? You've gone silent."

"When your divorce comes through …?"

"Nicole. You like me, don't you?"

"Of course. We've always been friends."

"Yes. And I don't want to lose that friendship. In Athens there was a little museum right in the grounds of Plato's academy. It was incredibly modern, a digital museum, but it was all about this ancient philosophy, from nearly two and a half thousand years ago."

"That's old."

"Yes, but … Nicole, did you know that Plato believed that the strongest love can grow from friendship? Philia is the deep love of friends for each other. The Greeks believed that when it led to Eros, to physical love, it created the strongest relationships of all."

"Have you been eating too much ice cream in Greece?"

"Yeah. Because I'm hot. You have to agree Plato knew a thing or two."

"So what are you saying?"

"I say let's date, Nicole, as soon as I get back."

"Okay."

"Yes!" Scottie beamed and punched his fist up into the air, startling a cluster of pigeons. They shot off the edge of the parapet and up, into the sky.

He returned to his room, studied his laptop, booked his return flight and snapped it shut. He knew exactly where he needed to be, and who should be beside him.

When a joyful Scottie texted the tour guide to find the party, he turned up to bid them all farewell. He told them he'd just fallen in love again, and he shouted them all a round of champagne.

They insisted he join in another dance to *Zorba the Greek* and Melodie took the place next to him.

"I'll be sad to see you go," she said into his ear.

He gave Melodie a chaste goodbye kiss on her cheek and wished her luck with the rest of the tour. She'd make someone very happy one day, but it wouldn't be him. Scottie had other plans.

At the airport, his flight couldn't come soon enough. He paced and waited and paced and waited and scrolled on his phone. He ordered a dozen long-stem red roses for the woman he loved. He was just about to press "buy" when he changed his mind, and upped it to three dozen. Yes.

He'd never been more pleased to return home to Australia. Nicole was waiting for him when he got off the plane, her face eager, flushed with joy, to see him. He was bedraggled from the long flight, though he'd done his best to shave and put on a fresh shirt. He stood before her, speechless.

It was Nicole who made the next move, hesitating only long enough to detach his hand from his bag and step into his embrace. Right there in the fairway, in the full view of a hundred strangers, they kissed.

When they pulled apart, her eyes shone. Tears caught in her eyelashes. She glowed, his Nicole. For him. He touched her cheek with tenderness; with awe.

"Come home, flatmate," she said, placing her hand on his and threading her fingers through his own. She pulled on his hand. They were at her car in moments, then back at the apartment, coming through the doorway.

"Now where were we when you left me?" said Nicole as she leaned against the inside of her front door and pulled him close.

And she kissed him again, right there in the hall, kissed him till he couldn't think, till he couldn't remember what day it was, what year, what decade, what country—only that finally he was in the right place at the right time, with the right person.

"Coffee?"

"Uh. Yeah. Coffee. Yep. I'd love that, Nicole." He stood and swayed as she dashed into the kitchen. "I need to take a shower."

When he emerged, he followed the fragrance of the coffee out to her verandah, where she waited for him, along with two of his mugs—"*It's accrual world*" and "*Be audit you can be.*"

A tiny jet lagged voice in his head told him she'd only agreed to date him, that what he was about to do could backfire. But how could he wait a moment longer? Hadn't he already waited most of his life for this moment?

There on the tiles, with the hot Sydney sun as witness, he went down on bended knee. In one hand, he held out a small blue and gold box.

"Nicole Huntley, will you marry me?"

"Oooh!"

"Nicole, let me do this properly."

Onto her ring finger, he threaded a gold band with a coin on top.

"What's this?" She pushed her thumb across the disc and examined the intriguing series of concentric squares and other parallel lines.

"Call it a place saver," he said. "It was the only good ring I could find at the airport. It's a reproduction of an ancient Greek coin. That's a labyrinth design from the myth of the Minotaur, I think. It's gold, but you might have your eye on one of Jim's rings, or one from my family. We haven't had a chance to discuss what you'd prefer, so you can wear this one for now. It's supposedly a reproduction from antiquity."

"The Minotaur? Gymnasts danced on the horns of a bull and then got lost in a maze?"

"A labyrinth, I think. There's a difference, though I'm not sure what it is. I dropped Ancient History before I learned everything," said Scottie.

"I love it, Scottie! It's beautiful!" She held the ring up to the light, where it shone in its slim simplicity. "But aren't we missing a few steps?"

"I missed you so much, Nicole. When you agreed to date me, I didn't want to waste another minute. I've already wasted too much time. Beck targeted me and I was too flattered to realize it. She had her own reasons for being a gold digger, and in the end, our marriage wasn't enough for her either. I was reckless to marry Beck. I thought when I gave her the things she wanted, she'd be happy, but she never stopped wanting more— even a different husband, thankfully! Living with Beck was hard, but living with you is easy. With you, I can be myself. I love you and I know I can love you forever. We're good for eachother. Don't feel you have to give me an answer yet. I just want you to know exactly how I feel about you, how I've always felt about you. Though it'd be great if you said 'yes' so I could stand up."

They laughed as she nodded and he rose and held her close in the warm Sydney sun, and they kissed each other, again, and then again.

Their coffees grew cold.

Chapter 7

Work was more exciting after Scottie's proposal. Everything was more exciting. When Nicole met Stella and her sister, Jeannie, for their monthly catch up to discuss Huntleys' growing online business, it didn't take long for the conversation to switch to weddings.

Still in its infancy, Shop Huntleys Online was experimental, and Nicole loved the way she, Stella and Jeannie bounced ideas off each other and decided in a heartbeat to make them happen. With her marketing nous, Nicole wove in social media opportunities and insights, and Jeannie's analytics allowed them to test the interest in their new, more affordable lines from week to week.

Stella's contribution was her endless imagination and experience of making and wearing jewelry. She dreamed up new products nonstop, though, to her frustration, she rarely had time to make them these days, so busy in the store, completing her own advanced apprenticeship with Jim, and supervising the younger apprentices. Through James's contacts, production was outsourced, but she longed to get her hands on tools and materials. She missed her days of pure creation.

With Jeannie's eldest, Lucy, now in Kindergarten, and little Sienna in tow, the three women met at a coffee shop in the plaza so that Sienna could enjoy the outing, too. Sitting on Jeannie's lap, she finished her babycino then toddled into the nearby fenced play area while the meeting continued. The day was windy and another child banged blocks on the fence. Sienna joined in.

"Lucky it's all indestructible," said Stella.

"As long as they're not hitting each other," said Jeannie. "Gentle, Sienna!"

"I can't imagine working out here in the wind and rain all day on a stall, Stella," said Nicole as she drew her coat closer around her shoulders. "Good move to select that position outside Huntleys, target James and end up snug inside our store!"

It was a running joke between them. In fact, it was the council which allocated Stella the space for her stall. She knew nothing of Huntleys when she set up Stellar, her own business. She and James clashed, and Nicole had been so hostile she'd almost closed Stellar down.

"I don't miss the storms, that's for sure," said Stella. "But sometimes I miss seeing the clouds, and the wind in the trees. We're so busy now, the days blur into months."

"How are the apprentices?" said Jeannie.

"Oh, it's great to have more hands on deck, but Divandra's a bit entitled. Fair enough. Her family in Malaysia has their own jewelry empire. And Shawn's a bit variable. Put it this way. He suffers from an amazing amount of food poisoning, especially on Mondays and when the surf's up."

Nicole and Jeannie laughed.

"Actually, that's given me an idea," said Stella. "Huntleys is so close to Bondi Beach, we need a new surfing line, with silver and mother of pearl and paua shell surfboards, waves and whale tails on chunky silver chains."

"Love it," said Nicole. "Weren't sharks' teeth a thing in the seventies? Jim always says jewelry ideas keep coming back because human bodies are essentially the same."

"When will you find time to design them?" said Jeannie.

"Well, at least the line will be timeless," said Nicole. "It's not like you need to rush it for Father's Day or Christmas."

"We could bring it to the main store in gold and opals if it's successful online," said Stella as a waiter collected their empty coffee cups.

"How are your wedding plans going, Nic?" said Stella.

"Actually, can I ask you two a favor?" said Nicole.

"Of course," said Jeannie.

"I need to find a wedding dress. I'm hopeless at fashion. Scottie's mum is lovely, and she's offered to help, but I'd really love your opinions, too. There's a shop just down the road. I'll only take half an hour of your time. Besides, Stell, you need to look for yourself. You'll need one soon too, won't you?"

Stella laughed awkwardly.

"James and I don't have a date, yet," she said. "But Jeannie and I just went through all this with our mother, Flame. We thought she'd stay single forever, but you know we went north for her wedding only recently?"

Nicole nodded.

"We practically had to hijack her," said Jeannie. "We took her to Brisbane the day before her wedding, and dragged her through a few shops, but all we ended up with was a length of green silk she wrapped around herself literally at the last minute."

"Oh! James showed me those photos," said Nicole. "She was stunning, and that was actually appropriate for the setting. It was all a bit hippy, wasn't it?"

"Bare feet and mango daiquiris in the farmhouse garden," said Stella, as she reached down to extract her niece from the play area.

"Well, Scottie and I are a bit more traditional," said Nicole as she led the way down Oxford Street. "Come and tell me what you think."

The noise of the street faded away as they closed the shop door, and set off a series of chimes which summoned a shop assistant. Sienna was fascinated. She ran her chubby hand along the display of gowns, testing the textures of all the satins and laces and pearl bobbles. The shop assistant glowered, so Stella hoisted Sienna to her hip and distracted her by pointing out glittering headpieces in a glass cabinet.

"What do you think of this dress?" said Nicole as she pointed to a traditional number with a cinched-in waist and puffy sleeves.

"I like the shape, but the white is too stark for your skin color," said Jeannie. "Trust me. As a redhead, I know about these things."

"How about this one?" said Stella. "I like the way it's a little bit daring, showing one shoulder, but also very elegant, and the smooth lines will suit you. Jeannie's right about the colour. This fabric is much creamier."

"Can you wait while I try it on?"

The sisters nodded and stepped out of the shop to walk Sienna backwards and forwards, each holding one of her hands. They swung her up in the air every five steps, to her squeals of glee.

"Why are Nicole and Scottie getting married before you and James?" said Jeannie. "You've been engaged for ages."

"She and Scottie have known each other all their lives, I guess," said Stella, but she frowned.

When they re-entered the shop, Nicole was up on a podium, the soft drapes of the gown hanging gracefully. Jeannie was right about the color. Nicole glowed.

The assistant bent two large mirrors on doors towards her, to show all angles.

"Just right," said Stella, and they all nodded. When Sienna joined in the nodding they laughed.

"Nicole, would you let me design a headdress to match? I can see something in pearls and gold wire, with just a few diamantes on one side, rising up in a kind of fan or feather shape, to match your hair."

"Stell, you are amazing!" said Nicole. "I'd love it!"

"Oh no! Look at the time!" said Jeannie. "Sienna and I are off. Kindergarten pick up time."

Chapter 8

Now that Nicole and Scottie were engaged, Nicole's Sundays were transformed.

Before Scottie came back into her life as her flatmate—then fiancé—Sundays had always been about lazing about in pajamas all day, or taking up a new hobby with a vengeance, then dropping it. So much for windsurfing. Scooting across the surface of the sea with just the power of the wind had looked so easy, but when she couldn't even pull the sail up out of the water, she'd given up, lain on the beach all day with a good book, then regretted the sunburn.

For the Scotts, sunburn would never happen, and Sundays never changed.

When Scottie first invited her to his parents' home for Sunday lunch, Nicole was honored. She'd eaten at their house often in the past, when she, Scottie, James and Will were all children together, but back then they ate chicken nuggets and chips in the den, and watched kids' videos while the adults ate at the formal table.

Nowadays, Scottie's parents treated her like royalty. At their formal Sunday lunch table, they gazed from her to Scottie and back again as if, like Scottie, they could barely believe she'd finally shown an interest in their only son who'd adored her all his life.

Occasionally, Nicole hankered for a long, lazy sleep-in with Scottie and croissants, but over the weeks and months, the Scotts' formality and manners never let up.

Scottie would open the car door for her after they'd pulled up outside the neat picket fence, and he'd stand back to let her walk through his parents' garden gate. So much for men and women having to behave exactly the same way as each other. Scottie's manners, with that special smile, made her feel like he cherished her. He treated her like a princess, every time.

Ron Scott senior and Dianne—pronounced Deeahrn—always answered the door as if the whole thing was a surprise. Ron would take the bottle of red wine Scottie cradled as if it were a baby. He'd exclaim over the type of grape, then hand it back for Scottie to open and pour.

They sat at the formal dining table, Scottie's father, Ron at the head and Dianne opposite. Everyone smiled a lot.

The idea of dressing up again on a Sunday after a full week of work was a chore, until Nicole worked out she could simply wear her "Sunday best." Same was good. "Same" was what Sunday lunch with the Scotts was all about.

The aroma of roast—be it lamb or beef—with a hint of something caramelized to come, the baked dessert, a rare Scott indulgence, always made her stomach rumble.

It wasn't that the Scotts did without. Not at all. Their well-kept bungalow in Sydney's lower north shore was peaceful and picturesque, with every comfort and luxury—a neat rose garden in a bed of violets, a lemon tree either full of blossoms or budding with fruit, and, inside, tasteful, comfortable furniture in "as new" condition despite its age, and not one item out of place.

At the polished dining table in the formal dining room, with the grandfather clock marking time behind her, and her back straight, Nicole kept her smile as polite as Dianne's. But as Nicole offered the mint sauce to Scottie's father, on its saucer to catch the drips, classifications from her marketing degree dropped into her mind and wouldn't go away.

The Scotts were textbook "traditional values." They didn't seek novelty.

Nicole smiled with satisfaction at Scottie across the table and stretched one foot out as far as possible without it being too obvious, to nudge his polished shoe. He glanced up sharply to meet her gaze, the warmth in his golden brown eyes always such a balm to her soul.

"Thank you," he mouthed.

In fact, it was never an effort to dine with the Scotts.

If Dianne was disappointed her only son was going to marry at Cynthia's Southern Highlands home instead of at St Andrews Cathedral or their beautiful sandstone smaller church, St Michael's, where the Scotts had so many friends, they never breathed a word of it to Nicole.

If anything, Dianne was more than kind to Nicole, welcoming her as "the daughter I never had" and always showing an interest in her week.

Dianne's posy of rosebuds and violets in the centre of the table wobbled slightly as she bumped the table with her arm. Nicole smiled again. Dianne had few indulgences, but she adored her small old black and white collie dog, Missy, and fed her the juiciest morsels of meat when she hoped no one was looking.

Ron Scott senior didn't approve of Dianne feeding the dog on the sly. He raised his eyebrows and lowered them again and continued his conversation with Scottie, about one of their clients' family woes.

Such conversations were always "strictly confidential" and often Nicole let herself be lulled by the play of light into the curved bay window of the beautiful room, rather than try to decipher the financial language of drawdowns, collateral, credits and yields.

Today, though, she tuned in. Fletchers Storage, one of the Scotts' clients, had recently "free floated" and all hell had broken loose.

There'd been plenty of investors—people who saw the value of a company that stored stuff—in an age when no one could bear to throw anything out, always wanted to buy more, lived in smaller and smaller housing as gracious homes like this one were replaced by medium density and high rise apartments, and no one had time to sort their belongings, let alone move them on.

The Fletchers became richer than ever as investors' money flooded in, but then their troubles began. The Fletchers were like many of the Scotts' clients; three and even four generations of family members, some more involved in the core business than others, but each believing they deserved an equal share.

One of the youngest Fletchers had convinced two of the others to sell out, and now, with almost twenty per cent of the company, he was so well placed for a successful takeover that the older family members were distraught.

"It's greed that does it," said Ron senior. "As if that young man doesn't have enough already."

"So what will happen?" Nicole asked.

"Every six months, this 'shark' can legally acquire another three per cent, and in five years, if he keeps it up, he'll have the fifty per cent he needs to change the board and chair, none other than his poor grandfather who has given his life to the company."

"But that's ages away," said Nicole. "Who's to say it will actually happen?"

"That's part of the problem," Scottie said. "But it probably will, otherwise, why would he be buying up shares? They call it the 'creep' rule."

"Sounds creepy alright."

"The sad thing is it sets one family member against another," said Ron. "I've seen it happen too often when companies float."

"Then why do you float them?"

"We serve our clients, Nicole. We do what they ask, and over time, family companies grow so large it's only sensible they explore their options for the future."

Nicole glanced from Ron to Scottie. No wonder Scott and Sons was a solid company in its own right. They were knowledgeable and trustworthy. They weren't greedy. They were fine people who added up numbers and handled their clients' tax matters in such ways that fault was never found.

Afterwards, Nicole and Dianne washed and dried the best crystal and porcelain by hand. They discussed the wedding plans as Ron and Scottie cleared the table.

Then, as usual, Dianne packaged up a chunk of the cooling meat and half the pudding for them to take home with them, as if they'd only just left home and were struggling to make their way in the world. Still, the leftovers came in handy, with both of them working long days.

In the car, after they'd smiled and waved goodbye, Nicole asked.

"That thing with the Fletchers, Scottie. Could that happen to the Huntleys?"

"Yes."

"Seriously?" said Nicole. She turned to him, her sense of wellbeing after the relaxed meal shaken. The possibility had never occurred to her. "It's like Jurassic Park out there! Or Cops and Robbers at the very least. Poison pills and predators. Should I be scared?"

"No. It's an adventure. There's a lot of money to be made if you can play it right."

"But it's not a game to play, is it? I always thought Huntleys was my life and certainly all of our livelihoods. It's Jim's at least. Are you saying we should sell or buy out each other?"

"This kind of business behavior is common knowledge. It's always been a possibility for Huntleys."

"How do you know all this, Scottie?"

"I don't know. We grew up with this stuff. It was happening all around us, so I guess we talked about it with the other kids at school. So many came from families who were trading. Half their parents were investing in each other's companies or taking them over. What did you discuss at school?"

"Hair straighteners. Diets."

"No! You're in business. Your family's in business. You must know some of this."

"I guess I was never that interested in those aspects. Maybe if dad had lived … We deal in jewelry, Scottie. It's all about fashion! This item goes with that item—not 'this company goes with that company.' Living with you has been a revelation. I love it when you talk money. What if we were to buy out Jim, James, Mum and Will?"

"You tycoon, Nic! You mogul. You industrialist!"

"Well. Anything's possible. That's what you said, isn't it? Maybe I missed my calling, Scottie, but I do know how to build a brand. I know how to market Huntleys' stock. Have you seen our sales lately? Stella's amazing. I know we got off on the wrong foot when we first met, but I have so much respect for her now. She and Jeannie have so many ideas. Online, we're trying new lines all the time. I guess we have this micro focus. We don't see the business as a whole. There's too much else going on. Do you and James discuss the big picture?"

"Sure we do. Always have."

"So here am I with Stella, obsessing over whether we should use pearls or cubic zirconia in her next line of earrings, and you two are discussing whether we should sell Huntleys, or create another whole business and sell that too?"

"Well, it's an option. The online business, Shop Huntleys, that's growing so fast it's hard to believe. Who would have thought it a year ago?"

There was now "Shop Jim's rings"—a button at the end of each of his "Huntleys jewel of the week" podcasts, and on the main Huntleys site, customers could even select "Huntleys French Collection" for a selection of the antique jewelry Cynthia sourced from French markets and Stella repaired in Sydney.

There was ongoing discussion with Will in the US about whether his fledgling outdoor wear business, Huntleys House of Hearts, should be linked to the Australian and French stores, since the customers were likely to be so different, but Hearts was still a part of the growing empire, with a steady market for Jim's Australian opal rings, and Stella and the apprentices were trying their hands at setting some top quality Nevada Black Fire Opals to broaden their expertise.

The idea their business could be sold from underneath them was unsettling, but Nicole tried not to think about it. Instead, she sighed with quiet joy as she watched Scottie take Dianne's cold meat out of the cooler bag and place it in their refrigerator. She hadn't told him she'd already chosen her wedding dress. Jeannie was storing it at her place. The secret blazed beside her heart.

Her wedding to this perfect man was only weeks away.

Chapter 9

Nicole and Scottie married in Cynthia's Southern Highlands home, an hour and a half from Sydney, the French doors thrown open to the fragrance of wisteria for the afternoon ceremony.

Scottie was keen to keep it low key and avoid the extravagance and pomp of his previous wedding, and Nicole wanted something intimate rather than grand, with closest friends and family, so when Cynthia agreed to let them use the beautiful home she'd created before she moved to France, they were thrilled.

In the white marquee, Stella, Dianne and Jeannie spent hours arranging white tablecloths, candelabra, with white roses and lavender in Dianne's crystal vases for every table.

Just before the four o'clock ceremony, when all the guests had arrived and were knocking back beer and champagne, the music could barely be heard for all the chatter and laughter.

Stella tapped on Nicole's door. She entered quickly and closed it, then held out a cake box. Nicole shook her head.

"I couldn't eat another thing, Stell," Nicole said. "I'm far too keyed up. I don't want to be sick. Can you imagine that?"

"It's not food! It's for your hair," said Stella, and she opened the box. Nicole gasped.

"That's so beautiful, Stella! I've never seen anything like it. Is this for me?"

"Who else is getting married today, Nic! Here, let me put it on and you can see if you like it."

"You know I went back to that shop and tried a few of the commercial ones, but they all made me look like a wedding cake. This is so minimal. Do you think it will fit?"

Nicole perched on the end of the bed in her long gown as Stella rested the creation gently on her head and secured it with a few pins.

Nicole stood and moved to the mirror, inspecting all sides with the help of a hand mirror.

"Genius, Stell. All the shop ones were too symmetrical. This is perfect with this dress. I was so worried about my one bare shoulder, but this balances the whole thing. I owe you."

"Nonsense, Nicole. Be the bride. It's your special day. Oh, and I brought some matching earrings you can try. There are pearls or diamantes. Faux, sorry, but you'll get the effect."

"As if that matters! You're so incredibly thoughtful, Stella. I can't thank you enough. What do you think?"

"Pearls," said Stella. "They link the cream of the dress with the rest of you."

"Now I really do feel like a bride."

"Just as well, given the time. See you soon!" and Stella slipped away as Nicole reached for her cream ballet flats, her stomach churning with too many butterflies.

Tears lodged in Nicole's throat when Cynthia and grandfather Jim walked her between the guests to a waiting Scottie, but they were tears of joy. Yes, she wished her father was there to witness her happiness, but everyone's faces beamed encouragement towards her and best of all was the expression on Scottie's face—a kind of serious euphoria, if that were possible.

Even her mother was happy. There was a stab of dismay to see Cynthia with the new partner she'd found in France, Émile, but she could only be glad for her. The mother she'd visited for so many weekends in the Southern Highlands house had been stylish and accomplished but bored and lonely, once she'd completed the building and decorating project. This mother was as radiant as Nicole herself.

Cynthia and Émile seemed ideally suited. He even showed an interest in all her antiques. She'd seen him peering at the old writing chest in the entry foyer.

"Do you think it's French?" she'd asked him, more to be polite than out of real interest, but his response surprised her.

"Non. It has some similarities, yes, but this oak, it is English, I think. And it is far too heavy. In France, these chests were *a porter*, to carry, portable, yes?"

"Oh. Okay." She'd just spotted a surprise guest. "Sorry, Émile!"

Even the youngest Huntley, bad boy Will, turned up for the wedding.

"You made it," said Nicole. "All the way from the US!" Yes, Will was unpredictable and a cad for most of his life, but Cynthia assured everyone he was on the straight and narrow now, and Nicole loved him anyway. She gave him a hug that knocked her headdress sideways, then introduced him to Émile and the others before joining Scottie again.

"Hitched again already, mate!" Will said after the ceremony as he clapped Scottie on the shoulder. Trust Will to say the wrong thing, but Scottie was ready for him.

"Can't all get it right first time, can we?"

"What do I know, Scottie, except I've never seen two happier people, and long may it continue. Nic's a pain when she's unhappy, that's for sure. No, Nic, just joking. Welcome to the family, Scottie, finally, eh? Family. About bloody time!" And he gave Nicole a brotherly kiss.

Nicole bit her tongue to stop herself bringing up all of Will's own failed relationships. That list would take all night to run through and the party had only just begun, but she couldn't resist one jibe.

"You're the last person to point the finger about relationships, Will," she said.

"I deserve that, Nic. Fair enough. But I'm a changed man, you know. Working on it, anyway."

"Good luck to you, Will," said Scottie, as he held Nicole tighter around the waist.

James gave a wonderful speech about how he couldn't be more pleased to officially welcome Scottie into the Huntley family as a brother-in-law.

The music began, and Scottie held out his hand for her, for the bridal waltz. They'd practised for this moment in Nicole's kitchen, but nothing had prepared her for dancing without tripping on the hem of her long dress. Awkward, even on her wedding day! Embarrassment flushed her face and chest bright red, with all eyes upon them as they missed the beat

59

and stumbled. Scottie caught her in his strong arms and leaned close to brush his lips to hers. He kissed her again as their friends and family applauded.

"I love you, Nicole," he said, his voice a low buzz near her ear. "Just enjoy this, enjoy it with me."

She let him hold her close, tight around her waist, let him lead her around the polished floor, till joy bubbled up in her, and she relaxed and smiled, then laughed as he whirled her faster and faster and they settled into the swing of it.

Their single friends made bee-lines for James and Will, as if not much had changed since they were all in their teens, when her brothers were the hottest school formal dates in the whole of the Eastern Suburbs. They'd even scored a few invitations in the deep north, across the Sydney Harbour Bridge.

There was Stella at the side of the room, watching on as James danced with one old friend after another. It was old Jim who walked over to offer Stella a slow dance.

When James cut in, Jim headed towards Nicole, while Scottie approached Cynthia for a dance.

"Happy day, Nicole," said Jim. "I'm so proud of you, beautiful bride. Every happiness to you both."

"Thanks, Jim!"

And they were happy—overjoyed.

The guests' congratulations and best wishes swept her up in a cloud of ecstasy that lasted for weeks afterwards. Just being with Scottie was so right—pure joy.

They honeymooned in the wineries of northern Victoria, and then settled back into life in Sydney together, but then things changed.

And then the honeymoon stopped.

Nicole couldn't work out why her discontent began. Sure, she wasn't alone anymore, but Scottie was often late, or busy on the phone or computer when he was at home.

A couple of times, she tried asking him to leave his work at work so they could enjoy the evening together.

"I'm sorry, Nicole," he said. "This is important. You'll understand soon."

"Is it something to do with Huntleys?" she said, dread pooling in her stomach.

"I can't say too much, sorry. Please trust me."

Nicole booked them a snap holiday to Vanuatu, hoping it would bring back the magic, but when they returned, the secret conversations with James continued.

The next evening, Nicole insisted she and Scottie drop everything and go for a walk without their phones.

They trekked in step up the headland. Suddenly Nicole stopped and pulled on Scottie's arm till he spun around towards her.

"What's wrong?" he said.

"I never want to forget how much I love you," she said.

And he did it. He smiled down, his warm brown eyes taking in the whole of her. He held out his arms, and when she laid her head on his chest and closed her eyes, he wrapped his arms around her as if he cherished her. And then? He kissed her.

But even then he wouldn't tell her what it was he discussed with James night after night.

Chapter 10

A week later Nicole stood in the doorway as Scottie flicked the switch for the data projector on the far wall of the Scott & Sons Accountants boardroom and fine-tuned the image.

She balanced two takeaway coffees—one for herself, and one for Scottie. Slim and handsome in his business attire, he was efficient, focused on preparing for this surprise meeting. Was he also on edge?

He flicked his dark hair out of his eyes, then flashed her an apologetic grin that spun her heart sideways.

Scottie steadfastly refused to tell her why James had called this first ever "formal" meeting of the whole Huntley family.

"You understand, Nic," said Scottie. "As the firm's financial advisor, I can't say a word."

"Secret Squirrel," Nicole called it. Nicole had worked in the family business nearly a decade, almost as long as James, looking after marketing and branding, but Scottie, as the company's financial advisor, answered to James, and not to her. If she'd assumed marriage would change his attitude, she'd been wrong.

She loved Scottie. How could she not? He'd adored her for ever and she'd only recently discovered she could accept his love, and return it. But every time he said "conflict of interest" with that apologetic smile, her annoyance grew.

"You'll find out soon," he kept telling her. "Soon" was now in about two minutes, according to the old Scott & Sons clock, high on the wall above the screen. She placed the cup in front of him and found herself a seat, then stood again and reached out to help him set up. Someone had already placed a jug of water and some glasses at the head of the table. While Scottie fiddled with the videoconferencing controls, she slid a copy of the one-page agenda and a bright blue Scott & Sons pen in front of the other seats.

"Cynthia, great to see you!" There'd been no guarantees that Scottie's video conference installation would synchronize with Cynthia's House of Clubs laptop in the south of France.

"I told you our village was no longer a 'zone blanche' or 'dead spot,' Scottie," said the stylish Cynthia, fixing her French uptwist.

"Remember to phone me if there's any problem, please, Cynthia," Scottie said, holding up his mobile. "You'll still be able to hear what's going on, and I'll put you on 'speaker' so we can all hear you."

"Hi, Mum," said Nicole.

Cynthia stopped fiddling with stray strands of hair. She covered a small yawn with the back of her fingers and smiled back.

"Hello, darling," she said. "Sorry about all the yawns. It's only seven o'clock here. Our shop doesn't open until at least ten." Émile peeped into the screen, his hand on her shoulder. Cynthia patted it. She looked well despite the yawns—more content than ever. France must suit her, or was it Émile's influence?

"I have Émile to thank for all my technical expertise, don't I, darling?" said Cynthia. She smiled up at him. "It's okay if Émile stays for the meeting, isn't it, Scottie? Lovely to see you both! We're all just so thrilled the two of you are finally together, you know."

"Thanks, Mum."

"Is Will joining us? What time is it for you in Sydney, and in the US? Is Stella there? I have a new shipment of watch chains for her to repair, some truly beautiful ones we found near Toulouse! So how are you, Nicole? Scottie? Now, what's all this about?"

Nicole leaned forward towards the video camera to show off her coral pink nails. One side of her head was covered in tiny braids, secured with elastics with little frangipanis.

"We loved Vanuatu, Mum," said Nicole. "I wish we were still there. No point asking me about this meeting, though. I've been asking Scottie for days, and he won't say a word."

Scottie pressed "mute" and turned to her.

"We've been through this, Nic," he said. "As Huntleys' financial advisor I'm bound by strict confidentiality requirements. It's up to James to run this meeting. He's the CEO. I'm only your facilitator."

"Okay, okay," said Nicole. She tapped her pink nails on the shiny surface of the table and took a sip of coffee. But it wasn't okay. Not really. As surely as her holiday tan faded, her husband had become elusive.

Scottie exhaled again, just as old Jim Huntley entered the room. Nicole's grandfather had never appeared more dignified. Jim rarely left the top of the store in Bondi Junction where he still made most of the engagement rings, his one-off treasures which were becoming collectors' items. But today, he'd taken off his jeweler's apron and donned the suit he'd worn to Scottie and Nicole's wedding. With his white hair brushed and those blazing blue eyes, he retained a charisma that came over brilliantly on social media. No wonder his video clips on "gem of the month" kept gaining followers. Nicole credited Jim's videos with helping drive Huntleys' online sales.

Jim gave his granddaughter a hug. She offered him her coffee. She should have thought of him sooner, but it wasn't as if she'd even known he'd turn up. This whole meeting was a mystery to her.

"No need," he said. "I prefer instant, my way. Let me get my own."

Nicole watched closely as Scottie and Jim shook hands. Did Jim know anything more about the meeting than she did? Jim's grip was always firm and his fingers raspy from a lifetime of working with gold, silver, gems and sharp tools. Jim met Scottie's eyes, but there was nothing special about that. He was from the era when business was done on a handshake. He'd been the one to drill into her the importance of eye contact with customers. Jim released Scottie's hand and turned to make his own coffee along the side wall.

He took his seat and nodded at Nicole and Scottie, then squinted at the screen and waved at Cynthia and Émile, just as Will appeared onscreen, beaming in from his home above his own Huntleys store in Nevada, the desert sky dark out the window behind him.

"Hey, Jim! How are you?" said Will. Nicole and James's wayward brother was supposedly making a fresh start in the US. "Still punching out those beautiful rings, Jim? I love your podcast by the way. Stroke of genius. You've got quite a following here in the US."

"Will, my boy!" said Jim. "My fingers still work, don't they? I can still see. But I'm glad to have those apprentices. They're getting the hang of it. Especially that Stella, senior apprentice and supervisor. She has the gift alright. Now. You keeping your eye on the prize, son?"

"Sure am, Jim," His voice dropped. "Hey, I need to talk to you about a ring, for Lisa."

Jim's eyes lit up.

Scottie's phone rang. It was Cynthia.

"The sound's dropped out, Scottie. I can't hear Will or Jim."

"My apologies, Mrs Huntley. How's this? Can you hear us now?"

Cynthia nodded and smiled as they all swapped greetings.

In strode James, a vital, vibrant, younger copy of Jim, in a pale gray suit. He eased his finger into his collar and undid the top button. He pulled off his signature blue tie, then rolled and tucked it into his breast pocket. James scanned the room and screen as he took his seat at the head of the table, his eyes searching first Jim's and then Nicole's, before flicking to his mother and Will on the screen, and back to Scottie with a nod.

He looked at his watch.

"Where's Stella, James darling?" said Cynthia.

"She's still in the store, Mum," said James. "It's Thursday night shopping. Now, I'm conscious it's late in the US, and I don't want to waste anyone's time. Thank you all for joining us at such short notice, and my thanks to Scottie here for making this boardroom available to us so our US and French branches are properly represented."

Nicole smiled proudly at Scottie, then frowned. This was a fine room, with its rich wooden paneling and deep red carpet, old fashioned, yet, with its video conferencing facility, contemporary too, a bit like her husband. Actually it was a great analogy. What did they say about "if the walls could talk …"? But they didn't, and nor would Scottie. While she admired his strength of resolve, surely he valued his wife above his fiduciary duties.

Strangest of all was James's formality. It was sinister. Was he nervous? It was as if he were on a great podium giving a political speech, not shooting the breeze with his family, the people he'd lived and worked beside all his life.

An inkling of dread lodged in Nicole's stomach. Had something bad happened? Was he planning to close their business? She swallowed and sat up straighter.

"I'll be the first to say I'm still getting used to having Scottie as a brother-in-law as well as our financial advisor, but I'm indebted to him for helping me prepare for this meeting, and I'll be relying on him in the weeks to come," said James. Scottie nodded in acknowledgement.

"I've called this meeting not only because of the rapid growth of our company to include Mum's House of Clubs in France and Will's House of Hearts in the US, but for another key reason I'll go into shortly."

Nobody moved. James cleared his throat. Fear twisted in Nicole's stomach. Out of nervousness, she took a swig of coffee. It burned her tongue.

"I know this is not an ideal way to conduct a meeting, with some of you videoing in and others here in person, but there isn't time nor spare operating cash to fly you all in," James said. "I'll do my best to ensure that those of you joining remotely will have equal input. Most importantly, this meeting will give you equal time to contemplate our options in the short timeframe we've been given."

"So formal, bro," said Will. "How's things?"

"It's great to see you all but we'll leave general chit chat until after the meeting if that's okay, Will."

Will held up two fingers in the "peace" sign and James nodded his thanks, his face still unreadable.

"Ordinarily, you would have been given twenty one days of notice and a formal agenda," said James. "As it turns out, this is not an Extraordinary General Meeting. At the end of this meeting, however, I will give you notice of an EGM, to be held in twenty one days."

Now every Huntley sat up straighter. Nicole glared at Scottie, eyebrows raised, but Scottie's eyes remained on James, and his pen was poised.

"Scottie, thank you for taking minutes for us," said James. "I declare this meeting open. As far as I know, this is the first formal meeting of the whole family who are involved in Huntleys, and as you know, it's only in the past year or so that we've opened our French and US branches, rendering us international."

James poured some water into a glass and took a sip. Yes. Her confident brother was definitely nervous.

"From my point of view, this global reach and growth is a great development, and, along with the opening of Shop Huntleys Online, a great investment in the strength of our company. However, our rapid expansion hasn't come without cost. I thank Scottie for continuing to sort out the tax implications for us. You need to know there have been unforeseen expenses at a time when our earnings have been erratic. It's not necessarily cause for concern. All businesses face challenges as they grow."

James took another sip of water. Nicole wished he'd cut the formality and share a joke, but he ploughed on.

"Importantly, recent developments foreshadow the need for us to make some choices about our directions, to become more strategic. This kind of thinking has been lost in the detailed undertaking of our day to day duties and in making the most of our unusual opportunities to expand."

As the marketing manager, Nicole was always inventing strategic plans, most linked to the annual shopping calendar. Was James finally coming around to her point of view that strategy was worthwhile? She raised her eyebrows, but he didn't notice.

"I'll be the first to say that Nicole, Will and I have been extremely fortunate to have inherited the right to be part of Huntleys House of Jewels and to bring the business into the present day. This is a good time to formally thank Jim here for founding our business, and mother, Cynthia, for keeping it running so smoothly after our father died, and then for entrusting Nicole, Will and me with it when she stepped back to focus on her own interests a few years ago."

He took a moment to give eye contact to everyone as he mentioned them. The slow pace was excruciating. It was as if he'd prepared and rehearsed his entire speech. What could possibly be so important that he'd go to all this effort and be so careful?

"Come on, James. What's up? Just tell us, will you?" She couldn't help herself. He shushed her with one hand, palm down, as if to calm her and seek her patience.

"Now, however, we find ourselves with a great many choices to make about our future," he said. "While I could make these decisions on my own, it's only right and fair that we debate and make them together if we possibly can. And this might not be easy. All of us might want different things from Huntleys, and be prepared to invest differing amounts of energy, time and enthusiasm. We must also recognize that our financial advisor, Scottie, is more involved than ever in Huntleys—as he has now married into the family. You'll be aware I've been engaged to Stella for some time; and I hope I'm not out of line in mentioning that Will may also wish to marry and potentially start a family ..."

"Darlings!" said Cynthia. "Oh. This is wonderful news. Is this Lisa, Will?"

"Mum, can I ask you to follow up with Will about personal matters after this meeting, please? I shouldn't have mentioned it now. Apologies, Will."

Will gave a thumbs up.

"Sorry, James, darling," said Cynthia. "I've interrupted."

"The thing is, it's time that we made some of our casual structure and operations more formal," said James. "Huntleys is still a family company, but in the past, emphasis has been more on 'family,' whereas in the future, we need it to be more on 'company.' Are you with me?"

Everyone nodded. Cynthia pursed her lips. Nicole tried to catch Scottie's eye, but he was busy taking notes as James spoke. Nicole wasn't sure. She certainly didn't want James to behave like this in the future, like a bore.

"Again I apologize for the rushed nature of this meeting, but there's been a development I need to share with you." All eyes were on James.

"Huntleys has had a buyout offer," said James, his face unreadable. "I'm going to lay out the bare facts of the matter. Importantly, I still need to put information together with Scottie's help so that you all have the same relevant facts when you make your own decisions."

Around the table and on screen, expressions froze.

"Ultimately, we have to make a joint decision about this within four weeks, so we'll meet again in three weeks," said James. "If we can't reach a consensus then, we'll have to vote. If it's a split decision, as CEO, I'll make the call."

Everyone talked at once.

Chapter 11

"I don't like the sound of this at all!" said Cynthia.

"How much?" said Will.

"Seen it before," said old Jim in his gravelly voice. He finished emptying the sugar into his mug and stirred it. "Who's offering?"

"GGT International," said Scottie. "Gem and Gold Traders, headquartered in Switzerland. They deal in luxury goods. They say they want to acquire Huntleys to continue their global expansion. All terms are negotiable; stock, buildings, people and brand."

"No," said Cynthia. She sat straighter, eyes closed, shaking her head. "You can't seriously consider this, James. You know Émile was forced to close his family's hardware store in Brussels when he was bought out by just such a company."

"How did we even show up on their radar?" Will said.

"We don't know exactly," said James. "Our new international status? Web presence, Stella's non-stop ideas, Nicole's efforts on social media and Jim's podcast on the revamped website have really grown awareness of our brand, and the new online sales hub is sensational, thanks to the expertise of Stella's sister, Jeannie."

"My market research shows Huntleys is front of mind," said Nicole, tapping one of the plastic frangipanis with her pen.

"What poll is that, Nic?" said Will. "Your old school friends?"

"Haha, Will. Shop Huntleys Online runs evaluations after every online sale and about 10 per cent of our customers answer extra polls to give feedback on Stella's new lines in exchange for first dibs on specials."

"Is GGT even a legitimate company?" said Cynthia. "Of course Huntleys would be a great acquisition for any company, but we haven't even had ourselves valued. We can't just let them snatch it away from us. I for one do not want to sell, especially now everything is going so well. Huntleys is us. It's our lives—Jim's especially, and mine. And it's your future, my darlings—yours and your future children's."

"How much are they offering?" said Will again. "At least let's get the facts."

In the Scott & Sons boardroom, all faces turned to Will. Was he gambling again? Why else would he be so interested in the money?

"It's too soon to share that detail at this stage, Will," said James. "As Mum said, we need to be fully aware of our own value before we compare it with what we're being offered. I need to clearly set out all the details of our assets and liabilities so that all of us can judge whether the GGT offer has any merit. If there is an appetite for selling Huntleys, there may be better offers out there for us. Let's hear what Jim has to say. What happened last time, Jim?"

"Oh, some hopeful or other gives it a go every decade or so," said Jim, slowly stirring the sugar in his coffee. "Offers come. Offers go. Huntleys endures."

"I like that," said Nic. "We could use that as a tagline. It's good for jewelry. Diamonds last forever ..."

"Not much point if we're just going to sell," said Will. On the screen, half a world away, his eyes gleamed.

"Go on, Jim," said James.

"There was a bit of jostling back at the end of the fifties when the tram line was pulled up," said Jim. "And again in the seventies when the train line came, and again every time a new mall opened. Never stops really. Change happens. At one stage our building was going to be a pinball arcade, and then we had an offer from a video rental chain. These fashions come and go, but people still want jewelry."

"I vote 'no,'" said Cynthia.

"We're not making that decision today, Mum," said James. "We have to study the offer carefully. They want to tell us more about their company. Here in Sydney, they've offered to take us to dinner tonight, those of us who are available, so I'll have to close this meeting shortly."

"They're already telling you what to do," said Cynthia. "Please, James. Just say 'no.'"

"It could be in everyone's best interests to accept this offer, Mum. We need to see the details. I undertake to share with all of you everything I learn about them and all the details of their offer, alongside relevant facts about Huntleys, ahead of our EGM in three weeks, so we can work this out together. Scottie is already working on laying out a broad list of five-year options for us to discuss. We'll send you the information once we've finalized it. It will include financial statements, so that you can consider the ramifications of keeping the business, as well as where we would all stand financially were we to accept the GGT offer."

"But not everything comes down to money," said Cynthia. "Remember that. We're a family, not just a business!" She adjusted her colorful round glasses on her nose, and peered closer to check all were listening. Émile's hand disappeared from her shoulder and his face came into view again as he kneeled beside her and embraced her with one long arm.

"Who has voting rights?" said Jim. "Does Scottie have a say? And what about Stella, as your fiancée? Surely she deserves a vote. What about Lorna and our other long-term employees? Huntleys is a big part of their lives, too. What will happen to our apprentices? What about Émile? He and Cynthia both run House of Clubs, don't they?"

"These are good questions, Jim, and I don't have all the answers at this stage," said James. "I want to know what all of you think, and I'll answer your questions as well as I can, but right now I need to get back to GGT and let them know how many of us are joining them for dinner this evening. Nicole, Scottie, Jim?"

"Seen it all before," said Jim. "All that wining and dining. Watch out. They'll try to get you drunk and then take advantage. Listen, but don't say too much. Knowledge is power. The less they know about us the better, at this stage, anyway. The phrase 'none of your business' springs to mind. Nicole, Scottie and James, if you're eating at their table, remember that. They're not your friends."

"Great advice, thank you, Jim," said James. "We'll remember it. 'Keep your friends close; keep your enemies closer.' We need to understand them better, and scrutinize their offer. We'll be glad to have you with us this evening, Jim. Your experience is invaluable. We must wrap up the meeting now."

Nicole stared at Scottie. Scottie stared back. Beyond asking her to keep this night free, her husband hadn't mentioned a thing about GGT. That was weird. Even now, he dropped his eyes from hers and busied himself with the equipment.

Why all the secrecy?

Chapter 12

As Stella locked up Huntleys House of Diamonds in Bondi Junction that evening, the grand old building was strangely silent. Nicole was nowhere to be seen, and even Jim must be out, with no lights on at the top where he lived. His television was silent, and his design studio was firmly locked.

Stella knew without looking that the Huntleys office would be shut—James had told her he had a meeting—but she checked it anyway as she made her way down the stairs, turning off lights and ensuring no one was stuck in the lift. The old rattler was beautiful, but ancient and unpredictable.

James phoned as she walked home through the plaza to their apartment.

"Thanks for minding the store, Stella," he said. "How's it been?"

"Decent," she said. "Quite busy—a big day all in all. How was your meeting?"

"I need to tell you about it, Stell, but first, how are you placed this evening? Can you come for dinner?"

"Is this a date? I'd love that, James, thank you. It's been so long since we've been out together—just the two of us. It's been a bit 'all work and no play' to tell you the truth. It'll be lovely to have you all to myself across the table, and someone else doing the cooking."

"Ah, Stell. I agree, I agree, but this evening's not exactly going to be just the two of us. In fact, we'll all be there—Jim, Nicole and Scottie—and some people from Switzerland. I'll tell you about it as we drive. See you at the apartment?"

"Okay." A little stab of disappointment rose inside her as she quickened her step. She longed for time alone with her fiancé, and this was probably just a supplier event. If she was quick enough, there might be time for a shower, to freshen up. This day seemed to have gone on forever.

James was already showered and dressed for dinner when she arrived. He smelled of aftershave. He inserted cuff links into a dress shirt. There was just time to run her hand over his shoulder, and lean in for a quick kiss. He grabbed her fingers and kissed them.

"Swanky?" she said.

"Definitely. It's the degustation menu at the Bathers' Pavilion at Balmoral Beach."

"That's on the northside, isn't it?"

He nodded.

Stella rushed through the shower and pulled on an outfit she'd bought in Singapore when she'd sold off some of her Stellar designs at an international jewelry fair, just before James proposed to her. The emerald satin dress with a scoop neck, cap sleeves and a cinched-in waist was glamorous. She didn't normally do glamor. She was more of a sundress kind of person. Her dark, curly hair was wet. There was just time to twist it into a tight bun and secure it with a string of diamantes. That should do; and she grabbed her highest heels.

As they cruised down Syd Einfeld Drive into town and across the Sydney Harbour Bridge on their way to the popular north shore harbor beach, James was preoccupied. This evening he was even more silent than usual. Was he nervous?

"So who are they, and what are they trying to sell us?" she said.

"Oh. No. They're actually trying to buy us. GGT International."

"Pardon?"

"We've had a buyout offer."

Stella twisted in her seat to stare at James.

"This is huge, James," she said, her heart pounding. How could James mention it so casually? "When did this happen? When were you going to tell me?"

"Scottie and I were approached a few weeks ago, initially by phone, by the GGT lawyers. It's complicated, Stell. I had to tell the family all at once. I have to catch you up on this. I'm sorry you couldn't be at the meeting this evening but I had to be fair with everyone, and you were the best person to mind the shop."

It was Stella's turn to be silent. "Mind the shop." Is that all she was to James; someone peripheral; a salesperson? She gripped her seatbelt and tried to quieten the little voice of resentment inside her. Was she wrong to be so offended? Maybe, but weren't they a couple? Why had he not mentioned this to her sooner? Didn't he trust her to keep silent? Were they actually partners, or not? She eased one foot in and out of a shoe. The traffic crawled along Military Road. James kept checking his watch.

Stella's mouth was dry. Her voice came out small.

"And are you … going to sell?"

"I don't know yet. It's not just my decision. Mum's against it at this stage. Jim wants us to be careful and just listen to what they have to say without revealing too much tonight. Will's always been keen on money, so he might want to sell. I don't know about Nicole and Scottie. Well, Nicole's the shareholder. Whoever knows what Nicole wants from one day to the next?"

Stella nodded slowly. Eighteen months ago, Nicole and Stella had been enemies. When Stella set up her faux jewelry stall outside Huntleys in the mall, Nicole tried to close her down, but when she and James had fallen in love, and Stella joined Huntleys, they'd put their enmity behind them.

She and Nicole often worked together on ideas for Shop Huntleys Online, now run by Stella's sister, Jeannie. Their working relationship was healthy even if they weren't necessarily best friends. Only that week, in front of the apprentices, Nicole told Stella she respected her creativity and work ethic.

"Did Nicole know about this, James?"

"I don't think so. Scottie and I agreed to wait to let everyone know at the same time, in tonight's meeting, to be fair to everyone. We have three weeks now to do our research, look at our options and make a decision."

"Everyone but me," she said as a bus roared past. Did he hear her? She studied his profile, the sun bleached brown hair, the tiny worry lines on his handsome brow, less obvious than the smile lines at his eyes she'd fallen in love with. Did this explain his recent silences?

She sighed and studied the shops as they crawled along—shoe shops, dog grooming, exercise wear, a rival jeweler—then glared at James again. Surely he could have mentioned something to her sooner. He was a good man, but didn't living and working together mean anything to him? Surely he knew he could trust her to say nothing to anyone, if that was the issue.

Her appetite disappeared. James was admirable. One of the things she loved most about him was his loyalty to his family, but how could he have shut her out like this? When had he been going to let her know? If GGT hadn't invited them for dinner, would he have told her at all?

"And will I have any say in the decision?" Her voice was small. They zigzagged through the back streets of Mosman where bankers lived, past the jaw dropping mix of heritage, tastefully renovated and architect designed houses, each vying for the best of the harbor views.

"Turn right on Awaba Street," said the car.

"What was that?" said James.

"I know I'm not a shareholder or anything," she said. "But I care what happens to Huntleys."

They pulled up at the waterfront. The sea glistened silver ahead of them to the horizon, framed by the two headlands, North and South Head.

James slid the car into an empty space, unclipped his seatbelt, and gave her a dose of his blue eyes and one of those smiles that melted her heart. He sprang out and around to open her door. He held out his hand like a gentleman, which was helpful, given the height of her heels. His warmth was always reassuring, but he hadn't answered her question.

The Bathers' Pavilion was to their right, an art deco building like a wedding cake, separated from the beach by a promenade. Tiny waves lapped at the shore. A pelican floated nearby as an abandoned sand castle slowly dissolved into the sea.

In the pavilion, many meals were already under way at the candlelit tables, the fragrance of seafood and exotic spices a hint of the menu on offer.

Stella recognised Jim, Nicole and Scottie standing with tall strangers at one side of the building. As they approached, silent waiters offered them a tray of drinks in beautiful glasses.

James was in his element. For Stella, who'd grown up in poverty, this evening would be an effort. She would have preferred a barefoot stroll along the beach, with James to herself and simple fish and chips in a takeout box. For now, she accepted a glass of French champagne, determined to take small sips. She wanted to keep her wits about her.

She plastered on the smile she'd worn all day and allowed herself to be introduced.

"Call me Wolf," said the slimmest of the men, with a slight German accent. He practically clicked his heels together as he took her hand, as if he might kiss it.

Despite herself, she was impressed.

"Delighted to meet you, Stella," said Wolf. "Allow me to introduce Carl; and Eric."

Charming. Their grooming was impeccable. Stella noticed details. Their watches were slim and expensive—the brands she'd seen in an airline magazine. Their shoes were shiny, their suits hand stitched.

"Enchanted," said Eric.

"I believe we've met," said Carl. "Singapore."

Stella narrowed her eyes. She'd met a bewildering array of buyers at that international fair.

"Stella of Stellar, are you not?" His voice was lower, almost seductive. Carl touched his glass to hers and gave her a slight smile.

"I underbid on your designs. I pay the price now, yah?" He chuckled and touched her elbow. Stella shivered.

"I'd love to hear more about GGT, Carl, and why you're interested in Huntleys."

"And what exactly is your role with Huntleys, Stella?"

James appeared at her side.

"Ah, I see you've met my fiancée," said James.

"Enchanting. Yes. This is your talented Stella. I believe we met in Singapore. And see this view! It reminds me of Lake Geneva, but we are landlocked as you know, whereas you, you are connected to the great ocean. Are there sharks?" He laughed, revealing a gold tooth. "It is a privilege to be here. Shall we eat?"

Waiters reappeared and ushered them upstairs to a private balcony and a long white-clothed table sparkling with fine glasses and silverware.

Stella was seated beside Carl, with Jim on his other side, Scottie and Nicole opposite, and James at the head of the table, flanked by Eric and Wolf. Wolf nodded to her, then turned his attention to James as the waiters rotated, shaking out more crisp white linen across their laps.

"So how long are you in Sydney, Carl?" said Stella.

"As long as it takes," he said, all seriousness. And then laughed. His eyes didn't laugh.

"And what a wonderful role you must have, traveling the globe and snapping up jewelry stores and fresh designs."

"Oh no. Not at all," he said. He patted his stomach. "Too much good food and wine. It is a tax on the body, is it not?"

"I can't imagine," said Stella. Her mother had struggled to feed Stella and her older sister, Jeannie, for most of their childhood. How much small talk would be required this evening?

A waiter poured rosé into one of her glasses just as a white bowl was slipped in front of her. On it hovered a shaving of something black, floating in a teaspoon of pale pink froth.

"To Huntleys House of Jewels," said Carl.

"And to GGT International," said James.

"Bon appetit," said Eric.

Stella caught Nicole's eye as they lifted their glasses. There was much waving of glasses and eye contact and polite smiling on all sides. Nicole lifted her eyebrows at Stella, who mirrored her gesture. They'd discuss all this later, she hoped.

Wolf drained his glass and took up his fork with a flourish, the rest of them following suit.

Ten courses later, Stella's head was spinning, despite the fact she'd barely sipped from any of the many glasses of fine wines. The food had been delicious, it was true, but better still were the morsels she'd picked up about GGT and their companions.

The company was rapidly expanding ahead of listing on the stock exchange. They wanted stock and talent but mostly they wanted "global reach" both online and with properties—jewelry salons.

It was Carl who'd discovered Huntleys and researched Stella on the internet—or so he said. He learned of her winning the inaugural Huntleys

Valentine's Day design prize online, and discovered she was serving her full apprenticeship in goldsmithing with Jim Huntley the First.

As he turned to speak to Jim, Stella took herself to the restroom and contemplated "global reach." It was as if a great metal robotic hand had stretched out from GGT headquarters in Lausanne and clutched at the back of her neck to render her a helpless kitten in its powerful grip.

She shook her head, reapplied some lipstick and determined to grill Carl upon her return.

Carl had begun his career working in fine arts. He'd been headhunted to GGT from a well-known auction house.

"Jewelry is art, after all," he said. "True collectors know this. The value of a piece accrues. It is not just the value of the gold and the gems within it. Most importantly, it is the way they are positioned which enhances their beauty, like the exquisite beauty of a woman, which cannot be explained in any other way. All have eyes, nose, mouth, chin, neck, yet each woman is unique, is she not?"

She placed her fingers at her neck, where Carl had stared. Creepy.

"Oh you'd have no argument with Jim here, Carl," said Stella. "He even calls his jewels his 'ladies.'"

"I do believe we understand each other." Carl smiled. Stella's lips smiled back but she refused to be flattered.

Another course was laid in front of them, a square of caramelized pork belly on a bed of alternating strips of what looked like beetroot and gherkin.

"But I can't agree with you, Carl," she said. "For me, it's not the shape of a person's face which matters. It's the kindness of a smile, the ideas behind the eyes …"

"Ah yes. You must let me complete my theory, Stella. So a true judge of jewelry sees beyond even the shape of the piece and the positioning of the elements, to appreciate the history of it, the talent behind its creation, both the design and the implementation. And for the most valuable pieces in the world, here is the 'value add'—their provenance. It is the actual designer who is shown, for, like a great work of art, there are limited works each can create in their one lifetime, are there not? The value of a Rembrandt is not just the fact that every square centimeter of every work evokes such emotion in the viewer, and that each remains so lifelike century after century—it is the very rarity of these works which fetches millions. Great jewelry carries just such value."

Now he was trying to flatter her design expertise.

"But we can copy those pieces, even in plastic and glass," she said.

"Ah yes. You began your career in 'faux', did you not? And yes, there is much to be said of jewelry for the masses, but I speak now of masterpieces, Stella."

"Of course," she said.

Did she want Huntleys to be swallowed up by the grasping tentacles of giant GGT? Should she care that Huntleys might disappear forever?

A wave of anger rose in her gut that James hadn't done more to prepare her. She was out of her depth—just another tiny pawn in GGT's global game.

Why hadn't James said something to her? Why this sudden announcement from him about tonight's dinner? Was it already a done deal? Was everything she'd worked for since falling for James so expendable? What kind of idiot was she to be spending every waking moment building up James's business, only to have him sell it like this at the drop of an offer?

Stella had already relocated, from Perth to Sydney, to run away from a boss who'd taken her for granted. She'd set up her own business, Stellar, to take charge of her own destiny, only to fall in love with James and redirect all of her focus on him and his business. What kind of life was she living? Had it all been a terrible mistake?

As the dishes changed from savory to sweet, the GGT representatives rose in unison and rotated their seating positions clockwise around the table. The waiters stepped forward with fresh champagne flutes and presented a magnum to Wolf who now was seated on Stella's left after giving all his attention to James for most of the night.

Stella tried to catch James's eye, but his head was turned to Carl, on his right. They were nodding about something.

"No," said Wolf to the young waiter. "I said the 2007 Louis Roederer. The Cristal."

As the young man scurried away, Stella felt sorry for him. The noise of the other diners rose with the mix of their perfumes and surrounded her, cloying. She didn't want to be here. When the sommelier returned with the correct bottle, Wolf merely nodded, then insisted on tasting it first and taking his time to register his approval as the sommelier sweated. It was a fine performance of power, but if it was meant to impress Stella, it had the opposite effect. She left her glass untouched, even when Wolf proposed a toast to "Huntleys and to GGT!"

Her temples ached. She pinched the top of her nose and tried to focus. Wolf beamed at her.

"Brilliant designer," he said. "We can put you in touch with the best in the industry. Our investment in Computer Aided Design is the best in the world. We'll fly you across for training. We only take and keep the best graduates, but news of your talent precedes you, Stella. We could make an exception."

It was as if she wasn't even there, or as if she were some jewel they could simply trade at will—not a living, breathing human with a soul and agency and dreams of her own. Had James already agreed to sell Huntleys? Was she part of the package? Is that what they'd been discussing in such detail?

"Do excuse me," she said, pushing out her chair. "I just need some air."

She caught Wolf's patronizing smile at James as she fled for the door and the cool night. The waterfront beckoned and she kicked off her shoes and ran down to the edge of the waves. A disc of the moon rose from the plane of the sea. Soothing water lapped at her ankles as she wandered to the northern end of the beach, inhaling the briny freshness to steady her mind and emotions.

She turned and stared at the golden rectangles of all the houses with harbor and beach views, wondering at all the invisible dramas and intrigues inside these homes. The Bathers' Pavilion was no different, with her fate being debated by strangers.

Even if James was willing to listen to her views, and so far he'd told her precious little, would the rest of the family still want to sell out? Nicole had made no secret of the fact she'd resented Stella's little stall and unexpected success, seeing her as a threat from the very start, and Scottie was an accountant, a numbers man. Will had cash flow problems all his life, from what James had told her of his younger brother. You had to be brave to declare your soul was not for sale at any price. Stella had lived the reality of such freedom. As children, she and her sister Jeannie had been semi-nomadic, subject to the whims of their mother, Flame—free but not easy. Would she, too, become a wanderer? If James was taking her for granted, she'd do well to consider her options.

Those Swiss businessmen might think they knew everything about jewelry, but they didn't. Jewelry was about far more than money. It was about meaning. Working side by side with Jim in evaluations, repairs and remodeling these past few months, Stella knew every piece was far more than the sum of its parts, not just because of who had made it, but because of where it had been given, and by whom, and why. Jewels were loaded with emotion, especially heirlooms—jewels regifted. They carried stories—of lost loves, of relatives long gone, and of times past. The fashion of their era was an echo cast in gold or silver.

Now, she could almost predict a remodeling job. These jewels were handed over with frowns, with memories of grudging stepmothers, disapproving mothers in law, or husbands who'd turned their backs on a marriage or tried to buy forgiveness for straying. It was as if by redesigning the settings, by committing the gold to the crucible, the owner could melt and banish sour memories and start afresh with a jewel as shiny and full of promise as a new day.

How could GGT even hope to put a value on a service like that?

She arrived back in time for the polite goodbyes. So much bowing and smiling. So many secrets behind all their eyes, not just the GGT trio, but Nicole and Scottie, not to mention Jim and James.

Wolf took her elbow, leaned down and whispered in her ear.

"So glad to make your acquaintance, Stella," Wolf said. "GGT looks after talent."

She shivered, willing James to come to her side, but he was busy inviting Jim to travel back with them. At least that was the right thing to do. She loved the way James showed Jim respect. Surely James was still the good man she'd fallen in love with.

She headed for the back seat, like an invisible child. James opened the rear door for her and she collapsed into it. Despite the walk, she'd eaten so much she felt ill. All that food had been a particular torture after such a long day. Maybe that was part of the GGT acquisition plan—the twenty-first century affluent equivalent of starving out a castle in order to invade.

"What did you think, Jim?" said James.

"Plenty of talk. I'd like to see the paperwork. What did you think, Stella?" said Jim. "They paid you plenty of attention."

"I couldn't help thinking of vultures," said Stella. "Very refined ones. Well spoken, well dressed. Super polite. But vultures. Don't get me wrong. Maybe you want to sell out, Jim. I suppose I don't mind either way. I care about designing. But I don't even understand why they want us. What are we? Well, you're a star and that's for sure, Jim, and Huntleys HQ is charming, but the building is so old. You know there's another leak in the tearoom window? And Cynthia and Will's branches are so new, surely GGT could simply set up their own new stores for a similar price, couldn't they?"

"I don't know," said James. "It's early days, Stella. I don't know what I want, and I need to take into account what the others want. Your questions are great. We all need to explore all the options. I have to be honest. This offer is forcing us all to re-evaluate in a very short time. I'm glad Scottie's drawing up that list of five-year strategic plans for us. As far as I know, it's the first time in Huntleys' history. How far ahead did you ever look, Jim?"

"About as far as Eleanor's smile, my boy." Eleanor's parents had owned the building and run it as a department store when she and Jim had fallen in love. With hats and gloves going out of style, and Jim's growing reputation as a jeweler, together they'd created Huntleys House of Jewels.

Jim held himself tall as he got out of the car at the back entrance of Huntleys, but Stella sensed his weariness. He must be in his eighties, and what a day they'd all had, even before the dinner. For a moment a flash of anger burst inside her. What right had GGT to demand they all traipse out for such an extensive dinner on a working night? Maybe their plan was to weaken them all with exhaustion and then pounce on a bargain.

"See you in the morning, Jim," she said. "Or I can message the apprentices and tell them their session with you is canceled?"

"I'm an old man, Stella, thanks anyway. I don't need much sleep. Business as usual."

In the lift of the apartment building, James frowned, checked his watch and drew a hand through his hair, turning to yawn widely.

"Would you like the first shower, Stella?"

"You go ahead, James. I'll sit up for a little while. I need to let some of that food go down."

She grabbed her sketchbook and began to draw—a half pearl moon, a spider and a web of gold with a shiny black back of ebony.

When she'd returned from Singapore to Sydney so high on the knowledge that international traders wanted her designs, and James had gone down on his knee to her there and then, she'd had no hesitation in accepting his proposal of marriage.

She'd melted into his arms and embraced their future together. There'd been no chance she wanted to open her Stellar stall out in the mall once more, under the searing sun and storms, with the seagulls and casual thefts.

Sharing her inspiration with James and his family had been easy for her. She had no shortage of ideas, and to her delight, James, Nicole and Jim enacted many of them successfully. It was something to celebrate together.

But now that she was supervising the apprentices, doing extra time serving in Huntleys, and trying to finish her own final goldsmith qualifications, there'd barely been time for fresh ideas. She loved to create, and a life without creativity was hardly a life at all.

Had the sparkle of her relationship with James been snuffed out when she wasn't looking?

Stella thought back over the past months to the pattern of their days. There was so little spare time, and when there was, James was preoccupied.

She drew a silver horizon and a bird flying out to sea. Stella went to show James, but he was already asleep.

Chapter 13

Nearby, in her own apartment, Nicole hung up her evening purse as Scottie headed into the spare bedroom—now their study—without her.

She loved Scottie, no question, but why hadn't he told her in advance about the afternoon's meeting, the buyout offer, and the extravagant GGT dinner? Nicole knew things could happen quickly in business and one had to be ready to take a chance, but it was clear Scottie and James had known about this offer weeks ago. Why all the secrecy? She sighed. Nicole really needed to discuss this whole buyout thing with her new husband, and surely he needed to discuss it with her.

As she prepared for bed, her mind replayed James's announcement and all the snippets of conversation at that crazy excessive dinner.

Carl had mentioned something about opportunities in GGT's marketing department for her, before banging on about opportunities to ski in Switzerland. He hadn't done his homework on her. She'd never skied in her life and was afraid of heights. Even flying to Vanuatu had been traumatic, until Scottie had insisted she drink two pina coladas and go to sleep.

"I haven't had a chance to see your proposal yet, Carl, but thank you anyway," she'd said, trying to listen in on Eric and Scottie's conversation—something about "proportional representation."

The coach clock Scottie's parents had given them for their wedding struck midnight. Only twenty days now before decision time.

Did she want to sell? She enjoyed the pace of her days at Huntleys, trying out new ideas, endless research, objectives, planning and evaluation. She loved her evenings with Scottie, with ice cream on the couch watching rubbish television. He was amenable to everything. She adored loving him and being loved in return.

But the meeting about the buyout offer rattled her, and that fancy degustation dinner, even more.

She stood in the doorway of the study, caught his eye and asked.

"What will happen to Huntleys, Scottie?"

"What do you mean?"

"Surely you know what I mean," Nicole said. She respected his professionalism, but keeping a poker face with his own wife? She refused to back away from it. "Jim's not getting any younger. And you—as financial advisor, you're right in the thick of the decision making, and yet technically, you don't get any say at all, do you? It's not fair, when you contribute so much. Are you on a retainer? Shouldn't you have some equity? What's our structure, Scottie? As my husband, surely you're entitled to some share of our family's company. You're family now. What are our options? You and James don't tell me much, do you? I do my monthly marketing reports, but I never see any of yours. I want transparency. It's only fair. Without the Huntleys' brand—my department—there'd be so much less to sell."

"It's true the branding's important, and without your efforts Huntleys would be relatively unknown, Nic," said Scottie. "But you must know there's still plenty of value in Huntleys without the brand. There's the real estate for starters, and the value of the stock, and the human capital."

"Who owns the French premises? And the Nevada store?"

"It's complicated."

"Don't patronise me, Scottie. I just want the answers. It's not really a conflict of interest thing, is it? I'm a Huntley, too. James might be CEO, but there's nothing to say he's more important than I am. As marketing manager, I'm important, too. It was my father who told me that, before he died. He told me he was clumsy, like me, that he couldn't make the jewelry, but there's so much more to a business than product. 'You can make all the jewelry in the world but it's no use to anyone if they don't know where to find it; if someone doesn't plant the idea in their heads they might want it,' he said. 'It's the marketer's role to help create meaning around the sparkles.' I'll never forget what he said, that jewelry's a powerful treasure, that it carries love and promises, it creates and deepens the relationships people need in their lives, that it's the closest thing to magic.'"

"Your father wasn't wrong, Nicole, and I've never said your work's not important."

"It's not like we have a formal structure or written job criteria. It's not like we work in a bank or anything, with lines of delegation. Why can't you talk to me?" She hated the whining tone of her voice, but it was there, that frustration, and there was plenty at stake. How could she let "conflict of interest" become a wedge between Scottie and herself all their lives?

Scottie sat back and held up his hands, as if in surrender, but his words didn't match his actions.

"Maybe it's time you did all have formal job descriptions and lines of delegation. We all want answers, Nic, but it's never that simple."

"What's that supposed to mean?"

It was the closest thing to a fight they'd ever had.

"I love you, Nic."

"Well?"

Scottie yawned and rubbed his eyes. Was it fair of her to ask him, at this time of night? Scottie was a creature of habit, like his parents. Dianne had told her their lights went off at 11 o'clock every night. They had all their lights on a timer, so that on the rare occasions they did go away, burglars would never guess. Scottie had more client meetings tomorrow, and all the days after that. It was only Thursday, and Huntleys weren't his only clients. But she needed more.

Scottie stifled another yawn, beckoned her across, rose from his desk, opened his briefcase and pulled out his leather document holder, with a notepad and pen.

He offered her a seat on the edge of the spare bed and sat down beside her. Her pajamas and his suit and the document holder were incongruous. She really should let him finish whatever he was doing and encourage him to get some sleep. She scooched closer to him and gave him a cuddle as he opened the cover and began to draw on the lined paper.

His voice reverberated through his ribcage and into hers. He wrote "Shareholders of Huntleys Pty Ltd" at the top of the page.

"Jim Huntley; Founder," he said, and wrote her grandfather's name directly underneath.

Under that he wrote James Huntley the Third, CEO. Directly under James, he wrote Cynthia Huntley, House of Clubs, France; Nicole Huntley, Marketing Manager; and Will Huntley, House of Hearts, USA.

"What about Stella?" said Nicole.

There was no mention of Stella, James's fiancée. Where once Nicole had found Stella annoying, imagining her an enemy, now she appreciated her. Stella's creativity was essential to the business. She was the never-ending font of ideas Nicole and James could help make happen. Not only that. Stella worked harder than anyone Nicole had ever seen. She served in the store and liaised with her sister, Jeannie, who ran all of the Shop Huntleys Online jewelry lines for different kinds of customers. Stella also supervised Jim's apprentices, the colorful Divandra and shaggy, lackadaisical Shawn; and she was finishing her own apprenticeship with Jim, for full goldsmithing accreditation. Surely Stella should have a say in the future of their business, too.

"That'd be ideal," said Scottie. "Unfortunately, circumstances are rarely ideal in the business world.

"So who has final say?"

Scottie drew a circle around James's name.

"As Chief Executive Officer, James is responsible for the day to day operations of the business and its solvency under the Australian Securities and Investments Commission. In other words, the buck stops with him."

"So James will decide?"

"Yes. But I know James wants to make the best decision for everyone. He's a fair person. He'll want your input—wait and see."

"But …"

Scottie yawned again.

"Please, Nicole. All that food. All that wine. And believe me, James has been discussing this with me every night for weeks. I've got to rest. Let's talk again in the morning."

He was through the shower, into bed beside her and asleep within seconds, though Nicole's mind continued to buzz with possibilities.

Would they all get a huge payout? Or not much at all? Would Huntleys be swallowed up and disappear, her job along with it?

She loved her work. It was Nicole's role to market the company, to add brand value and spread its reach. Huntleys was in her blood and fingertips, even though she'd never create a jewel in her life. She would fold boxes, mail out catalogs, empty garbage bins and wash up the tearoom cups—anything but turn her hand to the painstaking job of creating one special item.

If GGT bought Huntleys, what would happen to her careful marketing plans for the online side of the business, ready to roll throughout the year? She was especially proud of the way she blended the in-store and online shopping experiences for customers, and the way she was just about to launch the exclusive tours to Jim's lair for the high-end customers, another of Stella's great ideas.

Despite Scottie's plans to let her in on more aspects of the buyout offer, both of them were flat out until Sunday. Each time she tried to raise the subject, Scottie held up his hand, begging time out.

"I can't really say too much yet, Nicole," he said. "James and I need to thrash out all the options ourselves before we present them to the whole family at the same time. It's the only fair way to play this."

"I know, I know," she said. "Conflict of interest."

He nodded.

"If it's any consolation, I'm not enjoying this any more than you are, Nic."

But what was she supposed to say?

Chapter 14

Stella had had another busy day in the store, run off her feet. The only surprise had been a visit from a tall customer far too formally dressed for an Australian—Wolf. Was he here to see James? Would he purchase their livelihoods on the spot?

Stella swallowed and forced a smile.

"Wolf," she said, extending her hand. "How can I help you?"

He nodded and surveyed the ground floor as if finding fault with every piece of worn carpet, every chip on the old cabinets and even the fact the ceiling could do with a fresh coat of paint.

"Jim said you have some Swiss clocks," he said.

"They're upstairs. Shall I show you up?"

"Please," he said.

Stella nodded at Lorna to mind the floor, and took Wolf via the staircase. His silence was unnerving.

"Are you looking for a gift?" She tried to make her usual small talk to connect with a customer, but he was preoccupied, critically examining the worn marble of the staircase, and, outside the windows, lacings of cobwebs she'd never noticed before.

On the next floor, their clocks were on the far wall. A smile still plastered on her face, she led him across, but he stopped at the bright display cabinet James had installed to showcase her own designs, recast from inexpensive paste and common metal into precious stones and gold.

Wolf studied the display carefully, then nodded at her with a half frown, half smile.

"Your designs?" he said. She nodded. "One of each, thank you."

"The whole set, sir? In emeralds, sapphires and rubies?" said Stella. These items were among their most expensive. Did he not understand the value of the Australian dollar?

Wolf frowned.

"The emeralds," he said.

"Perhaps you'd like to see Jim's rings, as well," she said. "His set emeralds are magnificent."

"No. Thank you." A man of few words.

She removed a set of emerald earrings, an emerald pendant and a matching rosette from the case, placed them in the H of H boxes and drew out a black bag with handles. When she'd slipped them inside, she stuffed the top of the now heavy bag with gold tissue paper.

Again Stella felt the need to fill the awkward silence.

"Jewelry's such a wonderful gift when you're traveling as it takes up so little space," she said.

Now Wolf gave her a forced smile.

"Or are these samples?" she asked. Jewelers were known to copy each other's designs.

Wolf nodded. Stella had bought one of these high quality rosettes made by Jim for her own sister, Jeannie, to thank her for hosting her when she'd moved to Sydney to set up her stall.

She'd nurtured a hope that jewelry was special, not just any commodity to trade to make money, but a form of communication between people, to show love.

Wolf and GGT would crush her sentimentality under their well-heeled feet if she let them. It was depressing, but she rang up the sale, glad for the business, knowing that turnover mattered whoever was purchasing their product, at least while they still owned Huntleys.

"The clocks?" she said.

He smiled as if she were an imbecile, but ignored her offer. He took his time to scan the room.

"How many floors?" he said.

"Four if you include Jim's studio and annex," she said. She had no obligation to tell him that the office, tearoom and VIP room were the next level up. He could make an appointment with James if he wanted more information.

Abruptly he shot out his left arm and regarded his watch.

"Thank you," he said, turned away and descended. He'd already left the building by the time Stella reached the ground floor again, the heavy Huntleys door swinging shut behind him.

Several more customers were waiting and she barely had a minute till the end of the day, when she peeped into the office, hoping to tell James about the encounter, but the door was shut and all was quiet inside. James must be back in the city thrashing it out with Scottie.

Seeing this floor with Wolf's critical eye in mind, she made her way up to Jim's level, and then, on a whim, she climbed to the very top of the building, up the ancient spiral staircase, and out onto the roof.

She jumped to find Jim up there already, a large gin and tonic in his hand. He nodded a welcome to her.

"Jim!"

"Great place to watch the sunset!" he said. "Gin and tonic?" He offered her his own.

"No, no. Thanks, but no, Jim."

"Cheers," he said. "Thank you. I only have one a week, and this is it. You know I used to be an alcoholic?"

Stella shook her head.

"Best place to watch the sunset, up here. I proposed to my Eleanor out here, more than sixty years ago. Back then we had one of the tallest buildings for miles. Now look at us! Dwarfed by skyscrapers and shiny shopping malls, but there's still a view of the horizon and harbor if you know where to look."

Stella nodded. To the east she made out the darkening sea and horizon, and to the west, Sydney's glistening harbor, already reflecting the first of the streetlights.

"Cynthia offered me an apartment in one of those new towers back when she sold Eleanor's family home on the waterfront and you all bought yours, but I would have rattled in one without Eleanor." Jim gestured at the vertical buildings with his glass. "What do I need with shiny new appliances, slick benchtops and windswept balconies? I'm happy here in my annex, next to my workshop."

The stiff sea breeze carried with it the smells of takeaway food. It ruffled his white hair.

"Yes, when I fell for my Eleanor, I was a drunk, a no-hoper with shrapnel in my ankle and no idea beyond the next drink. To win her love, I sobered up. I learned all I could about goldsmithing. And she accepted it, my first and best engagement ring!"

With Eleanor, Jim transformed her parents' languishing department store into the most popular jewelry shop in Sydney.

Since then, Huntleys House of Diamonds had sold Jim's custom crafted engagement rings to the rich and famous who's who of Sydney and the wannabes and everyone in between. Jim was an artisan. The business had nourished not just himself and Eleanor, but their beloved only son Jimmy, who'd gone on to marry their lovely young shop assistant Cynthia. The next generation—James, Nicole and Will—inherited their right to join the business when Jimmy died, far too young.

"Regrets," he said now. "The years haven't been without their struggles, but we've had much to celebrate over the years. I do miss Eleanor. She'd never believe all the changes. Not just outside, but inside. Well, it still looks the same, but there's so much more now. Social media. What would she make of that? Magic, invisible marketing."

He stopped and peered at his drink, the condensation wet on his fingers, as if anticipating the hit of sour astringency, as if his drink was better this way. Limited.

"So now I'm a minor star, Stella, with my own 'jewel of the month,' what will we feature next time? Rubies? Eleanor's favorites."

"Sure, Jim. Everyone loves rubies."

He nodded and took another sip.

"Ah, that online shop. Who ever heard of such a thing in our day? Now you dial it all up on the screen, give them your credit card number and it arrives by post. Extraordinary. No one can say Huntleys doesn't keep up with the times. I guess that's why they want us, Stella, the Swiss. We're doing alright, you know, though the old building's crumbling a bit—like I am."

He toasted a chimney pot and took a sip.

"Just this one drink, once a week, to commune with Eleanor's memory and clear my mind. I was tempted to give in to the drink again when Jimmy died, and especially when Eleanor left us too soon afterwards, but I'd wasted enough of my early years on the stuff and too many Huntleys still relied on me to keep my act together. Sobriety. Beats days of utter ruin, that's for sure. Ah, but listen to me. An old man's mumblings."

"I love to hear about the old times, Jim, and about life."

"You do," he said. "And you're like a sponge. I can't believe how much you've learned in such a short time, Stella. Our James is one lucky man. We're all lucky you've joined our business. I wouldn't mind betting it's your influence which put us on GGT's acquisitions map, more's the pity."

"You don't want to sell?"

Jim shrugged. "What do I know; an old man like me?"

"Plenty, Mr Huntley."

"Jim to you, Stella. Yes, well. So do you. I don't like this GGT offer. Not one little bit. But James might well have the right approach, letting everyone have their say."

Stella remained silent. She'd barely seen James since the night before, and he certainly hadn't said anything to her about having a say, despite her long engagement to him.

"What do you think will happen, Jim?"

"Who knows? I find 'business as usual' to be the best approach. James is a good fellow. Of course you'd know that, or you wouldn't be wanting to marry him, would you? Fancy the Swiss wanting to buy us out!"

Jim and Stella stood together and admired the view for a long time, the final glow of the sunset to the west, as streetlights, then lights in homes and apartments, winked on in every direction. Lights still blazed in the city's towers, with plenty of commuters and cleaners still at work. Jim worked all hours himself.

"It's good to pass on my skills to the apprentices, especially to you, Stella, not that I can teach you much. You already know it all. What luck for us all young James found a partner so attuned to the family business! I saw James lift his game when you turned up with your stall out in the mall. What Huntleys has achieved since you joined us is nothing short of miraculous. And to think it could all be gone in three weeks or so!"

Jim spun the ice cubes in the last of his drink, ready to savor his final sip, but he shook his head slowly.

"A shame you weren't there for the meeting," he said. "You deserve credit for our recent successes."

"Thank you," she said.

"Words are cheap, Stella. I've been thinking about this."

"Oh?"

Out on the harbor, navigation buoys winked red and green as the ferries and party boats wove between them.

"I've tried so many times to capture that glistening harbor in the beauty of a piece of jewelry, and failed." He chuckled. "You could probably do it."

He leaned down to place his empty glass on the balustrade, stood again and reached into the collar of his shirt. He pulled a chain up over his neck, then held it out to her with his gnarled fingers. The metal was worn smooth. It glinted in the evening light.

"This workshop key," he said. "It was Eleanor's. I wear it to feel close to her." He held it out to Stella, and it swung on its chain. "I'd like you to have it."

Stella balked but Jim held her eyes.

"Are you sure about this?" Stella knew Jim never played games, but surely this was too significant a gift.

"Never more certain about anything." His hand remained in the air, key dangling, as if he'd hold it there forever until she agreed to take it.

When Stella closed her hand around the key, it was warm. As her heart soared, it was all she could do not to throw her arms around Jim. He was a father figure to her, and the grandfather and mentor she'd never had. The fact he'd entrusted her with the key to his lair was monumental.

"Best keep this to yourself," he said. He gently placed both worn hands around hers for a moment as she'd nodded, speechless.

"This is huge, Jim. Do you really …?"

"You don't need me in there with you any more," he said, hushing her and fixing her with those Huntley blue eyes. "I've watched you, and you know exactly what you're doing. You're a natural. Duck to water. Just remember to lock the door behind you when you're in there. Work alone and you won't be distracted. No injuries. I learned the hard way."

Stella caught his eyes and nodded. Jim was a stickler. Everyone had to knock to enter the studio, even Cynthia, his own daughter in law, and even James and Nicole, and especially Will, and no one was ever allowed in there without Jim.

"But, isn't …"

"There are two keys," said Jim. "Mine and yours. And no one knows about yours."

"But why … not James?" Was Jim saying he didn't trust James?

"I trust you, Stella. We're jewelers, you and I. James is a businessman."

"And Nicole?"

"Nicole and Scottie now," Jim said.

Stella nodded, eyebrows raised, still questioning.

"They're not jewelers, either, though I love them both."

She didn't ask about James and Nicole's brother Will, with his fickle history. He'd been on the straight and narrow for at least a year, in love with his American addiction therapist according to James, and well settled in their town of Boulder City in the US, where his shop was a mecca for outdoor enthusiasts.

But the family and the media still remembered Will's wild years as an international playboy and there remained something otherworldly about him. Will was restless, as if he were made of a different metal.

"And the apprentices?"

"Definitely not the apprentices, not without me there too."

"Cynthia?"

"Cynthia has no need at all to be in the studio. She's in France now. She never liked the smell, anyway."

Stella caught Jim's eye and they laughed.

"But why now?"

"Who knows what the future will bring, Stella."

"Make jewelry while the sun shines?"

"Something like that."

Pigeons cooed and nestled in the eaves as they made their way down the ancient metal ladder and back inside Huntleys. No wonder the building leaked.

"I used to shoo them away," said Jim. He chuckled. "But why begrudge a bird a warm nest?"

Stella flew down the spiral steps ahead of Jim, her heart light, hoping to catch James in the office, but he'd already left.

Back at the apartment, he was locked in the study, chatting figures to Scottie once more, for all hours. She and her fiancé might have been strangers.

Chapter 15

Next morning, she and James walked to work together. Despite his silences, there was a spring in her step. Just knowing Jim trusted her with the key to his workshop thrilled her. Perhaps there'd be time today to create more jewelry.

If her leap from creating affordable steel and glass rhinestones to gold and precious gems was logical, it still thrilled Stella. Her time in Jim's lair—with its circular bench and array of tools worn from a lifetime of shaping and twisting and filing and blowtorching the precious metal into submission—was as rare and precious as the materials she transformed beneath her fingers.

She craved her rare afternoons of alchemy, when the politics of the showroom, the stresses of her coursework and an inkling of unease about her relationship with James melted away, and only the glowing gold and the flame at the centre of her vision mattered.

Cleaning and repairing Cynthia's French chains in the haven of Jim's workroom had become her escape and her lifeline, but even more, she longed to make her own pieces.

In the tearoom, Jim was making coffee. Stella grabbed a glass of water just as Divandra entered in her bike shorts and opened her locker to pull out her work attire.

Jim raised his eyebrows and Stella returned the gesture. She hated Divandra's bike shorts—so revealing. Jim couldn't know it, but she was worried James was far too interested in their bright apprentice and her eye-catching outfits. Shawn was straightforward, but while Divandra wasn't trouble, she was far too engaging, a live wire, only with them for another month or two till her coursework ended. From a family of jewelers based in Malaysia with their own international interests, Divandra was gaining experience and qualifications in Australia, before returning to Malaysia to take her place supervising a whole team of jewelers who'd worked with her family for generations.

Stella liked Divandra. Everybody did, with her engaging personality. She had a way of making everyone laugh, and every transaction was a great adventure, but still. Those shorts.

Her locker door banged closed.

"Just ducking to the ladies to fix my hair," said Divandra. "Bike helmet hair!"

"Okay," said Stella. "See you on the ground floor in five?"

"Five," said Divandra.

"Thank you, Jim," said Stella, pulling the key out from under her crisp white blouse, then hiding it again. "Does this mean I can use your workshop by myself after hours?"

Jim smiled at her, the kind of Huntley smile that turned over hearts everywhere—James's smile. James. Stella swallowed. When had she and James last shared a genuine smile?

"Exactly that," said Jim. "So thank you, Stella. I've seen how hard you work, and your designs are impeccable. You have a real gift. It's rare. Can't be taught. Oh, and there are a couple of extra things I need to show you, without the apprentices. Can you drop in tomorrow at the quiet time?"

"Of course, Jim."

More surprises?

Stella didn't want to be that woman, that jealous woman, the one peering over her shoulder and listening at doors, but just lately, she knew she was doing exactly that.

Later that morning, when James leaned over Divandra, one arm on the counter, peering closely at something, Stella's heart thudded with suspicion and frustration.

She could just say it, say "what are you doing, flirting with my fiancé?" but it was clear what they were doing, at least on the surface. James was pointing enthusiastically at Divandra's designs for her next assignment and asking about them.

100

Stella couldn't leave her customer, who was taking a long time selecting a pair of earrings for herself. Stella's patient smile was painted on. Serving was never her favorite part of working with Huntleys House of Jewels, on the shop floor, but it was part of her apprenticeship, and somebody had to do it, with Lorna on sick leave and James busy flirting.

The worst part of it was she really wanted to hear Divandra's responses. Divandra had a surprisingly deep voice for such a small person and the kind of laugh that drew people in. Yes. Stella was annoyed. Divandra should be the one serving this customer, not Stella.

Now in her purple sari with gold thread, Divandra was beautiful— fascinating. Stella overheard snippets. "Diwali … oh yes … of course." Divandra kept flipping pages as James listened, asking more and more questions.

It was clear Stella's customer wanted the more expensive earrings, but couldn't really afford them.

"Would you consider a lay-by?" Stella said. She sympathized. She knew exactly how it felt when every penny mattered. It was one of the reasons she'd started her own jewelry business, Stellar, determined to make something of her life and escape the poverty trap into which she'd been born, or at least to spend her time doing something she loved— creating jewelry.

Falling in love with James Huntley the Third had changed her plans. He'd welcomed her into his arms and business and life and she'd thought they'd live happily ever after, but lately she wasn't so sure.

Though she wore his engagement ring—a spectacular emerald with a sash of diamonds, created by Jim—there was no wedding date in sight.

Stella tried to quell her negative train of thought, but when James gave Divandra more attention than he'd given her in a month, that decision to drop her own business, Stellar, and take up the apprenticeship and lend her strengths to making James's dreams come true, assuming they were exactly the same as her own … it made a lot less sense than it had at the time.

She forced her mind back to the shop, to her customer.

"Would you like me to put these on hold for you for a day or two while you give it some more thought?" Stella asked.

The customer's eyes kept returning to the earrings. She really wanted them. Stella knew that hunger, that longing that wouldn't quite go away. It wasn't necessarily avarice. There was every reason this woman should have a beautiful pair of earrings.

"They do suit you," Stella said.

"They're actually for my twin sister. She's graduating. I'm so proud of her."

"Oh, that's wonderful. Do you know, I could do something unusual. I'm building up a new line of jewels for my apprenticeship. It's about sustainable jewlery, along the lines of ethically sourced materials."

"Oh?"

"If you don't have cash, but you have some old silver or gold jewelry you're not wearing, or that's broken and you don't want to get it repaired, I can take it and convert it for you, because I'll be able to reuse it."

"I do have a few things. A chain that keeps breaking and a few links that were taken out of this watch chain. I inherited it from my grandmother. Her wrist was much bigger."

"That would do it," said Stella. "It's all above board. I can give you certification for the things you bring in. Are you able to come in tomorrow? It takes a little while because I have to weigh it and do the conversion calculation, but I'll be here in the morning, then I have to head off to TAFE. I'm doing a course myself. What's your sister's field?"

"Nursing."

"Oh, that's wonderful. I'm Stella, by the way. What's your name? I'll put these away for you."

"But what if what I bring in isn't enough to cover the difference?"

Stella lowered her voice.

"We don't normally offer discounts ad hoc, but just in this special case, I'll give you a discount." Huntleys only offered discounts in connection with Nicole's marketing plans, but what was the point in working if you couldn't use your money to do good? Stella would chip in some of her salary to bring this sale over the line, for the sake of these beautiful twins. Stella's own sister, Jeannie, was her best friend, and she could tell these twins were just as close. She couldn't imagine her life without Jeannie.

The woman's eyes met hers, her gratitude a sudden zing of joy that banished Stella's blues.

"Would you really do that for me?"

"Just this once," said Stella. "Sounds like your sister's a star."

"Oh, thank you! I'll never forget Huntleys," she said as she turned and left, head high.

When Stella finished putting the earrings away, James and Divandra had disappeared. Together? She sighed. At least her customer was happy.

Stella picked up a dusting cloth from under the counter and headed for the row of clocks against the far wall, with their pendulums marking their own version of the beating of her heart.

She'd been going to ask Divandra to do this weekly task, but where was she when she needed her? She scrunched the dusting cloth as the cuckoo clocks and other wall clocks began to chime. Half past three.

She pulled out her mobile phone and texted Divandra. "Please come and mind the ground floor. I have an appointment."

Divandra turned up a couple of minutes later, laughing. She really was beautiful.

"Sorry, Stella. James always wants to know more about my family's business."

"Of course," said Stella, more to herself than to Divandra. Jealousy was a curse. Divandra's family's business was actually as fascinating as the woman herself. For her final assignment, Divandra was designing a set of jewels to celebrate Diwali, the Hindu five-day festival of light around October or November, a time of sweets and family feasts, new clothes and, for some, the new jewels that made it as major a boost to Divandra's world wide business as Christmas always proved to be for the Huntleys.

James was right to glean as much as possible from Divandra, as she was doing from them. Divandra's Divali ideas had inspired Nicole and Jeannie to work on a schedule of global festivals to feature on Shop Huntleys Online.

On the top floor, Stella popped her head into the office. As James glanced up from his desk and caught her eye, he leaned back and smiled. He beckoned her in. The room still held that faint scent of coconut, of Divandra, exotic and delicious.

"Been grilling Divandra?" she asked.

He nodded as he stood and moved away from the paper-strewn desk and reached for her. Stella stepped straight into his embrace, placing her cheek on his chest, right next to his heart. Here at least nothing smelled like Divandra. Pure James. These moments were gold, but they were far too rare.

"So what happened at the rest of the meeting?"

"Oh. That. You don't need to worry about it."

"Really?" Stella stepped back.

"Seriously. It's all very early days."

It felt like a brush off, as if her questions were of no consequence. She glanced up at him, then out the window, counseling herself to stop being so sensitive.

"Well, I'm just on my way to see Jim, but I'd love to know more about it all."

"So many options," said James. He gestured at his desk with flowcharts scribbled on writing pads. On his computer screen, a slew of spreadsheets lay open. "Scottie and I are sketching out scenarios. We'll share them with everyone when we're ready, Stell."

Maybe he was right. Maybe she should stick to the shiny stuff and let him worry about company structures. But maybe he was wrong.

But now, for the first time, Stella used her own key to enter Jim's lair, knocking first so as not to startle him. The roar of the blow torch and its sulfurous vapors enveloped her as she closed and locked the door again behind her.

With his binocular microscopic glasses, Jim was a squid-like creature from the deep as he exhaled oxygen into the flame to make it hotter, locked in a battle of life and death with his latest creation.

A few moments later, he grunted, twisted off the flame and turned to greet her. He removed the headset, rubbed the top of his nose and stood, his hands on the small of his back.

"Righteo," he said. "You've earned your stripes, Stella Rhys."

"I don't graduate for another six weeks."

"That's just a piece of paper. Your skills and talents are real. Step one. Never lend anyone your key."

"No sir."

"Step two. Never tell anyone what I'm about to show you, except when you're ready to retire."

"You're not retiring, Jim!" It was inevitable yet unthinkable. Jim was an institution—the institution. Jim was Huntleys. She couldn't imagine the place without him. Didn't want to.

"You think I'll live forever? You think I'm made of gold?" The light in his eyes was brighter than the light drawn into one of his jewels. His laugh as he threw back his head warmed her like sunshine.

"There comes a time," he said. "You know it in your soul. No. I'm not giving up making jewelry, but I'm getting a taste for this podcasting thing. I'm readier than ever to share what I've learned. I'll keep making jewelry till the day I die, but only a fool would take all his good secrets to his grave."

Were there bad secrets in Jim's life? Stella shook her head, to focus.

"Good secrets?" she said.

"You need to know where I keep the ladies."

"Jim! Is that sexist?"

"It's the truth. You can call them what you like. I call them my ladies."

Jim always had the gems waiting for them when the apprentices had their lessons, out on the open bench, staring out at them like eyeballs without lids, those semi-precious stones, like topaz and amethyst, citrine and garnets, with strips of silver of all gauges stacked up beside them like so many fiddlesticks.

"And then we dress them for a party," Jim would say. "Show me your sketches."

And he'd unlock the gold safe, and draw out the wire of all sizes, and, best of all, the sets of draw plates for creating wire of every shape and size.

"They're the real jewels, aren't they," Jim would say. "Can't do much with a big block of gold, can you?"

And the lesson would begin.

Sure, Stella had a headstart after working with other metals and acrylic crystals, the affordable materials with which she'd created stock for Stellar. Stella understood what Jim would do before he even spoke, while Shawn and Divandra stumbled, clumsier than children around the minuscule materials.

"Practice!" Jim said. "Do you think I was a master before I crawled?"

Shawn might get there one day if he turned up and watched carefully, but Divandra would not. Anyone could see her main interest lay in management, not craft, but in the vast global network of her family's factories, she needed to be able to give the right directions.

What was clear to the apprentices, but not to Jim, was that Jim's techniques were ancient. Their tutors insisted they do a few classes on Computer Aided Designs and three dimensional printing. Hands-free manufacture was the future for all but the highest end jewelry manufacture.

In this, Stella knew she disagreed with Jim, but she understood he was from another era, and he was content to be the machine. With decades of creating rings behind him, to watch him was to watch the rings create themselves. No wonder his YouTube videos were such a hit. It was as if he worked at double speed.

Stella was no slouch, sometimes even faster than Jim, her movements fluid and certain, and her technique needed no correction, but her mind was open to so many future possibilities for jewelry manufacture as well.

She asked him why he'd given her the key and this one unique lesson, one on one, without the junior apprentices—the instructions on where to find his gold and gems.

He shrugged, then bowed his head, his strong hands outstretched, cradling the air between them, as if awaiting fresh raw materials. When he lifted his head, he pinned her with those Huntley eyes, blue as a never ending summer sky.

"You're our future, Stella," he said, and smiled.

Chapter 16

James stared at the spreadsheets on his screen. He flicked between them again, as if the mere act of scrutinizing them one more time would unlock the funds he needed to make Huntleys great. The ambition was there now, unlike when he'd been brought into the business upon his father's death, but there was never enough capital.

James was the first to admit he'd been sleepwalking for years when it came to the business. Only his sense of duty had kept him there, going through the motions for the sake of Jim and his younger sister and brother. He'd watched his mother grow grayer at the helm, and knew he must step up to give her freedom, after all the years she'd sacrificed to keep the business alive while his father was dying.

It was only when Stella appeared in the plaza, her glittering stall of affordable treasures impossible to miss, and her bright eyes and determination even more compelling, that James had come to his senses.

To Stella, Huntleys had been a treasure trove, the real thing. Seeing his inheritance through her eyes jolted him. He had inherited a fortune—not just a means of making a living, but all the good will among customers that accompanied all the work that had gone before. Huntleys had a name. It was iconic. There were thousands of Jim's rings walking around on the left hands of more Australians than they could count, not to mention the tourists who'd bought their jewelry and clocks; and customers kept coming back for more.

Later, when Stella shared with him her ideas for modernizing the business, it was as if the lights had suddenly been turned on, and her ideas kept coming, all of them welcome, all of them likely to give them the edge on the competition and a robust future for decades to come.

But Will and Cynthia's drains on the finances also kept coming. James had helped support Cynthia's well-earned semi-retirement, then bankrolled her as she set up her House of Clubs with Émile in France, but Will had drifted for years. When Will staged his recent turnaround, from international playboy to steadfast shop owner and pillar of his Nevada community in the US, James had forked out again. To bankroll Will's House of Hearts, the US branch of Huntleys, James had been required to mortgage the business.

Huntleys was trading well, but the mortgage took its toll each month, and there were always extra costs. While bringing on the apprentices was meant to lighten the load on Stella and free her up from serving to do more creating, it just meant she was busy filling in for lazy Shawn who was too often "unwell," and the studio was always occupied by Jim or the apprentices.

James felt bad, so bad he found himself dodging Stella at times. If he returned her glances, perhaps she'd see into his soul and sense his shame—his fear he had so much less to offer her than when he'd first proposed. With their rapid global expansion, the mortgages and juggling the supply chain for the online business—any company would be struggling to balance their accounts, wouldn't they? He kept hoping Scottie would reassure him they were back on an even keel, but the signs weren't clear enough yet. Only when their future looked rock solid would he be free to make Stella a Huntley. To marry her too soon might tie her down to a sinking ship. He closed his eyes, pushed his fingers through his hair, groaned and stared at the screen again.

James wanted to give Stella the world, but they couldn't even afford to create another studio for her. She was stoic. She rarely mentioned what was on her mind, but he sensed she was tired and frustrated.

So many of Stella's ideas were excellent, but he hadn't the capital to make them all happen soon enough, and banks wouldn't extend further credit.

They needed to modify their windows and store entry to appeal to a greater range of customers, but that meant architects' fees and development application fees, not to mention the cost of labor and materials and the puzzle of how to keep business trading while the work was done.

Those "you wish" doors were fine for their wealthiest customers, but they alienated younger ones with less to spend. Bondi Junction kept changing, along with the rest of Sydney, Australia and the world. "Diversity" was the catch cry. Jewelry was for everyone. He knew some young men wore pearls these days. Why not? And why shouldn't Huntleys be the one to stock their choices? Yet every change came with costs. Different stock, different displays, more marketing.

Since opening their French and US branches, James found wrangling the finances increasingly time-consuming, and Shop Huntleys Online was growing so rapidly it also needed his attention.

He and Stella passed each other in the shop at a run; they shared takeaway meals and fell asleep exhausted each night. Any time together was spent talking business, rarely simply enjoying one another's company.

But the GGT offer would expire in less than three weeks. Perhaps somewhere in its fine detail, new avenues would open up, if not for Huntleys the company, then at least for the Huntleys as individuals, and for his Stella. He sighed and dragged his eyes back to the fine print, and the seventh spreadsheet, or was it the eighth?

A text popped onto his phone from Scottie.

"Tax statement due tomorrow. Chat tonight about the options?"

At least while he was interrogating the details with Scottie there was hope he'd choose the right path. James texted him back a thumbs up and set to work again.

Chapter 17

That evening, Stella emptied their letterbox and let herself into James's apartment as usual. She was about to throw the junk mail in the bin when a thick beige envelope caught her attention. The stamps were French. Yes! It was from France, from James's mother Cynthia and her Belgian partner, Émile.

She sat it up on the windowsill above the sink, where James would see it when he came in, and they could open it together. If it was what she suspected—a wedding invitation—it might spur a conversation about their own event, still to be planned. A little rush of adrenalin sent Stella spinning in a pirouette across the kitchen, imagining a wedding waltz, and she smiled as she reached up and took down the rice cooker, scattering in a cup of white rice and another of water, and switching it on.

She chopped the vegetables, hoping James would appear soon, but there was still no sign of him. She checked her phone. No messages. He'd been on the phone to Scottie again when she'd left. He'd waved at her distractedly then returned to his conversation, brow furrowed.

She didn't envy him his responsibility for the financial health of Huntleys House of Jewels. Poor money management had almost spelled the end of her own business, Stellar, especially when her takings were stolen. At least Huntleys had safes on the property, though Closed Circuit TV security would be sensible. She must suggest it to James.

Stella pulled up her final assignment on her laptop, bit into an apple and tried to fight the brain fog. She'd been working all day. She read the essay topic twice, then a third time, then gave up, and switched on the stove, stifling a yawn. She'd have to eat and go to bed, and James could reheat some when he came in.

Stella reached for the exotic envelope and turned its textured weight over and over in her hands. Maybe it wasn't anything to do with Cynthia and Émile's relationship. Maybe it just contained some photographs from them, or a sample jewelry catalog from a French firm.

She checked her watch. Ten o'clock! She messaged James.

"You okay, James?"

"So sorry, Stell. Caught up still with Scottie."

"S'okay. I've left some stir fry for you. Heading for bed."

"Thanks, Stell. C u tomorrow."

The pale envelope was a glowing temptation. It was beautiful paper, thick and creamy. She so wanted to know what was inside. Suddenly, she grabbed a knife, and slipped it under the edge to break the seal. Inside was a flash of gold, a slim ribbon, tied in a bow around a card. She drew it out. The card was embossed with the golden outline of a fine chateau. In the dark kitchen, Stella ran her thumb over the depiction, enchanted with the indentations. It was exactly what she'd suspected—an invitation, printed in a beautiful old fashioned script.

Please join us as we celebrate our wedding at Angelica's French chateau.
Rue Saint-Pierre
Val du Loire
Émile Laurent and Cynthia Huntley
14 août
Répondez s'il vous plaît.

Stella stared out the window, picturing the wedding. August. Late spring in France; late Autumn in Australia. It was very Cynthia. Top class. Expensive, if they'd booked an entire chateau. She closed her eyes and remembered her mother's recent wedding, to Ross Archer, the reclusive widower. It had been a modest affair in the garden of Ross's farmhouse on the northern New South Wales coast. She rested the card open on the counter, then padded across the kitchen and drank a glass of water.

Though she was thrilled for Cynthia and Émile, a little stab of disappointment settled in her gut as she prepared for bed and slipped between the cold sheets, alone. She and James were supposed to be marrying, too, but so far there was no date, no venue and no guest list.

Not for the first time, Stella wondered whether James had cold feet. Was he keeping his options open? Did he have regrets about their engagement? Was he stalling?

Next morning, the invitation sat on the bench exactly as she'd left it, as if James hadn't even noticed it, let alone thought about it.

As he stacked his breakfast bowl in the dishwasher and stooped to tie his shoelaces, he was saying something about his late night.

"Sorry, Stell," he said. "It's so important to get all this right. If Scottie and I don't get the numbers absolutely right it could change our company forever. After all our hard work together for decades—generations really—this whole GGT business could blow our family apart."

"Some of you have worked harder than others," she said, then bit her tongue. But it was true. Cynthia and Will had expensive taste, and from what she could see, neither had contributed much in the past few years, especially Will. They were very good at spending Huntleys' money but not so interested in making it.

James's loyalty to his family was admirable. As they ate their breakfast standing up, he and Stella discussed Cynthia's love of collecting French antiques, and, as they walked to work together, Will's old playboy lifestyle, the invitation forgotten.

"This GGT offer has come at such a bad time, just when they both seem so settled, with sales finally starting to pick up in both their stores," said James.

"Can't you just say 'no' to GGT, then?"

"I really wish it were that simple, Stell."

"Why isn't it?"

"We've made a lot of changes in a very short time, Stell. All your ideas for starters; expanding online; the new branches. It's all expensive, and the competition never lets up."

"And I keep coming up with expensive ideas."

"You're wonderful, Stell," he said.

She smiled up at him but he'd already pulled open the door for her and was staring up the stairs, as if his head was already in his office again.

At first when James had opened the grand Huntleys door for her and stood back for her to enter, she felt like a princess. But now it was as if they were both automatons. If only she could break them out of this rut.

She wanted James back. She stopped in the foyer to embrace him, but he was frowning at his watch.

"CCTV," she said.

"Hmmm?"

"For security. We should install CCTV."

"Good idea, but it might need to wait a month or two. Would you have time to investigate suppliers, Stell? Would you mind?"

Another day raced by, and that evening, before heading home, Stella popped her head into the office again, where James stared at his computer screen.

"Coming home tonight, James?"

"Gotta chat to Scottie again, sorry, Stell."

"I think I'll go see Jeannie, then," she said quietly, as he asked Scottie to excuse him for a moment and put his phone on mute to listen to her properly. She was grateful.

"It's been ages since the two of us did anything but talk Shop Huntleys Online, James, and I miss my nieces," Stella said. "Want to join me there later?"

"Sorry, Stell. Can't, but please give them my best regards. Scottie's come through with another scenario and we need to test it against the different numbers."

Already he spoke about it as if the sale were a done deal. Stella understood he wanted to explore all the possibilities thoroughly, but wasn't there more to life than money and deals? Her nieces were growing up, too fast. It was suddenly urgent she re-enter the world of their soft toys and children's books and listen to their chatter.

"You will tell me when there are some concrete options, won't you, James? I might also have some ideas, you know. Can I mention the offer to Jeannie? She's become an integral part of the business, what with all the online action. Surely she deserves to know as well."

"If you like, although, unfortunately there's not much point. Only shareholders can vote." James stared back down at his phone as he unmuted it, and then back to his computer screen. Conversation over. She was dismissed.

"See you later then," she said, miffed. So. Non-shareholders were excluded. Why did that hurt? She grabbed the car keys. Sometimes she walked, but she'd have to get there soon to catch little Lucy and Sienna before their bedtime.

Jeannie buzzed her up to their apartment.

"Great timing," said Jeannie as the sisters hugged at the door. "Haven't seen you for ages. Dave's still in Thailand and Lucy's scraped her knee at school. She won't go in the bath because she knows it will sting. Sienna's through already and desperate for some of your special 'aunty' attention."

Sienna, in pajamas and clutching a teddy, removed her hug from Jeannie's leg to Stella's, and Stella stooped and swung her up onto her hip.

"What are we reading, Miss Sienna?" She headed for the pile of cushions on the floor of their bedroom and reached into the stack of books. "Dinosaurs? Shapes? Libby's Great Adventure?"

Stella marveled at the girls' toys, and especially all their books. They'd been a rarity in Jeannie and her own childhood. Time flew as she read and reread them, first to Sienna, and then to Lucy as she arrived with her knee covered in fresh gauze, hugging a bunny with long ears.

The girls smelled of baby shampoo and fresh towels and their heads became heavier and heavier as they lay against her and listened.

Jeannie arrived, scooped them into bed and turned off the light.

"Have you eaten yet?" said Jeannie in the bright hallway. Stella shook her head.

"Share a tin of baked beans?"

"Perfect," said Stella. It was like the olden days with their mother, Flame, when baked beans were a favorite meal.

"You must have known I have something to share with you," said Jeannie.

"Oh? I've got news too, by the way. I don't suppose James has spoken to you yet?"

"No?"

"It's early days. Hopefully he'll bring both of us in on the details soon. I'm pretty in the dark about it, actually. Maybe that's why I decided to come and see you. I still love him but sometimes it's hard, Jeannie. Do you ever feel that way about Dave?"

"Of course. Oh, Stell. Wait till you hear the latest. You first."

"Huntleys has a buyout offer."

"What? Wow! Really? What's that going to mean for everyone? For you? For me and Shop Huntleys Online?"

"No idea at this stage. James is talking with Scottie some more this evening. I've barely had a word with him for days. I guess it's a really big deal. It could change everything for the business, for his family. Apparently the Huntleys will hold an Extraordinary General Meeting in a couple more weeks and vote on it all. You and I have no say whatsoever, no voting rights."

"Nice. Oops. I suppose we need to just see what happens. Super interesting! Who's made the offer? Know anything about them?"

"Gold and Gem Traders International, GGT, from Switzerland. Apart from a schmoozy dinner with three of them, Eric, Carl and Wolf, at Balmoral, where we were force fed, nothing much."

"Well, that sounds positive. Not. Let's look them up online, Stell. After all, GGT could be our bosses in three weeks!"

"Nice website," said Stella after their simple meal.

"Click on the branches. Look, they don't have one in Australia. Maybe that's why they're interested. And I suppose if they already have four in France they might as well have another. But they've got one in Vegas already, so why would they want one so close, in Boulder City, too? You said it's easy driving distance, didn't you? Do they have to take all three of Huntleys' salons, or are they only interested in Australia, or maybe just in the northern hemisphere ones?"

"No idea, Jeannie. You know what I notice?"

"What?"

"They don't have any online sales."

"Let me see."

Stella swiveled Jeannie's laptop towards her.

"Did they talk about online sales at the swanky dinner?"

"No. They just kept trying to flatter me about my design skills and saying how I could join their design studio."

"Well, your designs are really special, Stell. Your design skills are world class."

"Not that I get to design much anymore," said Stella. And yes, she sounded sulky because she missed being creative. A lot.

115

"Not right now, maybe, but that's because you're finishing your apprenticeship. You don't want to throw away all that work, do you? If uni taught me anything, it was the value of sticking with it till I'd got that degree. You're so nearly done, aren't you?"

"Just one more assignment, Jeannie. I suppose I should be working on it now, but it's so good to see you. Hey, let's not talk business. It's all I ever hear from James these days, and I live and breathe it all day. Sorry to be so grumpy. So, what's your own news?"

"It's funny how all these changes seem to be coming at once. Dave's been given an offer we're seriously considering."

"Oh?"

"They want him to move to Singapore."

Stella inhaled sharply. She searched her sister's face. She'd miss her terribly if they took up the offer. On the other hand, Jeannie was always having to cope on her own, with Dave away on business trips, sometimes for weeks at a time. As an electrical engineer he was in high demand retrofitting factories throughout South East Asia to make them more energy efficient. Customers loved him. Business was booming."

"And will you go, do you think?"

"Still working it out, Stell. You'll be the first to know, if we do. The company wants to fly us up there to look at apartments."

"Wow. Sounds like they're serious. So maybe you'd give up working for Shop Huntleys Online anyway. Would you keep working over there?"

"Maybe after we settle in."

Jeannie was talking as if they already planned to move.

"I guess it would be great if it means Dave can be with you all more often," said Stella. Her smile was fake. The news shook her. Lately James was never available. Now Jeannie would be gone, and her adorable nieces with them. She squeezed her eyes shut to stop tears. No need to be so emotional. What was wrong with her?

"I don't know."

"And I could always come and visit." Stella kept her voice cheerful.

"Not exactly like this, though. Dropping in. We'll miss you, Stell. If we go."

Stella kept up the brave smile. Something inside her turned upside down at the thought of Lucy and Sienna being so far away. She must take

116

time to visit them more often, whether or not they moved. How easy it was to take friends and family for granted.

"Have you told Mum and Ross?"

"It's a bit early yet. We've barely had time to discuss it ourselves." Stella stood to go.

"When's Dave back next? Let me come and babysit and you two can go out together and talk without distraction."

"Next Wednesday, Stell. That'd be lovely."

Chapter 18

It was early morning when Will rang James. James creeped out of bed and padded into the next room so as not to disturb Stella.

"How much, man?" said Will. "Tell me what they're offering."

"We're not ready to share all the options yet, Will. We're still working them out."

"Surely you can share broadly. You're shutting me out. Tell me. What have you and Scottie got up your sleeves? You selling us out?"

"Just give us another few days, Will. We've been working night and day on this. It doesn't help that you wake me up and demand answers when we don't even know all the questions. You're lucky I still answer the phone to you."

"Yeah, but you never tell me anything new. Tell you what. You keep up this silence, and I'll promise to vote against you whatever you propose. How's that?"

"What's that supposed to mean?"

"Joke, man. Where's your sense of humor? Look. Just tell GGT to give you another month. I want a brainstorming session. Stuff your EGM decision. Why work to their timeframe? You're the one who calls the shots. They want your company; they play to your rules."

"What makes you think that's the case?"

"Well, they want you, don't they? Maybe they have to wait. Took me a long time to learn it, but sometimes the best things in life are worth waiting for."

"How is Lisa?" said James. James had met the willowy Dr Lisa Bakker at The Peters Clinic in Vegas where Will was undergoing treatment for a gambling addiction. That Will was attracted to her was no surprise. A notorious womanizer, Will was attracted to many, and women everywhere reciprocated. The surprise with Lisa was that she was out of bounds, and while this would never normally have slowed Will down for a second, in Lisa's case, Will had told James he knew she'd lose her hard-won career if he did so. To pursue her would be no act of love.

Will surprised everyone, including himself, by vowing to wait the full two years before formally approaching her. In the meantime, he'd dedicated himself to setting up his House of Hearts adventure wear and jewelry business in Boulder City where she lived. Any excess energy was taken up organising his Black Fire Opal Boulder City Skyrun, to raise funds for young people with addictions.

"Lisa's totally changed my life, bro. Never thought I'd want to settle down like you and Stella, and Nicole and Scottie, but there you go. Lisa's special. So's Stella of course. How is Stella? Hey, what about Mum and Émile tying the knot? You going to the wedding?"

"I hope so, but frankly I have no idea what we'll all be doing then. This offer has really changed my view of the future alright. Anything could happen."

"You're not thinking of selling; my conservative brother, who always does the right thing?"

"But what even is 'the right thing,' Will? When dad died and I had to leave uni to help run the business with mum, it was pretty clear that was the right thing to do, but now? I look back at the last decade and wonder whether it's been worth it. Was that really what I wanted to do with my life, to carry on Jim and Jimmy's dream just because I'm James Huntley the Third? Don't get me wrong. I'm grateful to have a job and a great family—you excepted of course, Will; you gave us all the run-around for so long we can't quite believe you've finally come good. No. I shouldn't have said that. I take that back."

"Nah. I deserve it! I shock myself when I think back. You reckon you wasted a decade. What about me? That I didn't choose that 'bad boy' path hardly excuses me. It was all a media beat-up at the start, but I was the one who kept living up to my bad image.

"Well, I still regret rubbing it in. Your past is over. You've got plenty on your plate now, mate, and it's all good—the fundraising, House of

Hearts, Lisa—I only want the best for you. That's all any of us have ever wanted. But this offer? Will, the last thing I want to do is push you off track by selling your livelihood, unless that's what you want. Getting a large sum of money might seem like a great idea in the short term …"

"But you're worried I'll gamble it away."

"Well …"

"Yeah. Could be tempting. I see that. But you know I don't do that anymore."

"What? Gamble. Great to hear it. That's fantastic, Will. So, when are you and Lisa tying the knot?"

"Hey. What about you and Stella? That's quite an engagement."

"I want this all sorted before I offer her my hand."

"That's old fashioned, you know, James."

"Yeah, well. What I don't want to do is bring her into a life of working in the store all day, with no time to create. I don't want her to have to worry about the old building. It's more decrepit than ever, Will. Falling apart. Charming, yes. Weatherproof, no. We need a new roof, new windows, new power supply, new plumbing, new carpet and a new lift. There isn't enough room in the workroom for Stella and Jim to create at the same time, and the apprentices also need time with the blowtorches. It's one thing after another."

"And in rides GGT with an offer to take away all your worries and give you another shot at life."

"In a nutshell, yes."

"And old Jim could still create his rings somewhere, maybe even in his lair. Have you got a good lawyer? Even if you decide to sell, there can be caveats; you know, conditions. I don't know much about it. Why don't you phone Adam Li? Wasn't he in your year group? The last school magazine was full of all his corporate law achievements. He'd be just the guy. Might even chat for free if you offer him a watch or something."

"Lawyers are expensive, Will. We don't have endless funds. That's part of the problem. We expanded fast to set up Mum's House of Clubs as well as your House of Hearts. There are tax implications, business registration, IT costs, compliance costs …"

"Yeah, well what's it going to cost if you get it wrong, James? Could break up the family. Break Mum's heart, and old Jim's. We're young enough to find other business interests if we have to—maybe we even want to, though I'm fully committed to making this work for the long term if it all works out with Lisa—but what about Jim and Mum? Mum made it pretty clear she's against selling, didn't she?"

"Yeah, I know. I can't sleep worrying about it. As CEO, I'm trying to please everyone. I might end up pleasing no one."

"Heavy is the head that wears the crown, King James."

"Very good. Shakespeare. I didn't think you were listening in high school, Will. Surely all that alcohol dissolved your education."

"Impressive, yeah. I do think better now I don't party every night. What does Stella think?"

"Haven't had a chance to lay it all out for her yet. Trying to get my own head in order, work out all the options."

"Doesn't her sister work for you, too? Jeannie? Isn't she the mastermind behind all your online sales? Are you going to give employees any say? Will they get a cut if you sell?"

"Welcome to my world, Will. How do I know?"

"And what do Nicole and Scottie want?"

"Scottie's trying to stay neutral. He won't get a vote, though he could influence Nicole of course. I haven't spoken with Nic in any detail yet. Same issue I have with Stella. I need to understand it all myself first, before I try to explain it."

"Well, here are the options as I see them. Sell none of the business. Sell some of the business. Sell all of the business. Pretty simple, really."

"Yeah, but there are buildings, stock, people, brand value, online assets."

"Well, good luck. Keep in touch. I won't disown you whichever way it rolls, if that's any comfort."

"You've really changed, mate. Thank you. Now, when are you sending us those Black Fire Opals? I told the apprentices about them and they can't wait to try setting them. There could even be a market in Malaysia. We've got this apprentice at the moment, Divandra ... Hang on. That's another call coming through. It's Mum. I'd better take it."

"See you."

"See you."

James ran his fingers through his hair. So much for his plan to creep back to bed. He pressed "answer."

"Mother? Everything alright?"

"I'm so worried, darling. What if you, Nic and Will want to sell? I did the wrong thing giving you all equal control with Jim and me, didn't I?"

"It's a bit late now, Mum."

"I was just trying to be fair, but you've always been the most sensible, James, the most responsible. You're really the one with the business head on your shoulders."

"Well, Nic's been quite committed."

"Of course. And you know, I always thought that giving Will more responsibility might bring him around, anchor him somehow, in all those years he was drifting. Do you think he's really changed, James? Or not. All this business with his Nevada store. You see the numbers. Is it starting to pay its way? Or is he just bluffing, do you think? I hate to think this way, but it really matters now, darling. If we end up selling, it would be the worst thing for him—setting him free in the world again with no responsibility, wouldn't it?"

"Yes. I can see that, but he really is hoping to make it work. And I do know that his donations are going through to that organization for troubled young people. He's at least serious about that, about other people, for the first time in his life."

"But this business about the doctor…"

"Dr Lisa Bakker, the gambling therapist?"

"Well, it's so unlike Will to wait for anything, or anyone for that matter. And to wait for two whole years …"

"I agree it sounds unlikely, for Will, especially."

"But I've thought of something even worse, darling."

"Yes?"

"Well, suppose the two years comes up, and he approaches this Lisa doctor, and … Well, what if she rejects him? That's a real risk, isn't it? Imagine what it would do for him? And if he had all that money at his fingertips … Well, it would be understandable for anyone to go off the rails for a while, let alone someone so vulnerable."

"Will's not vulnerable, Mum."

"Nonsense. Everyone is; at some level—especially someone who lost his father at such an impressionable age."

"Mum, let's give Will some credit. He turned a corner at that clinic, and from what I can tell, he hasn't looked back. He's set up his store. You saw what a great job he did on that. And you met Lisa, at the opening. She wouldn't have gone along if she wasn't interested, would she? And he was respectful with her. Normal, for the first time. You know how he always was with women. And sales are coming in. If anything, they're growing, though we'll have to get used to your northern hemisphere seasons."

"But James. You don't think he's bluffing? Will can be very charming. I see that now. I forgave him for so long. I was blind to his bad behavior for too long, just because he reminded me so much of Jimmy. I hold myself responsible to an extent."

"You're a great mother, Cynthia. We all know you did your best in challenging times."

"Well, Jimmy didn't want to leave us, and we did want to give you all the best start in life, and to keep the business strong for you all. We discussed all of this, you know, before he died. Not that any of that will be relevant if you all just sell up."

"Well, we'll see what happens."

"You say that, but it's not as if you don't have a choice, James."

"Thank you, mother. Thank you for the call. It's late over there now and, talking about the business, I'll have to head out shortly. Try not to worry. Scottie and I are working out the numbers. We'll be in touch with you all again soon."

"Thank you, darling."

He sighed and groaned. It was payday. With everything else on his mind, he'd almost forgotten he had to line up all the payments. How long had it been since the GGT offer appeared out of the blue? It felt like a lifetime.

Chapter 19

Drrrrrr. Drrrrrr. The incessant drill of the alarm clock. Stella nestled towards the centre of the bed, hoping for a cuddle, but James's space was already growing cold. He'd leaped out ahead of her.

Wednesday. Would this week never end? Another long day in a long week in a too-long month of duties.

The day's major events scrolled through her mind, more real than the steam and splash of James in the shower as she rose and began to dress; the meetings with the pest inspector and lift mechanic, and hopefully an hour or two off when Shawn's shift began, so she could make a start on that assignment that was already overdue. With some luck, Jim would give her extra time in his studio to finish repairs on the latest shipment of antique gold chains Cynthia had sent across from her provincial hideaway in the south of France.

Last time Stella had time in Jim's studio, Nicole jumped in ahead of her, insisting she record Jim's jewel of the month podcast. It was now so popular that listeners were tweeting suggestions, and a representative of the US embassy had brought in samples of unusual gems found in America. It was social media gold for Will Huntley's US branch of Huntleys, even though his store stocked mostly adventure wear and just a few jewels.

That was a brilliant episode. Who would have ever dreamed of "Hiddenite," a gem discovered by a geologist named William Hidden in the late 1800s in North Carolina and also found in Madagascar, Brazil and China?

Stella couldn't recall all the details, something about lithium and aluminum and silicon, but the green, blue and yellow colors at different angles fascinated her, as well as the long, elegant shape. She'd love to create a Hiddenite ring, but how could that happen when she couldn't even get on top of all the repairs, let alone finish her assignments? And she needed to speak with Shawn again to see how his own assignments were going.

Breakfast was hasty, the milk too cold and the coffee too hot. James frowned into his phone.

"James?"

"Mmmmm?"

"Silverfish."

"Sorry?" His eyes were miles away.

"Did your Mum ever say anything about silverfish?"

"Nup. Don't think so. Ask her. Better still, ask the pest inspector. That's why we pay him."

Stella couldn't remember when she became the building manager. Maybe it was just after she became the Human Resources officer, in charge of shifts.

"Could you check with James if I can take an extra week at Christmas?" Lorna had asked. "My sister's visiting from Adelaide."

"Of course," Stella said, and let her know James's response, an emphatic "yes" for their longest serving employee. Stella hadn't minded working twice as hard in that extra busy week without her, but from then on, she'd become the "go to" person for all things HR.

As James rinsed out his coffee cup and jangled his keys, Stella gulped down the rest of her own and rushed to brush her teeth. Her own phone dinged.

"Unwell. Soz." From Shawn. Again. Great. So much for nailing her own assignment this afternoon. She'd have to ask for an extra extension. The only good thing was that this time Shawn had given her advance notice. His usual style was to simply not turn up.

She grabbed a couple of wads of frozen leftovers from the freezer for their lunch and rushed down to join James in the foyer. He was unusually silent, preoccupied again.

"Everything okay?" she asked.

"Mmm." He gave her a perfunctory smile. They caught every "walk" sign and the chance to talk was lost.

They entered the building and she switched on the lights and took their lunch up to the tearoom fridge, while James went straight to the office again.

A bright laugh told her Divandra had arrived and had probably stopped at the door to the office for a chat with James. Stella liked Divandra. She really did. But did her favorite apprentice have to wear such alluring outfits to work?

Sure, she slipped on a fresh white shirt and a long black pencil skirt as soon as she'd secured her bike in the basement next to the safe, but being the fitness freak she was, this involved running up three flights of stairs to the ladies' room near the VIP room on the top floor.

Divandra turned heads. Yesterday morning, Stella and James entered Huntleys just as Divandra sprinted up the stairs in front of them. Stella couldn't help but notice James's eyes following her fit form as if she were some kind of Indian-Malaysian goddess.

Later in the day, entering the first floor, Stella noticed a conservative older woman staring at the display of earrings in one of the cabinets. Divandra stopped folding boxes and approached the customer expertly, engaging her in conversation. Moments later, the woman was laughing and pointing at this and that under the counter, while Divandra unlocked the cabinet and drew out a tray of the earrings. With her dark velvet skin, Divandra's white smile was eye-catching and her sparkly personality was infectious.

Suddenly Divandra glanced up and beckoned her across. Had she caught Stella staring?

"Our customer is admiring your earrings, Stella," said Divandra.

"Oh, did you design these?" said the customer.

Stella nodded.

"She's an amazing designer," said Divandra. "We're at college together. Stella's by far the star apprentice."

How did Divandra do that? By complimenting her, she'd placed them at the same level, even though technically Stella had employed her and was already more qualified. Stella bit back her own bitterness and forced herself to smile graciously.

"Divandra's a star in her own right," said Stella. "And sadly, she'll leave Huntleys once she finishes her apprenticeship. Her family runs a huge jewelry emporium in Malaysia."

"Oh?"

"So Huntleys is lucky to have her on board."

"Nonsense," said Divandra. "The honor's all mine."

"Oh how lovely. Now, about these earrings …"

"Stella, may I show this lady the more valuable ones? You see, she wants to wear something truly special to her granddaughter's wedding."

"Of course," said Stella, noting the customer's very stylish walking stick and ignoring the vague insult that Divandra had just dismissed her own designs. Ideally, Divandra would be showing her to the VIP room for a high-end purchase, but it was true there was another option—to make Stella do the walking.

"Of course I'll bring another selection. One moment, please."

"Can we offer you a seat while you wait a few moments?"

Divandra steered the customer to a sitting area at the side of the floor while Stella ran up the stairs, unlocked a cabinet, drew out a tray of her designs in real emeralds, sapphires and rubies, and brought it downstairs.

When she returned, Divandra had the customer under a spell as she described the Malaysian crown jewels.

"My dear I had no idea," said the customer.

"Oh yes! Oh thank you, Stella!" Divandra took the tray and turned back to the customer, effectively dismissing Stella.

Churlish. That's how she felt. Divandra was doing her job as pleasantly as always. And at least she was here and working hard, unlike Shawn. So why was Stella so riled?

Maybe it had something to do with the way James's eyes tended to follow Divandra's race upstairs a little too eagerly.

The previous night, Stella cooked a special meal for him, hoping they'd sit together at the outdoor table, look out at the city lights and hold hands again, as they'd done in their first few months living together in James's apartment. He'd thanked her, but he plonked both their meals on trays and switched on the television as usual. She was going to bring it up with him, but he was already laughing along to a show. He needed this release.

On days they both worked late, they often brought home takeout and arrived home just in time to flop in front of whatever rubbish was screening. She didn't begrudge him the escapism—just wished he found her as riveting.

For the fourth night in a row, James was fast asleep by nine o'clock. He'd been right there beside her, warm and dear and strong, but not with her. His long legs stretched out in front of him. One arm lay along the back of the couch, the other on the armrest and his head rested slightly backwards, that sun-bleached wave of brown hair as ruffled as if they'd just made love, which they hadn't for longer than she could remember.

Her heart ached for his company as her skin shivered, remembering his caresses. How long had it been since those long limbs were wrapped around her?

He'd been so peaceful she'd no wish to disturb him. Too many of their days started early and ended late, and often he was out at meetings or on the phone with Scottie until all hours.

The best she could do was snuggle in close and finish watching the movie, something silly set in Los Angeles about a wedding that went wrong. So much for discussing their own wedding plans.

Only when she'd switched the television off did James stir and blink beside her, disoriented.

"Ah," he said and yawned and unleashed his gorgeous blue eyes on her, on all of her, until she smiled. "Guess I missed the best bits," he said, as the subtitles ended and an advertisement blared.

Was this what it was going to be like, married to a minor global retail giant? Would they miss the best bits?

"What's wrong?" he said.

"Nothing," she said. "I'm tired, too."

"Let's take a run down to Kangaroo Valley this weekend?"

"I'd love that, thank you, James, but I've got another assignment due on Monday."

"Can you do it tomorrow? Take the day off?"

She shook her head and he lifted his eyebrows.

"College," she said.

He frowned, then smiled and held out his arms. It had been James's idea she gain full credentials, for jewelry manufacture, for goldsmithing, gold trading and everything else that went with the life of a top jeweler, and he was proud of her, she knew it, especially when she'd come top of her class and won the major prize last year.

128

He'd accompanied her to the ceremony, snapped photographs for Nicole to share on socials, and had taken her out to dinner with champagne, harbor views and the works. When the waiter brought them tiny glass bowls of sorbets she'd stared at them for too long.

"Some problem with the palate cleanser, Stell?" James's concern was considerate, but how could she explain to him that as children, she and Jeannie once ate ice cream for entree, dinner and dessert, when their free-wheeling mother, Flame, hadn't managed anything better.

Huntleys was sponsoring Stella's studies, and she was lucky to work with Jim, such a master craftsman, who never failed to praise her for her creativity, precision, speed and dexterity.

"The future's in good hands," Jim had told her only that week, that day he'd grabbed both of hers in his own gnarled ones, his blue eyes twinkling, and given her the only other master key to his studio. "I know you'll keep it safe."

While Jim's faith in her was reassuring, in truth, Stella rarely felt at ease in Jim's studio. She knew better than to leave his tools out on the bench—each had to be returned to its exact correct place in the semicircular rack—and she never let the other apprentices up there on their own. She longed for her own space to work, where she'd never fear breaking something irreplaceable.

After sixty years of continuous use, Jim's tools were worn with the shape of his hands, and even though he was becoming more stooped by the day, he was much taller than diminutive Stella. Her shoulders ached from reaching out for the most distant tools and working with the materials above optimal height. She longed to amass her own kit for the trade, but there wasn't even time to look online for what she needed.

Jim's studio was almost a relic, a stage prop for Jim's popular "jewel of the week" podcasts. She and Nicole had spoken of how special it was, and planned the customer loyalty program might offer studio tours to deepen customer relations, perhaps ahead of Christmas time, to strengthen word of mouth recommendations.

Enough thinking about the business! Here was James, awake and with his arms out, for her!

Stella leaned in for a hug, joy evaporating her blues. She tipped back her head for a kiss and was rewarded with the soft brush of his lips. James Huntley the Third was a catch, asleep or awake, especially awake.

His phone rang.

"Sorry," he mouthed, breaking away. "Yep? Nope. Really?" He covered the mouthpiece. "It's Scottie again. Sorry, Stell. I have to take this, with the board meeting coming up. See you in bed?"

Next thing she knew, this morning's alarm had rung.

She shook her head. Here in the basement of Huntleys, the pest inspector wanted to talk. He'd known this building all his life. His own grandfather had chased out the rats when James's grandmother Eleanor's parents owned the store and ran it as an emporium, with shoes and hats and gloves and suits and evening gowns, until Jim had married Eleanor and transformed it into Huntleys House of Diamonds half a century ago.

Stella loved this building. The musty basement could tell its own stories, though mostly they only ever visited the extra safe down here. Now, she was becoming an expert on silverfish.

"They head for humidity, right? You'd never think the top of a hill would be damp, but this whole ridge is sandstone. Even when it's dry here on the coast, the water runs in from the mountains. It's lower, right?"

Stella nodded.

"And with all the leaks in Huntleys, well, you're going to get damp. Especially down here."

"Yes. That's why we've called you," she said. "So what can we do, please? We have to do something. They're getting into the gift bags and I even found some in the VIP room, under the old linen. They're revolting—creepy and they're so destructive."

"That's damp for you. Fix the leaks. Ventilate." The pest inspector's hands were on his hips. He frowned at the building's foundations.

"Well, you've got your diatomaceous earth, but that's a health hazard now. Deadly if you inhale it, even if you're not a silverfish—joke—and you've got your traps, but if you want a real solution, you're going to need a new building, right?"

"Ah. That's not part of my brief, and Huntleys is beautiful."

"True. True. Heritage?"

"Pardon?"

"Does this building have a 'heritage' listing?"

"Oh. I don't know. I should find out. I will find out. But we're certainly not wanting to rebuild, not right now. Surely there's something you can do for us now. Just to get rid of a few?"

"Well, there are your dehumidifiers. I'd get one down here for starters."

"Can you recommend a brand? What's it likely to cost?"

Stella planned to tell James about it at lunch time, but ended up snatching hers alone—partially reheated Thai take-away—not a highlight. She had a sudden flashback to her life as an office manager back in Perth, working non-stop for that creep of a boss who had her under his suave thumb for nearly a decade. Was she repeating history here at Huntleys? At least James was nothing like Damian, and she loved working with jewelry.

It was a gray day and custom was slow in the afternoon, but just as she was about to take herself back to the tearoom to make a start on her assignment, the lift man turned up.

Lorna buzzed Stella, and she bounded down the stairs to meet him. Another trip to the basement. Another trip down memory lane for the representative.

"It's an Otis!" he said. "You don't see many of these any more." He lovingly caressed the brass control panel. "I can see it's been well maintained. They go forever if they're looked after. So what seems to be the problem?"

"It's stopped a few times between floors," said Stella. "We can't have that. Fortunately no customers have been trapped, but it's a worry." She didn't add that James and Divandra were stuck inside for nearly an hour late last week and hadn't seemed the least bit worried; Divandra chuckled in that inclusive way, and James insisted they'd used the time profitably, discussing precious metals, and they'd laughed again. If Stella had been paranoid, she'd be worried. Anyone would be. James was gorgeous. Should she be worried?

"So you're going to need a retrofit," the rep was saying. "It doesn't meet current regulations. Should really have a two-way communications system in it. It's fifty fifty whether you just replace it, but it has a certain style, and the shaft isn't large enough for the current regulations. You don't get them like this anymore."

"So what's that likely to cost?" Stella said.

"Lifts aren't cheap. I'll get some quotes to you."

"Give us a range of options, please. Surely a service would help. Clean the cables and connection; that sort of thing?" She'd seen it before, the upsell. Was he trying to pull the wool over her eyes because she was female? Would he give the same answers were he consulting James? How could this person be praising the condition of the classic lift at the same time he was suggesting a replacement?

"Of course we'd need to consult other companies if it's going to be too expensive," said Stella. Her years as an office manager had taught her a thing or two. She didn't really want to see three lift companies. She didn't have the time. She just wanted a solution, and a quick and fair one.

The flash of recognition in the consultant's eyes told her he understood.

"Huntleys looks after its contractors," she said. She hoped for sensible quotes so they could get on with it. "We pay quickly."

Not for the first time she wished James's mother, Cynthia, was more accessible. She'd run Huntleys single handed after James's father died, until James and Nicole took over in recent years and she'd moved to France. It was the middle of the night over there now—not the best time for a chit chat about elevators.

Three customers were waiting when she saw the rep out the door, and she forced her mouth up at the corners.

"Now, who can we help first, please?" she said.

It was only when all were satisfied that she allowed herself time to reflect. What she really wanted was to be stuck in the elevator with James. The fantasy made her smile all afternoon. She'd share it with him at the end of the day.

"Tell Jim to send us more Boulder opal rings." The message flashed to her phone straight from Will in Nevada. Oh. So now she was becoming the servant of Will Huntley, James's younger brother, the scallywag come prodigal son of the family, so insistent on his own rise to fame and fortune with his own branch of Huntleys after a lifetime of wasting his opportunities that he couldn't even use a "please" or a "thank you" or bother to ask her how she was. Clearly he'd had trouble communicating with James, too, but why did that suddenly make her the best contact?

132

She pressed down the hunch that her good will was being used and taken for granted by the Huntleys and told herself she was glad she could be the glue in this special family.

She made her way up to Jim's lair at the top of the stairs and rang his bell.

"Who is it?" he shouted through the door.

"Stella."

"Use your key!"

Fair enough. She'd momentarily forgotten he'd given it to her. Jim's arthritis meant the journey to the door and back to unlock it was best avoided. She should have been more thoughtful.

"Jim, how are you?" she asked.

His blue eyes lit up to see her.

"Where have you been all my life, Stella?"

"Busy selling your beautiful work, Jim Huntley, and supervising the apprentices, and trying to do my assignments. Don't forget you canceled our last session. Hiddonite. Remember?"

"Yes, yes. What's up?"

"Will's apparently having a run on your set Boulder Opals." Stella filled in the niceties on Will's behalf. "He'd love some more if you can find the time."

"Hmm. Good to hear he's doing well. I did that too, you know. Found my feet. Eleanor found them for me, in truth." Jim gave a big sigh. "You don't want to hear all that again."

"I do," she said. "Tell me again."

So he did—all about how he'd bumped into Eleanor when he alighted the Bondi tram "a hundred years ago," knocked off her hat and fell in love with her on the spot.

"I was in a bad way after Korea. Had to clean myself up big time before I could buy her a new one. And look at me now."

"King of a global empire and a social media celebrity to boot!" Stella finished his sentence.

They laughed together.

"And how are you getting on, young Stella?"

Stella noticed the time over his shoulder.

"I have to go and lock up."

133

"That time already? I tell you, Stella, the days disappear like seconds when you're doing what you love," he said.

"Or almost love," said Stella under her breath, coveting his tools and bench space. What she wanted to do—needed to do—was design and make jewelry, not lock up the store.

"Good to see you," she said and he nodded.

"Get out the Boulders for me while you're here, and the strip wax, would you?"

"Of course. You're not starting on them tonight are you?"

"No time like the present," said Jim.

"But what'll you do for dinner?" Stella took the key from around her neck and stooped to access Jim's secret safe beneath his bench.

"Oh. That time already. No shortage of food in Bondi Junction. Run down and grab me some noodles, would you? Ah, to be young again, with all the time in the world."

She pulled out the tray of opals. The package of Boulder opals was on top and she took it from the stack and brought it to Jim.

"Of course I'll bring you your dinner, Jim, but I have to tell you that even though I'm younger than you are, it doesn't feel like I have any time at all, either."

"Yes, busy days when you're learning and serving, alright. A busy day's a good day. Challenges create achievements. Ask James to order more of these Boulders too, please, Stella."

Released from their box, the gems glowed on his bench under the bright lighting—bluey greens with flashes of gold and orange, and the occasional deep red. No wonder Will's customers wanted them. Each was completely unique and always would be, these fragments of former living things trapped in time, the water in them transformed to solid beauty.

Unlike other opals, Australia's Boulder opals could not be sliced or cut. Each pebble shape had to be set as it was, hence the need for the wax to be shaped around them, set in a mold, then replaced with molten gold. Jim Huntley created his rings from scratch. He refused to use premades— mass produced blanks. Jim's policy was to create each ring as unique. It was time consuming and expensive work, but rewarding, and Stella longed for an opportunity to set her own designing mind loose around the stones as surely as the glowing gold.

"I'd love to set some too, Jim," she said as she locked the safe and stood back.

"Mmm." He was already wrapping the first with wax, grabbing a scalpel to carve off the excess, his mind on the job.

Before turning off the lights on this too-long day, she'd fetch his dinner.

She stepped out for the first time all day and breathed the fresh evening air, hopeful for the first time that her assignment was achievable. If she could stay awake tonight, she'd nail it—her final one; the culmination of eighteen months with the Huntleys, a goldsmith's ticket of her very own, a shining credential to take her anywhere in the world to ply her trade.

As she slipped back into the building, the spice of Jim's steaming noodles through their packaging made her stomach rumble.

The lights were still on in the office. She'd pop in and ask James to order more Boulders.

Jim grunted his thanks and she left him to it. Soon, surely, he'd give her more design time. It had been his suggestion she gain her qualifications.

As she rounded the corner to the office, she heard the shuffling of paper.

"Hi, darling," she said, as she entered.

James was not alone.

James and Divandra were huddled close—too close. Heads together, they were murmuring, completely in their own world. Their heads snapped up in unison as they locked eyes with her and then with each other.

Chapter 20

Stella was no intruder. She was James's fiancée, wasn't she, and an integral part of his business? Her heart banged against her chest.

There were no smiles for her in this office—just silence. Divandra moved away from James and stared at him again, and then at her. James's smile came too late, forced.

Silence. Too much silence. She waited.

Stella's pulse drummed in her ears as memories of similar scenes with her old boss back in Perth rose up. Damian "unavailable" and the sound of another woman's laugh in the background when she'd phoned him those nights he was supposedly "working late," and the smell of another's perfume in his apartment when she came to stay. Damian had kept Stella on the blind leash of hope for years.

This time she wouldn't be so stupid.

When she shrank back around the corner and flew down the stairs, she couldn't escape fast enough.

Never again. She wouldn't stand for this. What a fool she was. How blind could a person be? All the excuses she'd told herself about her old boss over and over leaped to mind, and she dismissed them. There was no point fooling herself any longer.

She'd wasted enough time with James Huntley the Third and his entitled family. She was out of there. Jim was alright. Jim was a gem, and she loved him, but there was no point assuming James was like Jim and would adore her forever the way Jim still adored Eleanor, even though she'd died nearly a decade ago. Stella's eyes told her otherwise.

Evidence James's ardor for her had faded was everywhere. He ignored her in the evenings, ignored her in the mornings and ignored her all day. James was using the GGT offer as an excuse to avoid her, while he clearly still had time for Divandra.

Was James no better than his philandering brother Will, breaking hearts all over the world? If so, then Stella's heart was no longer available. It told her so, hammering in her chest as if it was about to crack her ribs wide open. She could barely think, her body in panic mode. Flee. She must flee. She'd done it before and would do it again, but this time, surely she was wiser. She wouldn't throw everything away. She'd send that assignment in if it killed her, to finish this never-ending apprenticeship. At least she'd have something solid under her belt for all the effort she'd invested.

Jealousy was a poison but it focused her mind.

Out the grand doors of Huntleys she flew, out into the mall, past the stalls where her own stall, Stellar, had once stood, its sparkles attracting crowds, including James, who'd brought her an ice cream one hot day. Those days were gone.

Her back to the impressive Huntleys facade, Stella clenched and unclenched her hands and forced herself to look up at the sky, at the harmless puffy clouds. She willed her heartbeat to steady and her breath to return to normal.

It didn't work. She took a few steps and checked on her emotions. Fury. Dismay. Pain. She tried to talk herself out of it. She was wearing James's ring. Surely that meant something. Or did it? It wasn't like the Huntleys had a shortage of engagement rings.

She swallowed. Was she being fair? Maybe she'd just imagined something special between James and Divandra. She swung her arms and breathed deeply as she walked home. She tried to corral her panicking mind. Maybe she was being paranoid. Either way, if James wouldn't make time for her, she'd just have to create a fresh opportunity for the two of them to reconnect.

Chapter 21

For Scottie, living with Nicole had been easy. Right from the moment he'd moved in, and throughout their engagement, and especially since their wedding in Cynthia's Southern Highlands home they'd been inseparable, but there was no question this GGT offer was a source of tension.

Nicole insisted on bringing up GGT again and again, despite the fact he'd explained so carefully why he wasn't at liberty to share any of the details until James gave him the go ahead.

She just didn't want excuses. She wanted answers, wanted to dissect every last little possibility and all the pros and cons of selling out to the glittering giant, to the point he felt trapped in the labyrinth of her questions.

At first he'd tried changing the subject. When that stopped working, Scottie had to simply leave the room. If he glanced back, her stares of bewilderment and rejection ate into him like the horns of the Minotaur.

Worst of all was the nagging fear—if Nicole's love for him had blossomed only recently, could it equally rapidly wilt and die?

He and James had to play their cards right, for the sake of everyone, himself and Nicole included

Scottie could ill afford time away from the Huntleys project, but his father loved a game of golf early in the morning, come rain hail or shine. They only played once a month, just the two of them.

"Golf?" said Nicole as he pulled on his golfing shoes. "Really?" Clearly she was still mad at him.

Since Scottie's return from Europe and their marriage, they'd had a dream run, each day happier than the last—until the last few tense weeks.

Had it all been too good to be true? Was this marriage following the same arc as his previous one, to Beck? Was he not cut out to be a long-term husband after all? Was he failing in some way? He didn't believe that. His own parents were still happily married. Most marriages were successful. While "conflict of interest" had always been a risk in their relationship, due to his privileged insight into Nicole's family business's finances, surely their love for each other was greater than anything else. Why was Nicole giving him such a hard time?

"Nicole, he doesn't ask much of me. It'll only take a few hours."

In truth, Scottie was glad of the break, glad to free his head from the figures and discuss the issues with his father, Nicole's resentment included.

"Well," said Ron Scott senior as the father and son walked from the second hole to the third, when Scottie raised the subject. "They don't call it 'conflict of interest' for nothing, son."

"More like 'interest' that never drops, and 'conflict' that keeps on building," said Scottie. "I keep explaining to her I have to follow James's instructions. He wants all details released to all shareholders at the same time, to be as fair as possible."

"Mmmm," said Ron.

"She keeps saying she's James's sister and she deserves to know just as much as he does."

"It can certainly be difficult."

"Surely you've had similar situations like that with mum, dad? Nicole's not happy, that's for sure. She just glares at me."

"Hold your ground, son. Dee and I had the same problem in the early years. She was always wanting to discuss the clients, but we just can't do that, not in any kind of detail. Generalizations, yes. Specifics, no. We had to learn to discuss other things, like food and decorating, and then of course, when you came along, that solved a lot of that problem. There was barely any time to discuss a thing, we were so busy with your nappies and feeds and trying to get you to sleep, and then watching you learn all those wonderful things that babies do, rolling over, crawling, walking, playing golf."

Scottie punched his father on the arm, bent to push his tee into the moist soil and place the ball on top. He took a careful swing and his ball bounded up the fairway. He loved Nicole with every fiber of his being, but he wouldn't have swapped this time with his father for anything.

...

Back in the empty apartment, Nicole fretted. Since that meeting and James's revelations about GGT, Scottie always had time for her brother, but never for her. Was she imagining things?

Maybe Scottie should give up on her and just marry James, she laughed bitterly as she emptied the dishwasher. Gay marriage was legal in Australia after all. Not that she imagined there was anything physical between them. But there was no question they kept shutting her out.

She'd tried to explain the way she hated being excluded and they'd made some progress, but one sweet Scottie kiss on a headland was not enough.

Why did "commercial in confidence" mean that James could talk to Scottie, but neither of them could talk to her? It was infuriating. She had plenty of information they needed, if only they bothered to ask her.

Had Scottie and James even considered the online side of the business? Did he and Scottie fully appreciate how well she, Stella and her sister Jeannie had worked together to launch Shop Huntleys Online?

And did they know about the Facebook posts tracing some of the stories of Jim's old rings, with families encouraged to send in pictures? They were in the middle of a three-month campaign to showcase Jim's rings that were already out in the community, to tell the love stories behind them ahead of Valentine's Day. She heard these rings were fetching double and triple their current day value changing hands on eBay.

And she had questions, useful ones that might not have occurred to them. If GGT bought out Huntleys, would they keep the right to use the Huntleys' name?

Were Scottie and James aware of the recent success of "Shop Jim's rings" which she and Jeannie added to Shop Huntleys Online a week ago? Social chatter was building. Would GGT buy all these sub brands of their business as well? The button at the end of each of Jim's "Huntleys jewel of the month" podcasts had accounted for more than half the traffic to online sales last month when he'd featured sapphires, one of his favorite stones.

And they'd just launched "Huntleys French Collection" for a selection of the antique jewelry Cynthia sourced from French markets and Stella repaired.

And as for what might happen with Will, all options were still to be explored.

When Scottie came home, the cut grass of the fairways was still wet on his golf shoes. Nicole met him at the door.

"Can we just not talk about this now, please, Nic?" said Scottie, as he slipped them off and reached for his business shoes. He smelled of fresh air and sunshine. How could she have begrudged him this time out of the office? Just lately the rings under his eyes told the story of his series of late nights thrashing out details with James, and Will kept waking him too early each day with fresh questions he wouldn't answer. At least he was consistently silent with Will, too, and not just with her.

"What?" he said, when he caught her staring at him.

"I'm glad you're happy, Scottie."

"Just a bit longer, Nic, and everything will be better for all of us."

"Hope so."

Chapter 22

Nicole picked up her mobile to phone Will in Nevada. Her pink nails were starting to chip, her tropical holiday a distant memory. She must remove it and accept that the blissful uncomplicated days with Scottie were over. She sighed, and prepared to leave another message.

"Hey Will. I know you never answer this thing, but I really want to speak to you. It's Nic again."

"Nic! How are you?"

"Will?"

"You rang me, didn't you?"

"You never pick up."

"Want me to hang up?"

"No. No. How are you?"

"I'm okay. Great really. Got a plan for the first time in my life. Working through it. Not there yet, but I'm hopeful. How are you? You and Scottie, eh? Our old friend finally won my sister's hand. That gives me hope, for sure. You two still deliriously happy?"

"Fine. We're fine, Will. Well, actually I've barely seen him lately with this GGT offer. He won't discuss it with me. He's a good man, Will. Too good. But don't you think if I was married to the financial advisor I might get a bit of insight? Turns out his lips are sealed. What have you found out?"

"Nothing. James is the same. Says he's got this plan to share more info with us all at once."

"Well at least they're consistent. But what are you thinking, Will? This whole GGT thing totally unsettled me. I'm restless for the first time in my life. Just as everything was going so well, being in love with Scottie, the marketing so much more interesting with the online sales and you and Mum coming on board with your US and French stores, and then GGT turns up. And Scottie won't even discuss it with me. It's driving me crazy. I don't know how it is for you, because you're the opposite of me, but Will, don't laugh at me. I actually don't know who I am anymore."

"What? I'm not really laughing. I'm listening, Nic. What do you mean?"

"You never cared about Huntleys, Will. You just did your own thing for years. It drove us all crazy the way you went from party to party and barely gave us a thought. I've never done that. I've turned up for work every day of my life. Huntleys has always been part of me. It was just there. I've never known anything else. And now I wonder what I've been missing; whether I shouldn't just sell up my portion, even if the rest of you decide to stay and fight it out."

"Nic, take it from me. Independence is overrated. You haven't been missing a thing. Don't toss it all away, Nic. I know I'm new at actually accepting responsibility for anything, but that means I know what it's like to have no reason to be alive. I'm not exaggerating. The last thing you want is to lose your reason for getting up in the morning. I've only just found mine, and I love it. I was just like an animal before, completely at the whim of my addictions. I thought it was fun, but I look back and wonder how I could have wasted so much of my life on nothing. I was drunk half the time, and looking for the next drink the other half. You don't want to lose your mojo. And for God's sake, sort things out with Scottie. Don't let something like this get between you. He's a good man, and you two are right together."

"Well you've certainly changed, Will. You're sure you're not bluffing?"

"Yeah. I'm a hypocrite. But I know what it was like. Are you really thinking of selling?"

"Yeah. I'm seriously considering it. Maybe it would free me up. Maybe there's something more out there for me than working in the family business forever. Mum talks about it as if it's a great advantage to be a Huntley, as if we're the nicest poorer version of the Royal Family, but I've just never known anything else. I just accepted that Huntleys would always be there. And now I'm excited that my life might turn out to be something different. I need to ask you—would you be interested in buying out my share?"

"You're not serious? I'm the last person with spare cash after the life I've led. But Nic. You don't want to sell."

"Why not? And what if James and Scottie advise us all to sell?"

"Nic, I'll be arguing against that. I know you might not believe me, but when you've drifted for so long like I did, being part of something bigger than yourself—having a few responsibilities—is actually a gift. Knowing I've got customers out there who rely on seeing me every week; who need my shop to be open. I like knowing I need to face the world every day and unlock my doors on time. I know it might sound boring, Nic, but I'm loving it. It's exactly what I need right now, and I'm giving it everything I've got. I need to make this store a success. The last thing I want is a bank account full of money and to be cast adrift again, with no place to call home. I'm committed to Boulder City for as long as it takes, so Lisa and I can get on with our lives."

"Lisa, huh? You know how rarely you mention her name? We all wanted to meet her at our wedding, but you turned up alone, bro."

"It's really complicated, Nic. Actually it's simple. We can't have a relationship for a full two years or I'll throw her career under a bus. So if I went ahead and dated her and did everything I really want to do ... Man, don't even get me thinking that way... The point is, I love her. Nothing would be more selfish than for me to pursue her before those two years are up. I need to wait, and I'm going to do it. She's worth it, Nic. She's amazing. She saved my life. And let's not underestimate Huntleys' role in saving my life, either. If it hadn't been for Mum, recommending the clinic where Lisa works, and for James, who backed me to go ahead and set up my House of Hearts here, I'd still be drinking, gambling my way to zero, or dead."

"But isn't waiting for Lisa also a gamble? What if Lisa doesn't love you back? Sorry. Shouldn't have said that."

"That's my sister alright—straight talker from way back. You're right, Nic, it is a gamble. But it's the only hand I'm prepared to play when it comes to Lisa. The media made this big thing of me on the arm of so many beautiful women, but I know that kind of life is not what it's cracked up to be. I only want Lisa. She's my anchor, my center. She's the only one I want, and it's not just for me. I want to be here for her, always. But don't get me wrong, Nic. I really want this for Huntleys, too.

People talk about giving back and I want to play my part. With my US branch, we can truly make Huntleys global. I want to pay my way and invest my efforts in the family business for the future."

"Hard to believe from my wild little brother, Will."

"Yeah. Well, maybe I finally grew up. Nic, don't throw away what you have. How many people can say they have a network of opportunity like we Huntleys do?"

"That's true, but right now, Huntleys is tearing Scottie and me apart. I hate not being able to discuss GGT with him. Seriously. He just walks away from me."

"Get real, Nic. I saw you give this guy the cold shoulder for six years, all through high school. Sure, we were all in our own worlds back then, and me for many more years longer than the rest of you, but even I saw the way you treated him back then. Big fail, Nic. So the fact you two are actually together is brilliant. You two were so happy at your wedding. This guy is good for you. You'll never find anyone who loves you as much as Scottie does, and all he's asking you to do is hold off discussing it all for another six days!"

"But Will, back then it was just a teenage crush. Scottie didn't even know me."

"He did, Nic! We all grew up together."

"Whatever. Anyway, now he keeps going on about a 'conflict of interest'. The GGT offer is now, and it's true it might pass, but every single time something comes up like this in our business, something 'commercial in confidence' or whatever, it's going to drive us apart. I hate it. It's like he's two different people. Scottie off duty is my Scottie. No problem. But Scottie on duty is this poker-faced automaton. Try living with that."

"Nic, I'm living by myself here. If I'm lucky, I see Lisa a couple of times a week. She walks her dog past my shop and waves, and that's it. My heart's pumping like a machine. Talk about a crush. I dream of Lisa night and day. And I have to be happy with that. So life's not perfect for you and Scottie every living minute? Suck it up."

"'Suck it up.' Right. So you won't buy my share?"

"You're not seriously still considering selling out of Huntleys, are you, Nic? It's nuts. Be restless. Fine. But don't do anything rash. If you're bored, come and see me. Come and do some brand work for me. Meet Sondra and the skyrun team."

"You're not just saying that because you don't have the money?"

"Nic. Don't sell. I know I'm the last one to give advice, given the fact I never followed anyone else's advice, but don't."

"Sure you did, bro. We could always count on you to do the opposite."

"Yeah. That's about right. So I do know I'm in no position to dish it out. But at least think about what I've said, Nicole. Don't let this GGT offer rattle things. For all we know they target family companies on purpose, to drive us apart and pick up a dysfunctional bargain. Let's give James and Scottie the time they need to prepare their response and see what they come up with. Let them put their cards on the table. Then let's talk again."

Chapter 23

Next morning, when Stella entered the kitchen, James was already on the phone in the other room. His mother's invitation still sat on the bench, untouched. Didn't James care about his mother's happiness? Did love and marriage mean nothing to this man?

She poured cold milk on her cereal and tried to block out the bitterness, to stare into the distance at the glittering harbor and focus on the morning ferries as they glided to Manly and back to the Quay, to Mosman and Cremorne, and under the bridge.

She breathed and held her head high. That was better. She came up with a plan. Easy. If James wouldn't invite her to dinner, she'd invite him. They'd go somewhere different and talk about something fresh, like when to get married. In fact, she'd take him to that wedding venue at Watson's Bay. Plenty of engaged couples went there to try out the food and check out the spaces. Why not them?

During her late lunch break, she googled "Eastern Suburbs wedding venues". Many popped up. And if James was worried about the cost, maybe they could marry at Cynthia's Southern Highlands house, as Nicole and Scottie had done, or just go to a Registry Office and have a cake in the Huntleys tearoom. They had to at least talk about it.

That moment, James came into the tearoom, opened the fridge and frowned.

"Leftover Thai takeaway, bottom left hand corner," said Stella.

"Thanks, Stell." He grabbed it, rustled in the top drawer for a fork and disappeared back into the office, without even heating it up.

Stella followed him in and closed the door.

He stared at his computer screen as usual, and tapped at a key or two.

"Mmm?" he grunted.

"I'd like to make an appointment with my fiancé," she said. "For dinner this evening. Out. Just the two of us."

He sat back and gave her a smile, as if seeing her for the first time.

"Great," he said. "Yes. Okay."

His blue eyes blazed into hers so hard she almost blushed. Why hadn't she thought of this sooner?

"It's been so long since we've had a change of scene, James. It'll do both of us good. We can both work late and go straight there. I still have to finish my final assignment. No business talk tonight. The sky won't fall in if you give it all a break for one night."

"You're right, Stella," he said. He gave her a wry smile. "Sorry I've been such a bore."

"I love you, James." Stella swallowed. How could she bring up his relationship with Divandra without accusing him outright?

"I love you, too."

Why did it still sound like he didn't mean it? His eyes were back on the computer screen already.

"Collect you in the car downstairs at eight tonight?" she said. Maybe it would be easier to speak to him as she drove, without eye contact. "Mystery destination."

"Great. Thanks, Stell. It's a date."

Stella rushed home after work, showered and washed her hair. She'd planned to work on her assignment, but instead, she dressed carefully and put on fresh makeup, adding a spray of the perfume James had bought her for her birthday. He really was a caring man, and a generous one. They must never allow themselves to get in such a rut again.

She hummed quietly along to the car radio as she waited outside Huntleys back door for him to appear.

Appear he did, but he wasn't at all relaxed.

"Stell," he said. "Forgive me. I just had a call back from Adam Li, a top corporate lawyer. Will and I were at school with him. Long story short, he's agreed to see me at no cost to chat about our buyout options, but the only time he can see me is right now. He's still in his office in town. Can you book again for tomorrow? I hate to do this to you, but ..."

"You're going to do it anyway."

"Stell, don't be like that. Please. Look. I'll phone him. I'll tell him I can't make it."

"Forget it. What's dinner anyway? I can eat anywhere, with anyone, except you, of course. I'll go see Jeannie. I was going to tell you she and

Dave are looking at moving to Singapore, so I'd best see them and the girls while I can. Will I pick you up after your meeting?"

"I don't know when I'll finish, Stell. There's a reason these guys earn millions. They work all hours."

"So do we, James."

"Yeah. Lately. I'm so sorry, Stell. Thank you. You're wonderful."

He went to open the car door then turned back to her.

"By the way, Stell. Do you know anything about some missing rubies?"

"What?"

"Jim reckons some rubies have gone missing. He mentioned you're the only one with a key to his workshop safe, apart from him."

A car tooted behind them as they stared at each other. It tooted again.

"Look I've got to go, Stell. Don't worry about it. We'll talk about it later. Thanks for the lift."

"What's that about rubies?" said Stella, but he stepped out and closed the car door on her words. He strode away and was eaten by a lift that looked like an enormous transparent vacuum cleaner stuck to the side of the city's newest skyscraper.

Chapter 24

In the lift, James's phone buzzed.

"James, darling," said Cynthia. "I'm so pleased to catch you. Can you talk?"

"I'm just in a lift. I have an important meeting, Mum," said James. He checked his watch. "I've got two minutes. How are you?"

"I'm so worried, darling. I barely slept. Nicole wants to sell. And Will may wish to sell, too, I'm sure of it, though a whole heap of money is the last thing he needs. I'm so worried about him. If we sell, James, my whole life is a waste. I will have kept our business together for nothing."

"Let's see, Mum."

"That's exactly what Émile says, James. He says 'on verra'—we'll see. But I don't want to see. I'm so tired of this GGT company. How can they just ride in and derail everything we've worked for. They're destroying our family, setting us against one another. How dare they! Can't you just tell them to go away?"

"I'm sorry to hear this is hard for you, Mum, but to be fair, we need to explore our options."

"But darling, every time I try to discuss it with Nicole and Will, we just disagree. Will sounds distracted. No, not like the old days when he could only see as far as the next party, but his mind is on other things. I can tell. His skyrun, and that Lisa. He seems so far away. It's never the right time to phone him. He's either busy at the shop, or volunteering to organize that run. And Nicole! Nicole has no imagination. Well, that's not fair. She's very good at marketing. But she can't see how valuable the business is for her future, more valuable than ever now she's married, though she doesn't seem to see it that way. And now she's mad at me. She thinks I'm the one who's stubborn."

"It'll be okay, Mum."

"When did you become the parent, James? I'm the one who should be comforting you. But do you know, not one of you has replied to our wedding invitation. I've been saying to Émile, we might as well call it off. No one will turn up. How ridiculous to have planned to hold it in that whole huge chateau. There'll just be the two of us there, Émile, and his friend Angelica, and we both know she wishes she were the bride. It's silly. A waste of money. An indulgence. And really, darling. When are you and Stella going to marry? You're the young ones. You're the ones who should be getting married. I do worry, darling. Why wasn't she at that meeting? Do promise me you're consulting her. I'd feel very left out if I were her. You know Jimmy and I were married within two months of his proposal. We couldn't wait."

"Mum, it's because of Stella that we need to make this decision so carefully. At the moment, I don't have as much to offer her as I'd like— a secure future."

"But darling, you should know there's no such thing as security. Not really. You just have to go forward and give it everything you've got. What do you mean you have nothing to offer her? You have yourself, don't you?"

"Look, Mum. I need to get to this meeting. I have to hang up now. Please don't worry. I'm doing it this way so nobody has to worry. Scottie and I will send everyone the same information shortly and you can stop trying to guess what might happen. Not much longer now... I have to go. Sorry."

Why was he having to apologize to all the people he loved? Hopefully Adam could bring some clarity.

Corporate law must pay well. Adam's office was on the thirty second floor. The artful reception desk was empty at this hour, but for an enormous display of Bird of Paradise which picked up on the orange wedge under the name of the company backlit under the counter and repeated behind it on a smoked glass screen.

"James," Adam appeared at the elevator, hand outstretched. His collar was undone. No tie. He'd had his teeth fixed.

"Adam, so good of you to see me," said James.

"Not at all, James. Come in, come in. This way."

Adam's office was right at the edge of the building, above the Royal Botanic Garden, looking east to South Head and the horizon. James could almost make out Huntleys, high on the ridge of Bondi Junction, and their old school to the left, and, at the far left, the iconic Sydney Opera House.

He looked down then took a step back. Not for Nicole, these giddy towers of industry. She hated heights. Where would Nicole end up if Huntleys sold out? Marketing for a company like Adam's? He sighed and ran his fingers through his hair. He hated being responsible for everyone's future like this. Well, before GGT, he'd had that responsibility, but this was different. His actions could spin members of his family off in all directions against their will, in a matter of weeks.

"I can't thank you enough," he said.

"Whisky?" said Adam, offering him a casual seat at a setting in one corner.

"If you're having one," said James. "Quite an office."

The amber liquid nestled itself around a stack of ice cubes in the chunky glass.

"So, how are you, Adam?"

Adam spoke of his new wife and two-year-old and another child on the way.

"Congratulations! You should be at home with her."

"It's okay. She's used to it. I speak to clients in the UK most nights, so I don't come in to work until late each morning. It's workable. So come on. What's this about a take over?"

"It's not that complicated, or simple for that matter," said James. "It's not as if Huntleys is listed on the stock exchange or anything. But in some ways it makes it harder that every shareholder is a member of my family."

"Yeah. I can see that. Family expectations, eh. You took over when we were all just out of school, didn't you?"

"Yeah. I suppose it was always expected of me, and my mother did most of the hard work in the early years, keeping it together for me while I got my head around it, but this offer has caught me totally by surprise. Made me realize I haven't been strategic enough. If we're going to sell, we'd be in a better position if there were multiple offers, wouldn't we?

"Maybe. Maybe not."

It was a relief to talk.

"It's just… I was going through the motions for years, trying to take my father Jimmy's place for everyone."

152

On his empty stomach, the whisky relaxed his body and his tongue.

"Will went totally off the rails. I suppose you read about him. Well, the media made it all out to be worse, but there was some truth to it."

"Yeah. Not that I read gossip columns, but he's a bit of a celebrity bad boy, isn't he? Didn't he break off an engagement to someone famous in Italy?"

"I never did hear the truth of all that, but he's on the straight and narrow now, or so we hope. He's opened a branch of Huntleys in Nevada, and he's raising money for kids with addiction."

"Good for him. He was such a champion at school. He won everything. Could have been an Olympian in any sport he'd chosen. We were all in awe."

"If only crashing parties was an Olympic sport, he'd win gold for sure." They laughed.

"Yeah. Well it was actually Will who suggested I call you."

"Sensible man."

"We can't afford you, Adam. We can offer you an engagement ring. Or how about an eternity ring for your wife?"

"Not necessary."

"Seriously. Come and see me in the salon. In the next two weeks while I'm still CEO of Huntleys. After that, who knows?"

"It doesn't generally happen that quickly, James, even if the sale does go ahead."

"This is exactly what I need to know. And would you have any idea why they're even interested in us? We're small fry. We say we're global, but we only have three salons, and the one in the south of France, run by my mother, is also very new. We're not global like GGT, anyway."

"Who knows? There's a lot of bluff in business. Maybe GGT just want to tie you up in an option so you can't sell to their competitor. There's a lot of that goes on. Great for lawyers like me. Untangling the promises and side clauses and fine print can take years."

"Better to just say no?"

"Or you could launch a counter bid, to buy out GGT. Anything's possible. What do you actually want? Have you thought of listing Huntleys publicly?"

"Scottie's drawing up some options for us. We hadn't thought of either of those ideas."

"Scottie, eh? How's he? I remember you were best buddies. Didn't you two win us that cross country trophy in your final year? I remember you up on stage at Speech Night."

"Yeah. Scottie's welded on. The Huntleys and Scotts go back three generations now. Oh, and Nicole finally worked out Scottie was a good man. You know they married recently?"

"No, but I'm pleased to hear it. That's great news. More whisky?"

"Can I get you some dinner, Adam? Call up some take away?"

"Let me do that. Welcome to my life. We could drop down to the club, but the walls have ears. What do you want? Pizza? Chinese? Thai? Korean? Steak sandwich? Hamburger? Remember the chicken shop?"

"The chicken shop! I reckon we were all made of chicken back in those middle years. Every day after school I had one of their huge chicken burgers with mayo. I used to dream of them. Couldn't wait to chow down."

It was good to remember the past with Adam, and laugh.

"What happened to Helene?"

"No idea. I guess jewels weren't as glamorous as she imagined. I don't pine after Helene. You know I'm engaged."

"Tell me."

"Her name is Stella. She's an incredibly talented designer." James described Stella's skills, her productive relationship with Jim, and the way she'd breathed new life into their business.

"And what does Stella think of GGT?"

"We haven't talked about it much. They took us all to Balmoral for a big feed. She called them cultured 'vultures'. The buyout is such a great solution in some ways. It would free us from the aging Bondi Junction building and all the costs associated with setting up the other branches. We could start again with just her talents, do anything we want."

"Do they want your staff as well as property? Will they let you keep trading as Huntleys? Where's the fine print? All this should be negotiable. If Stella's that good, maybe they just want her."

"No. That would be like selling her. This is impossible. We're in an impossible position. I can't be responsible for other people's lives like this, for the people I love."

"It's okay, James. It's just a game. Call it a long cross country run with a hurdle or two. Sounds to me like you don't want to sell Huntleys, don't want to lose control. Family companies are always like that. Sell the present and you lose the future and the past, all of that."

"But what if Nicole wants to sell? What right do I have to force her to abandon a new and better future?"

"She could walk out tomorrow and work for someone else, couldn't she?"

"I suppose so."

"Send me across their offer in writing and come and see me again in a couple of days," said Adam.

They ate chicken burgers sent up from one of the hotels, reminiscing, and when they shook hands at the end of their meeting, James was walking on air.

When he let himself into the apartment, Stella was just a lump in the bed. He slid in beside her and slept solidly for the first time in days.

But when he woke next morning, Stella was gone. She must have left early for work. There was no sign of her, just her engagement ring, twinkling on his white kitchen bench in the morning sunshine.

Chapter 25

Alone in the car, Stella didn't feel wonderful. Disappointed. Unimportant. Overlooked. Overworked. Underappreciated. And now, angry. Had James just accused her of theft?

There was no way she could drop in on Jeannie in this mood, especially with Jeannie and Dave still deciding whether to stay or leave. She'd just weep and beg them to stay and complain about James.

So, a meeting with an old school friend was more important than dinner with his fiancée. Stella tried to be understanding, but it hurt to be sidelined. Why couldn't James have included her in the meeting? Brought her up with him, introduced her as his partner. Wasn't that who she was, in business and in bed. She'd thought so.

If it hadn't been for all these secret meetings and the way James paid so much attention to Divandra, she wouldn't be so furious.

And what was that just as he left the car? Had she heard correctly? Did James just accuse her of stealing Jim's rubies? Surely not. But his words replayed themselves in her ear.

"Jim reckons some rubies have gone missing. He mentioned you're the only one with a key to his workshop safe, apart from him."

Her blood ran hot, then cold. She clenched her fists. Should she call him now and insist they talk? No. He'd made it very clear this meeting was important, more important than spending time with her right now.

Stella fought to rein in her emotions. She had an assignment to complete. Whatever the future held, it would be madness to throw away all her hard work of the past months. She might as well complete her certification, as Jeannie had advised.

Up in James's apartment, she turned off her phone, turned on her computer and wrote like a demon. She knew her trade. She knew it through and through. She didn't know people, but she knew her jewels and gems and gold. She knew durability and rarity; she knew her four

Cs—the color, clarity, cut and carats—and all her crystals, even the orthorhombic, though she was never sure exactly how to spell it.

Yes, she knew some inclusions, too, though she had to look them up. Moss and star effects were straightforward, but the gas bubbles, liquids and minerals trapped in the stones that changed their colors and created other optical effects were more complicated. The varieties were part of what she loved about her work—they created an endless fascination.

She wrote about the cleavage of gemstones, about tenacity, and specific gravity. What had she forgotten? Pleochroics which changed color; and luster, and fire. Surely that would do.

No. Why just give the basics. This was her world, her passion. Let them see what she knew.

She did a rapid word count. Two thousand four hundred words. A bit long. Tough. If it was all about passing, she'd at least convince them she knew what she was doing.

References! Her old art teacher had taught her the importance of referencing her work. She pulled up her two previous assignments and copied their reference lists, then scanned the books beside her bed, the ones Jim lent her right back in the beginning; an old encyclopedia of goldsmithing, and H Wilson's Pitman classic handbook, in hardcover.

There. Now. A conclusion. She had to write a conclusion. But she needed to flee. Fast. She'd already more than fulfilled her word count. Didn't they take marks off if you went over? Nobody really wanted to mark this stuff. If they were anything like her, they'd gone into the industry because they were desperate to create, not to mark assignments.

Conclusion: *The jeweler enhances that which occurs in nature by combining elements, selecting shapes with regard to the effects of light and the shape of the human body, to create lasting beauty and meaning. It is the duty and joy of the jeweler to take the raw material of the earth and add as much value as possible to justify the cost and environmental damage caused by mining and to create value for the employer and satisfaction for the purchaser.*

That would have to do. She'd attended every lecture and workshop, she'd finished every practical exercise and assignment. They'd have to pass her. Surely.

She emailed her essay with a polite explanation of why it was a couple of days late, then sat in silence.

"Stop feeling sorry for yourself," she said, as she snapped the laptop shut and wandered around James's apartment alone.

She showered and went to bed. Ten o'clock arrived. Still no James. Eleven o'clock. Midnight.

Was he even with Adam Li? Visions of James and Divandra laughing together haunted her.

Only that morning she'd seen them deep in conversation again, heads together. When James patted the young woman's shoulder, jealousy erupted, a poison so bitter it hollowed her out. Her heart hammered hard in her ears, but not hard enough to block out a new truth, that the future was unwritten.

So much for her solid commitment to James and the Huntleys. Where was his commitment to her?

It wasn't like she had to go through with any of this.

And anyway, wasn't that what an engagement was for? To test out an intention? Engagements fell through all the time. How many months ago had she rushed back from Hong Kong and James had gone down on bended knee? At least eighteen and there was still no wedding date.

They'd discussed online sales, Mother's Day specials, Father's Day lines, catalogs, what takeout food they'd snatch for dinner, whether to hire someone permanent in case Lorna retired or bring in new apprentices, but nothing as trivial as when and where they'd marry.

For the first time, Stella understood her mother Flame's aversion to relationships. There was something pathetic about begging your partner to be faithful; something so demeaning she couldn't even imagine it. No.

Until meeting that reclusive widower with a heart of gold, Ross Archer, her mother had begun again countless times, turned her back on another school and community and uprooted Stella and her sister, Jeannie. Jumping on another bus or into another old claptrap of a car and heading out for a fresh start was normal. Stella knew exactly how to do it.

There was no way Stella would sleep tonight. The way ahead was pure and simple. North. To the wide open spaces of Ross's old farm in the Byron Bay hinterland and her mother. Flame, of all people, would understand.

Chapter 26

Before she left, Stella ran around the apartment, grabbed essential items, shoved them in a bag and scanned James's view of Sydney Harbour, beyond the kitchen counter. Farewell, said her heart.

She swallowed a sob.

It only took an instant to yank off her engagement ring and leave it on the bench. So much for Jim creating beauty and meaning. The ring glinted in a shaft of light from the bedroom, casting blue light across the white marble surface. Exquisite. Solitary. Just minerals. Devoid of meaning.

Then she fled, off, down to Huntleys to grab a few things, and then to the railway station.

She caught the first train north, north to her mother, Flame.

Should she tell her sister Jeannie? Of course she should. And she really should let Flame know what was happening. She reached for her phone, but her pocket was empty. No! She must have left it on the desk next to her computer. And she should have left a note for James, shouldn't she? Didn't she owe him that?

But the vision of his head so close to Divandra's hovered again, and his words about Jim's rubies—as if she would steal from Jim!—and fury exploded in her gut as the distance unraveled between Sydney and the gently rocking train seat that held her.

Angry tears flowed and the anger oscillated to a wretched ache at all she'd lost, and back to fury again. No. Let James think what he wanted. It no longer mattered to her. Nothing mattered to her but fleeing.

After an hour or two, the racketing of the wheels against the tracks soothed her enough for sleep to claim her, her exhausted head against her pack as the coast flowed past in a blur outside the window, and Huntleys House of Jewels and James Huntley the Third retreated, further and further behind her.

She'd missed the day train, so she headed north as far as she could anyway, to Newcastle. To anywhere. They'd often stopped in Newcastle when they were girls. Flame loved the beach, and Newcastle had plenty. As she stood on the platform, Stella debated her choices.

Already the sea air was clearing her mind of the worries of the past few weeks. The world was bigger than Huntleys. She'd forgotten how huge it was, how full of possibility. If she caught a night coach she'd be in Mullumbimby in the morning. A walk along the river to the lighthouse would help her relax. The sound of the waves soothed her soul. She had coffee and a snack, and later, a swim in the baths. The sea was cold at this time of year, cleansing. She found a park bench in the sunshine, out of the wind, and watched seagulls swirl.

Time passed. She made her way to the coach station, bought her ticket and stepped up and inside, exhaustion overtaking her as the engine started up.

When she woke, head against the window and a crick in her neck, dawn was breaking over green fields. The ache in her heart quenched any hunger, though she'd love a hot cup of tea.

As she studied other slumbering passengers, she wondered what she'd done. The image of her engagement ring glittering on the benchtop back in Sydney stayed with her, mile after mile. Silent tears flowed. She ached for James, for his blue gaze and that wave of hair at his brow, his shoulders, the warmth of his hand in hers. Every memory scrolled through her mind—the first time they'd been in the old lift together and couldn't keep their eyes off each other, the ice cream he'd bought for her on his way back from the beach that day she was wilting in the heat of the plaza, the way he'd saved her in the storm, their harbor picnic …

Her reflection in the dark window was all frowns and misery. No wonder he'd fallen for Divandra instead. She cried again.

Just as well this coach was headed north. There was no way Stella could turn around now and go back into Huntleys, especially if they all thought she was a thief.

Flame was in the farmhouse kitchen when Stella arrived. Her mother's red hair was piled high on her head, secured with a chopstick. She hummed to herself as she made sandwiches. The place smelled like onions.

Stella caught a glimpse of herself in the mirror above the old fireplace—wild eyed and bedraggled. She'd hitched a ride up the winding mountain road with the postie. A childhood traversing Australia with the happy-go-lucky Flame had developed Stella's practical skills and adaptability, if nothing else.

"Stella!" Flame dropped the butter knife and ran to the doorway, to ease her pack off and wrap her in a hug. Stella dodged the chopstick but endured the hug for the first time in years. Her mother smelled of patchouli and onion.

"You didn't tell me you were coming! Now where's that lovely James?"

Stella clenched her jaw and left hand at the same time, hiding her empty ring finger a fraction too late for Flame's quick glance.

Yet what did it matter? What did anything matter?

That James and Flame had hit it off at Flame and Ross's unlikely wedding here last year was irrelevant. Flame of all people would understand why Stella had fled. She'd done it herself at least a dozen times. Flame and Stella hadn't always seen eye to eye, but she was still her mother.

"Ah," said Flame. "Take a seat. Cup of tea?"

Stella nodded and collapsed onto a kitchen chair, her head heavy in her hands.

The ache that had stolen her sleep for weeks, that slug of heavy metal in her gut, spilled over into tears, or was it the sharp, oniony steam?

She sniffed.

"Toast?" Flame said, and she nodded.

"Vegemite or honey?"

Stella shrugged. She wasn't actually hungry.

"If I'd known you were coming, I would have made something you like, Stell. There are plenty of eggs if you feel like something later. I'll be out most of the day, sorry. Ross headed out early."

Her mother made toast anyway and spread it thick with orange marmalade. She sliced it in two and left it within Stella's reach, lifted the lid off the onion pot and stirred the concoction within with a huge spoon.

"Makes a beautiful orange color, this," Flame said. Flame tie dyed scarves and sold them at markets. "I wish I'd known about these natural

162

techniques earlier. Carrots also make a lovely shade, but it's a bit of a waste of good food. You need quite a few to get a decent color. At least everyone throws out their onion peels. Always good to learn something new, isn't it? How are your own studies going, Stella?"

Stella shrugged. Here in the sanctity of Flame and Ross's old kitchen, her life as a jeweler was a world away.

"I'm hoping I'm done. I sent off my last assignment before I left."

"Well, that will be good, won't it?"

"I guess so. I still have to send in a final collection of designs. I'll get to it."

"Want to tell me what's going on, Stella?"

Stella shook her head.

"We're a bit short of spare beds at the moment, Stell, but tell you what. How about you have my old caravan? The sheets are clean. We were going to have a bush regeneration workshop last weekend, but it was washed out and we cancelled the guest speaker. He was going to use the van, so the bed's all made up. Come and go as you please. Sleep all day if you want. You look like you could do with it. Sorry I have to rush off. Want me to cancel?"

Stella shook her head and sipped her tea. A stream of sunlight through the kitchen window hit the toast, turning the marmalade to shiny amber, and Stella's stomach grumbled.

Flame bustled out and returned again with a towel.

"Plenty of water in the tanks, at least, so you can have a good long bath or shower."

"Thanks, Mum."

"Always good to see you, Stell. I'll be back late this afternoon. Pop your head in if you'd like dinner with Ross and me, though the caravan's full of the basics."

Stella finished the toast and had a wash, weariness overtaking her.

Just as she was going to head out to the caravan, Flame and Ross's phone rang. It flicked over to voicemail.

Jeannie's voice! "Mum! Is Stell with you? James is frantic. Stella's disappeared."

Stella snatched up the phone.

"Jeannie?"

163

"Stell? Thank God. We're worried sick. Why didn't you tell us you were heading out? What's going on?"

"I'm sorry, Jeannie. I wanted to call you, and James, but I left my phone behind by mistake. I left in such a hurry."

"You didn't even leave a note! I don't know what's going on, but that's not fair."

"What would you know about it?" Stella snapped. "We've had a buyout offer and he won't tell me about it; I … I worry he's having an affair with one of the apprentices, that Divandra; and he's practically accused me of stealing some rubies. How fair is that?"

"Hey! I'm just trying to find out what's going on, Stell! I can't imagine James having an affair, Stell. He's mad about you. You're engaged for goodness' sake. And why would he think you'd steal from him? There must be a sensible explanation."

"Look, Jeannie. I traveled all night. I don't really know what's going on. What I do know is I can't put up with any of that again. You remember how blind I was with Damian? The truth was staring me in the face for years. I just needed to get away. I haven't had a break since Mum and Ross's wedding. All I ever do is work. I'm so tired."

"Well, I'm glad you're safe, Stell, and I'm not planning to tell you how to live your life."

"Good. Because there's a pattern here, Jeannie, and I'm a sucker. They're exploiting us, those Huntleys."

"Stell! You're not yourself. You don't mean these things."

"What would you know, Jeannie? We're just employees. I've given up on my dreams and my own designs."

"Why? You can have your cake and eat it, too. In fact you're meant to, aren't you? Where are you at with that apprenticeship? Don't you need to design some final works and have an exhibition or something?"

"Sure I do. Tell me when I've got time for any of that. I know I shouldn't be up here, hiding. I should be on the Huntleys' floor again, polishing the cabinets and selling their stock. For ever and ever."

"Stell! Don't give up on your gifts like this! Even if what you say about the Huntleys is true—and I don't believe it is, by the way, but we can discuss that later. You've come so far! Even if James is in love with this Divandra person—and I just don't believe that either from the way he

164

looks at you, but even if… Stell, don't let some man spoil your life. At least finish your full apprenticeship and get your goldsmith's license. Then you can work anywhere you like, doing what you love. And please don't write off James. He's a decent man and he loves you. You might have it wrong, you know, about him and Divandra, and what's this thing about rubies?"

"You tell me, sister. I know nothing about missing rubies."

Stella stared into a dark corner near the telephone table. She changed the subject.

"I don't suppose you received that wedding invitation from Cynthia and Émile, did you, Jeannie?"

"Hang on, Stell."

"You should see it. It's so … 'Cynthia'; the raised gold lettering; at a chateau, as if she's some kind of royalty. It's more of a summons than an invitation. Who would dare decline?"

"You don't want to go? You're not just jealous, Stella, because you and James don't have a date yet?"

"It'll cost a fortune."

"It will be something to remember for ever, Stella."

"A wedding on the other side of the world?"

"It's just a flight away. Take a holiday. Come and see us at the same time. Get a flight through Singapore. Stay with us a few days on the way there or back, or both."

"So you're definitely leaving Sydney?" Anguish sliced through Stella afresh.

"Looks like it. Sorry, Stell."

Stella was silent. Had she ever been so miserable?

"You're okay then, Stella?"

"I am," Stella was surprised she could still speak. "I'll be fine; I'm just so tired. Can you tell James I'm okay? I don't want to talk to him. Tell him I'm sorry I just left like that. I know I should have organised for a casual to come in. But why should I always take responsibility for staffing as well as everything else? Other staff take leave or get sick. Call this sick leave. Jeannie, Damian always made the staffing my problem, too. I'm over it all. I can't do this anymore … tell him I had to have a break. That's the truth. Am I having a breakdown? I'm too angry to phone him myself."

"Take it easy, Stell. I have to take Sienna and Lucy to preschool. Give my love to Ross and mum. I'll phone James. I'll tell him you're okay. Go to bed, Stell. Everything will be okay. Phone me again later and we'll talk some more."

"I will. Thank you, Jeannie. You're the best."

Stella took herself to the caravan and slept like a baby.

She awoke a few hours later, confused. Where was she? Bird calls greeted her instead of the drone and roar of traffic. She threw open the flimsy caravan door to green grass and mountains and air so fresh it hurt her lungs.

What had she done? Fled the city, fled James, fled her future. In a sudden panic, she pulled on her clothes and shoes and fled again, downhill, away from the caravan and the farmhouse, away from her thoughts and fears and misgivings and regrets and guilt at leaving James. Faster and faster she ran, trying to forget.

Deep in the rainforest, when her chest ached from running, when perspiration dripped between her breasts and chafed at her thighs, when she could run no further, at the edge of the rippling stream, as it tumbled over moss and rocks, Stella sank down on her haunches, gasping for air.

She rested her back against an edge of giant fig and closed her eyes, the ache in her chest deep as an ax between her ribs. This was heartbreak. She was lost, lost in the woods, lost as a leaf adrift in the stream, running through the rapids.

What was she doing here, so far from Stellar, the business she'd created so she could never feel this lost again?

Why had she run to her mother, of all people, the mother who ran from every broken affair, who'd even run from her when she'd put her foot down in Perth and refused to pack up and move again.

She was utterly lost. She opened her eyes and stared into the canopy, that patchwork of leaves of every shape, straining for the sky. A slight breeze moved through them, ruffling their patterns as a hand smooths a rumpled tablecloth, as fingers push through a head of hair.

Instantly, James sprang to mind, that gesture of his, pushing one hand through the top of his hair, pushing back that wave that flopped forwards at his brow.

She squeezed her eyes tight again, and let herself sob for all that was lost, that wonderful dream that she and James were made for each other, that her skills would complete his business and together they would rebuild the Huntley empire stronger than ever.

She was a mere apprentice, replaceable, and James was already on to the next one, exotic Divandra, his infatuation with Stella over within eighteen months, their engagement meaningless, their love life a memory so good it only made her ache again for the loss of him.

Gradually her sobs died down. She took a deep breath, and another, and before her eyes she disappeared. Motionless as the tree trunk behind her, she sank into the forest till the forest creatures forgot that she was there. A bot fly lighted on a tree, a chain of ants resumed its march, a constellation of native bees formed and reformed on their secret mission.

A kingfisher swooped and scooped up water, its blue wing more dazzling than the sapphire engagement ring she'd left behind on James's kitchen counter.

What was an engagement ring when you owned a shop full of them? To Stella, the symbol had lost all meaning, as surely as she had lost her own purpose.

Stella melted into the fabric of the forest, scarcely breathing.

After weeks of frantic rushing, from college to Huntleys to James's apartment for another hasty meal and evening of assignments, flopping into bed long after James had hit the sack, longing for his body to show hers some attention, staring at his beautifully formed shoulders and jaw and chin with its shadow of a beard as he slumbered, as if it were a precious sculpture, untouchable; now, she stopped, motionless, and willed herself to forget, to let him go, to let her assignments go, to let her roster go, to simply be; to breathe in and out and blink, and nothing more.

She had no idea how long she sat, her back at one with the buttress root, her heartbeat slowing, her breath more shallow, her skin a mere continuum of the life around her, her toe the shape of a leaf, her arm another limb.

A group of wrens bounced in and pecked and tweeted and moved on.

High above, three black cockatoos shrieked, their red tails festive.

As the sun shifted above in its never-ending arc and the world turned beneath her, Stella emptied her mind until the ache in her stomach was her only sensation, and surely even that was just another shadow that would pass, as rain evaporates, as a frog in a staghorn might jump away.

Dragonflies, water insects, a ring of ripples at the edge of the deep water, a beak? At the splash of a curved brown tail, Stella stood and peered. It was. A platypus; shyest of creatures.

She crept closer to the water, squatting on her haunches, mesmerized. The marsupial's fluidity was molten gold, and another rose and swirled with it before they disappeared.

The flash of reflections as the water burbled over the river rocks, the laminar flow like polished jade.

Stella's designing mind burst alive again and would not be stilled. She must find her notebook and capture the shapes.

Back at the caravan, heart and lungs on fire from the effort of racing uphill, Stella reached for her sketchbook. Her heart lurched again as she threw open the box of colour pencils. This had been James's first gift to her, that Christmas he'd gone away. Back then, he'd been so attentive, so thoughtful; back when everything was new.

She cherished his gift even now, the way the pencils channeled her designs without her having to think, directly from her imagination, onto the page.

She ignored her hunger, laying out one design after another across the book.

A crack had opened in the crust of her imagination. After months of repairing Cynthia's antique watch chains, and demonstrating her skills acquisition for her course, and nothing actually creative beyond duty, beyond fruitless effort, wooden and clumsy—now, ideas flowed like molten gold through her pencils.

Inspiration tumbled onto the page, forcing her hand to ache with the speed and insistence, the design imperative as she emptied her mind.

Only when darkness came did she stop, to switch on a light, and still she drew. Her hand cramped. Her stomach rumbled. She rubbed her eyes, grabbed a banana.

A half moon rose and she drew that too, lacing it with cobwebs and vines, dripping with diamond dewdrops.

Just before dawn, when every empty page was full, as the mopokes called, one to the other across the valley, sleep overcame her, and she slept the sleep of the unburdened, hugging her pillow.

Chapter 27

"Come on, Scottie," said Nicole as she pulled open a packet of corn chips and sat on the side of Scottie's desk chair in their spare room. She waved it in front of his nose until he took one.

"Beer? Wine? It's Friday night," she said.

Scottie sat back and stared at her.

"Yes," she said. "It's me. Nicole. Your wife."

He smiled thinly.

"Beer then," she said. "I'm sorry I don't have the choice of five I offered you back when you were just my flatmate, and I had designs on you, but there's doubtless something in the fridge."

She returned with the beer in a couple of his coffee mugs—*"for caffeine a tax"* and *"Never lose balance"*—and Scottie smiled again. She leaned forwards to kiss his dimple and he caught her lips in his. He really was quite handsome, even when he was tired like this.

"That's better," she said. Could she risk it? She had to. She couldn't wait any longer.

She offered him the packet again, then said it through salty crunches.

"Enough 'secret squirrel,' Scottie."

"I knew I'd pay a price for my beer and chips," he said. He held her eyes.

"Well, I want to know what you and James are discussing. Honestly, I don't blame Stella for running off. We're both feeling so left out of this whole thing. Hear me out. I know James insists you two want to do things right so this offer doesn't break up the family, but the way I see it, the way you're doing things is already breaking up the family."

Scottie finished the corn chip and tried to stand, but Nicole pinned him down by offering him another.

"It's my turn to cook, Nicole," said Scottie.

170

"Forget it. You are not getting out of this conversation so easily. You've dodged me all week. Let's order in pizza." Stella grabbed a notepad and pen and took Scottie's hand. She led him to the living room and sat on the sofa, pulling him down beside her.

"Huntleys House of Jewels," she wrote at the top, then added "'Assets.' "It's not like it's rocket science, is it? We have stuff to sell, and GGT wants to buy it. If you can't tell us how much they're offering, at least let's work out exactly what we can sell and how much we think we're worth."

Scottie sighed as she wrote a list.

- Huntleys House of Diamonds Bondi Junction store
- Stock
- Jim's home and studio (above store)
- Huntleys brand
- Shop Huntleys Online
- Supplier relationships
- Huntleys House of Hearts Nevada store
- US stock
- Will's house above his store
- Huntleys House of Clubs store (and home above it) in France
- French stock
- Huntleys' talent and industry knowledge.

Her pen hovered to the right of the first item.

"So, what's the building worth?"

"It's not that simple, Nic."

"It's worth something, isn't it?"

"Depends on the condition it's in. At some point, a building becomes a liability, as it has to be knocked down and replaced. Huntleys is old now, more than a century. Systems become obsolete. Building codes change. You know yourself the roof and windows leak and the lift is shonky. Fire alarms are minimal. There should be a ramp into the building from the plaza …"

"But it's worth something, Scottie. There are plenty of buildings in Paris three times its age, and nobody's knocking them down. Even our land is valuable! It's so central. It's close to the railway station and buses, and there are more residents than ever living nearby. And it has a rental value, too, doesn't it? Even if we closed the business and just rented the place out, it would be worth something to someone."

"Alright. Let's put three million on it."

"And the stock?"

"It's insured for one and a half million."

"Jim's apartment and studio? I know they're tiny but you can't buy anything in Bondi Junction for less than a million now."

Scottie kept his lips shut, but she added it to the tally.

"Huntleys brand value," she said. "That's my department, but I have to admit I have no idea what that's worth. But again, it must be worth something, Scottie. It's brought GGT to our door from Switzerland. Let's measure 'brand' by repeat custom—customers who come back again and again. Do you know, it wasn't until we started Shop Huntleys Online last year that we created a customer list? It was all in Jim and Cynthia's heads."

Scottie shook his own head.

"I tell you, that Stella, Scottie. She has so many bright ideas. It was Stella who suggested we ask customers their birthdates and offer them birthday discounts. It's so simple, and so effective. We've been able to send them emails about our specials. It's brilliant."

Scottie nodded and drank more beer.

"Stella really should be included in our meetings, shouldn't she? I don't understand why she's being kept in the dark even more than I am. Don't you agree?"

"It's not about whether she's deserving or not," he said. "I agree she's a great asset, but she's not a shareholder. She's an employee, and employees don't own the company. It's not unusual."

"Well it's wrong."

"Business structures often lag behind reality. Companies rarely update such things. Usually only after someone dies or sells out."

"Could we sell out?"

"We?"

"Well. Me. Could I sell out? If not to GGT, then could I sell out to say Jim, or James, or Will, or Mum? Not Mum. She wouldn't accept my share. She wants me to keep it. Says she wants the whole family to stay involved forever. I don't understand why."

172

"Well, she put in a huge effort after Jimmy died, from what dad says. She held it together until you all finished growing up, so you'd have something of Jimmy's, he told me. But yes. I suppose you could sell your share to any other shareholder, or even someone outside the family. Would you sell out? To GGT?"

"I don't know. I don't even know what my share would be worth yet, do I? So, getting back to our brand value, if you look at our social media followers, there are several thousand across all the channels, and if each one of them bought just one small item for say a hundred dollars every year, you'd have half a million dollars. That's something. And what if we sold franchises? We could do that, couldn't we? Help people set up branches of Huntleys all over Australia. All over the world for that matter, and they could trade under our brand and reputation, with me still doing the marketing."

Scottie frowned.

"That's not a bad idea, Nic. I have to admit I've never considered that."

"Exactly. I've been trying to tell you and James you should discuss things with the rest of us, Scottie!"

Scottie nodded as she hovered her pen over her list.

"What's Will's place worth, Scottie? Did we lend him money for it?"

"It's a lease. He hasn't purchased it. So really it's a liability."

"Well, that's his problem isn't it? Would it be cost neutral, then? What about his stock?"

"You're making this difficult for me, Nic. James and I agreed to keep all this close."

"Oh, come on Scottie! We've nearly finished."

"Alright. Cynthia owns her French property, so she'll make her own decision about the Australian headquarters and her interests. And as for 'talent and industry knowledge,' your last point, all employees are actually liabilities. You know what you're paid each year, so multiply it out for the rest of you, if you must. I suppose you'll get a payout of some sort if GGT fires you."

"You don't believe all that stuff about them taking us to Switzerland?"

"I'm a conservative economist, Nic. No. I don't. It's very complicated. It's all very well saying we can just sell Huntleys and Jim's apartment, and all the rest of this, and divide up the money and you'd all get a few million dollars, but would you really put your own grandfather out on the street? I'd never have thought you were so mercenary, Nicole."

"So you don't think we should sell to GGT?"

"Depends what's important to you." Scottie's dimple disappeared.

"I'm just trying to piece together some facts, Scottie! Do I have to make an appointment with the financial advisor as the marketing manager?"

"I answer to the CEO, Nicole." He sighed.

Nicole narrowed her eyes. Scottie avoided them and stood up.

"I'm going to get the pizza," Scottie said. "What sort do you want?"

"I'm not hungry now. I don't want to argue with you, Scottie. I just want answers. You choose the pizza."

When he'd closed the door behind him, she spoke again to the empty room.

"Why should I have to put up with this lack of transparency, never knowing where we stand? If we sell, we can start over, without all these complications."

When Scottie came back, she ignored the pizza, turned over the page and wrote "ownership" on the top.

"I'm afraid the only owners are the actual Huntleys," said Scottie. "With you, James, Will, Cynthia and Jimmy, there are five of you, so you divide a hundred per cent by five and you end up with twenty per cent each."

"Well, that's easy enough," said Nicole. "If we just sell up and take the money, maybe I could pay off my apartment. I could get a job anywhere. Does Scott & Sons need a marketing manager? I could set up my own company, contract out to small businesses. It's kind of freeing to think I could create a whole new life."

"You're the shareholder, Nicole. It's your vote that will count, not mine."

"You don't have to be so poker faced, Scottie. You know the financials. You're the expert on a balance sheet. How much is Huntleys in the red? You and James keep talking vaguely of tax implications and compliance costs and the state of the building. What's the worst case scenario?"

"It all comes down to risk appetite, Nic. The company has fared better in the past. Dad explained it to me. In the early days, when Jim first set it up and society was more conservative, you could bank on everyone getting married. They all wanted engagement and wedding rings, and Jim's business boomed. Eleanor's family did well with property. They had their department store, and they bought their waterfront block back during World War Two, when no one wanted to be torpedoed by a submarine in the harborfront suburbs. As real estate prices kept climbing in Sydney, the Huntleys could always inject cash into the business by mortgaging their home, then pay it back when the profits rolled in."

He placed the pizza box on the table.

"Things are more complicated now," he said. "Not just because Cynthia traded in the old home for all your apartments, but because there are so many of you involved."

Scottie topped up their beer and brought in a couple of plates.

"In the early days, Jim and Eleanor made all the decisions together. Now there are five key decision makers, the way James wants to run it anyway. You're lucky James is such a fair person. He could be the dictator, but he's never been like that. He really cares what the rest of you think. That's what's making this so hard for him. Many CEOs wouldn't give you the luxury of considering your own wishes. They'd just push through their own agenda. So, really, my love, it comes down to what you think you want for your future."

"Hmmm. A life of luxury, to lie around in your arms, Scottie."

"Just as well I've worked out when you're joking, Nicole, or I might take you seriously. And the honest answer to that is that Dad and I've looked after the financial affairs of a few lottery winners and people who've inherited a small fortune, and the money never lasts nearly as long as everyone expects. There's no substitute for working at something you enjoy. Not just for the money, but for your happiness; for your health and peace of mind."

"You're not an accountant. You're a philosopher. I married a genius, Scottie."

Nicole opened the lid of the pizza box and the aroma filled the room.

"Did you see mum and Émile's wedding invitation?" she said. "Will we stay over there for a while and see a few other things? You can take me back to some of those places you saw on your tour."

"I'd love to, Nicole. But Huntleys will need to hire some new staff if you're all going to be overseas at the same time."

"Such a practical philosopher, Scottie. Not if we all just sell up. Let's sell, Scottie, and get rid of this rotten 'conflict of interest' once and for all. Then we'll actually see what the future brings."

Scottie took a huge mouthful of pizza and did not reply.

Chapter 28

Stella slept late. She dreamed of jungles. Spider webs clung to her arms, and vines wound around her ankles as she tried to climb high into the canopy, up towards the sun.

She woke in a tangle of bedclothes. The van was hot. She kicked off the sheets and threw open the door to encourage some breeze for her sweat-soaked limbs.

While it was a relief to discover her panic was only part of a nightmare, the sense of doom and entrapment continued, her estrangement from James a tragedy. Her drawings were scattered on the little dining setting, and she flipped through what she'd created in last night's frenzy.

Her designs, at least, were strong. The skill hadn't deserted her after all, though the uncertainty of her future made her frown.

"One step at a time," she said.

Barefoot, she walked to the outside tap, to splash her face and take in the day.

The shining wedge of a car was an intrusion on the rustic landscape. It represented airplanes and cities.

She made her way into the farmhouse kitchen, dreaming of eggs for breakfast. Maybe that bush regeneration expert had turned up after all, or some other friend of Ross or Flame.

A man was in the kitchen, his back to the door. She knew those shoulders, the sun bleached hair, the long legs. Longing and caution hit her with equal force and she hesitated at the doorway.

"Stella?" James's eyes were red. He hadn't shaved. As if reading her thoughts he ran one hand over his cheek and chin and pushed his hand back through his hair. James, always so perfectly groomed, had never appeared more disheveled. Had she done this to him? Guilt corkscrewed in her gut. She loved him—hated to cause him pain.

She wanted to run to him, to comfort him, to tell him everything was okay, and be held in return, but her heart was wary.

Hadn't she seen with her own eyes the way he and Divandra had leaned in towards each other, and then pulled away, as if guilty, when they noticed her? She wasn't going to play that game anymore, to beg for his attention. Maybe Flame was right, and all men were fickle.

But then her mother had proven most fickle of all, upturning her life philosophy by finally marrying Ross the widower. While she hadn't yet spent much time with them, by all accounts they were perfectly happy turning this farm in the Byron Bay hinterland back into wilderness.

"Why are you here?" she said, her tone neutral.

"I drove all night." His voice was angry.

"Doesn't Huntleys need you?"

"I don't care about Huntleys."

"How can that be true?"

"I've never lied to you, Stella. What is this? Why are you here? I was worried sick about you. If you hadn't spoken to Jeannie yesterday, I'd still be at the police station."

"You went to the police?"

Stella's heart hammered and her blood ran cold. Flame had had a bad stint with the police. They'd targeted her for crimes of poverty, for driving without a license and sleeping in her car. She'd spent time in jail simply because she couldn't afford bail, before her charges were dismissed. Her hand on the door jam, she stared back out at the rectangle of golden daylight. Where else could she run?

James's voice, more gentle now, drew her attention back to the kitchen, to him.

"What was I supposed to think, Stella? You left your ring. You left your phone. You could have been killed or kidnapped for all I knew."

Anger and panic ruled her tongue.

"Oh. So now I'm the one who has to say sorry, am I? As if I'm the one who did something wrong." She knew she should apologize for scaring him—it had never occurred to her he would fear for her life—but bitterness was a venom.

Anger flashed back at her from James's eyes, and then hurt. How she longed to go to him, to pull him into her arms, to take away this pain. But the distance between them was unbreachable. What point was there in clinging to his body when so much was wrong with every other aspect of their lives together?

"What have I done wrong, Stella?" James slumped into a chair, head in his hands. "I've driven all night, insane with worry. I've been bending over backwards to do everything right." He looked up at her and she slipped inside the kitchen, a little closer, and sat opposite him, the big old table between them, still wary, head high.

"Thank God you're safe," he said. "Tell me what's wrong. If you don't talk to me, I have no idea what you're thinking."

"You're right, James. We stopped talking. I could never get a word in edgeways. In case you didn't notice, you were with Divandra most of the time. Have you conveniently forgotten that?"

"There are reasons, Stella."

"Are there? It takes two to talk, you know. You could have told me why you were spending so much time with her. Tell me now. Tell me what it is that meant the two of you had to have cosy little chats all day and half the night for all I know."

"There are lots of things we discussed. And yes, I was keeping some of it from you, because you looked so anxious and tired, if you want to know the truth. I try to keep my business worries out of your life. You have enough on your plate. I could see that, and I didn't want you worrying about even more."

"Really? Like what? Like how you and Divandra had fallen in love?"

He sighed. He pushed his fingers through his hair again, searched her face, deliberating.

"What's that supposed to mean?" he said.

"You know what I mean, James. I saw you. More than once. I saw you again and again, and if you didn't notice what Divandra was up to, she certainly knew exactly what she was doing."

"If you're implying Divandra and I have any romantic interest in each other you couldn't be further from the truth. Divandra is having an arranged marriage, with the heir to a diamond cutting empire in India, which she's ecstatic about for the record, and I'm engaged, to you—or at least I thought I was, until I found this on our kitchen bench." He reached into his pocket and held up her ring, the exquisite sapphire, blue as his eyes, focusing the light of the clear blue sky from the window and

179

doorway, from out there in the open air, where she longed to be, far from this altercation with the one she loved. But he'd crossed a line with Divandra.

"What's one ring when you have stores full of them, James?"

A muscle in his jaw moved as he clenched his teeth, his eyes taking her in.

"Is that what you think?"

"Well, it's true, isn't it?"

"Actually, this ring means a lot more to me than that, but if it means nothing to you, I'm wasting my time here."

She wanted to sooth his brow, to offer him breakfast, but her whole body ached with tension. The space between them was solid and impenetrable as Huntleys' counter.

"Am I?" He laid the ring in the center of the table and stood, towering above her.

"I don't know, James." She stood too, her hands on the smooth wood of the table. She wanted his honesty, nothing less, but she also wanted him, desperately. The table stood between them, the ring the only object on its scrubbed surface.

"There is nothing between me and Divandra, Stella," said James. "But if you won't believe me—if you don't trust me—then my words mean nothing."

"It's your actions, James. I saw you together so often."

"Did it ever occur to you there might be another explanation? Divandra's knowledge of gems is extraordinary, incredible. I was lucky she told me. These are close-held secrets because each technique adds value, and you of all people should know how our industry is all about adding value.'

"So it was all about her knowledge." She hated her own tone, so jaded.

"Cynicism doesn't suit you. Stell, I don't understand. What makes you think Divandra and I have any interest in each other beyond our businesses? Hasn't she shown you the picture of her diamond mogul yet, with his turban and distinguished beard? She's wild about him. And Stella, you're the only one I want. We're getting married!"

"Are we? When? Your mum and Émile are getting married. I kept trying to show you their invitation but you were always asleep or in a meeting."

"Is that what this is about?"

"We've been engaged for more than a year, James, and we still haven't set a date. Does that sound like a healthy relationship?"

"We've been busy. We've been too busy. I'm sorry, but retail is like that. I've been working hard, and now, with everything up in the air—Stell, I have to have things squared away so I have something solid to offer you for the future. That's the only reason I didn't leave straight away once Jeannie told me you were here. I submitted the Board papers before I left, as I said I'd do. Our whole future relies on the GGT decision."

"Oh yes. GGT. But there's always another drama, isn't there? Things will never be perfect, James. And if you want 'perfect' you certainly don't want me."

"So you want to throw away what we have, after all we've achieved together? You'll finish your apprenticeship and move on?"

"You can find someone else to manage your apprentices. How about Shawn, or Divandra, or … this is an idea … use a recruitment company and hire someone." It came out acrid. She hated her words, but they were better out than in.

"I thought you loved that role, Stella," James shook his head, dismayed. "I thought you loved Huntleys. The reason our stores are so busy is because your designs and ideas have brought in so many new customers. I thought we were a team, rock solid, and then I came home and found this on the bench! Why didn't you tell me you were unhappy?"

He pointed at the ring.

"I tried, James, but you were always on the phone with Scottie, or chatting with Divandra, or asleep. Tell me this, James Huntley. What's even so special about family if they shut you out? I might as well go work for GGT where at least I'll know I'm worth exactly as much to them as they pay me—nothing more and nothing less."

A shiver ran through her. Working for Wolf and Carl and their ilk, so charming, but cold and manipulative, was the last thing she wanted. She wanted to be with no one but this man, James, but not the way it had been lately. She owed him this truth, however much it hurt them both to hear it.

His face was twisted, tortured, but she may as well lay it all out now—all of the resentment that had been building for months.

"There's so much about Huntleys you don't know about, James, and I could tell you, if only we still talked. I'm lonely. Lonely for you. You're never available. You put everyone else first."

"Oh. What is it? What is it you want to tell me about Huntleys?" Why was he so defensive all of a sudden. He stood taller than ever as she began.

"Everything, James. Divandra might know things, but so do I. I have ideas every day. You used to listen to me."

"Tell me."

"Did Will tell you about my Men's Geometrics line idea? Signet rings and pendants on woven chain chokers, and half pearl half gold wrist bands?"

"No. Tell me. I want to know."

"Men's jewelry is all the rage in the US right now. Jeannie and I want to try a Shop Huntleys Men's Geometrics line in the online store. Jim scoffs at it. Says it was the briefest of fashions in the 1970s, but men's chains have always been big in Europe."

"You're right. I've never thought of any of that. Great idea."

"Good. Well, you might also like to know that Shawn's already doing his final assignment on the idea. Jim gave him some onyx and jade for his signet rings the other day, for the lost wax technique."

Stella knew Shawn had been back to Jim's lair more often than scheduled. Shawn left a smell of bubble-gum everywhere he went. She'd tried to discourage him from chewing it when he was serving. Let Shawn set the tone of his own establishment one day. Huntleys was clean and classy. Not that bubble-gum was a bad fragrance—many large department stores added fragrance as part of their branding according to Nicole—but Jim wouldn't have a bar of it. Jim's lair always smelled like bubble-gum when Shawn had been there. For Stella, it was a distraction.

"Huntleys Men's Geometrics. Yes. It's a great idea."

Her eyes flicked to his wrist and throat. Men's Geometrics would look fabulous on James Huntley. She ached to go to him, to encircle his wrist with her fingers and run her fingers through his, press her face to his neck and inhale him. How she missed him. She ducked her head away as tears stung the back of her eyes.

"Well, I don't know when I was supposed to raise it with you, with you always at the computer or on the phone."

Or chatting with Divandra, she wanted to add, but bit her tongue.

"Well, this is sure one way to get my attention. Running away. I've been sick with worry. I had no idea where you were. You didn't even leave a note. How cruel is that, Stell? It's just like, suddenly, in your head, you're breaking off our engagement and setting off to the middle of nowhere without me."

"My family's always done that."

"Well, my family hasn't. It's not mature; it's not sensible and it's not fair."

James was right. Yet her fog of hurt and anger still lingered. She wouldn't add guilt to it.

"You might be prepared to run away from what we have, Stell, but I'm not," he said, his voice more gentle.

"I already told you I'm not perfect."

"I don't want perfect, Stella. I want you. That didn't come out right. You're perfect the way you are. Except, please trust me. If we don't trust each other, there's not much point is there?"

"How can you talk about trust, James! You practically accused me of stealing Jim's rubies the other night! How could you think I'd steal from Jim? I love Jim from the bottom of my heart, as if he's mine, all the fathers I never had, and all my grandfathers. How can you think I'd steal from him, let alone from your precious family company? You think no one is holier than a Huntley, and nothing more important than your business. But you won't even talk to me about the options for the future, for what was to have been our future, James."

She stood and curled her fingers into fists in front of him, then hurled at him more words of fury.

"While we're talking about theft, you're the thieves. All of you. Your company has stolen all my time, every bit of it. I had a business too, a year ago. Remember that? Stellar. And I was too love struck to even think of selling it to you. There was no fancy buyout offer for Stellar from

Huntleys, was there? Yet you—you swallowed me whole, and I gave myself to you willingly. I thought we were in this together, James, in life together. What a fool I was."

Chapter 29

How could he have forgotten Stella's pull on him, her hair dark, wild and curly around those eyes as they flashed with anger and hurt and dismay as she flinched at his accusation. Why was he hurting her like this?

He reached out a hand across the table, to hold one of hers, to broach this painful distance, to help her remember how much he loved her, but she pulled her own away before he could touch her. With her back against the wall, she was like a wild animal, assessing escape routes.

"Say it," said Stella. "You think I stole those rubies, don't you?"

James's phone pinged. He pulled it out of his pocket and turned it to silent, without looking at it. Whoever called would have to wait. Only Stella mattered. None of this had gone as he'd planned, as he'd hoped. He could never have guessed the depth of her alienation, the pain he'd caused her. All her points were valid. Could he ever forgive himself?

"I didn't, Stell. I'm the CEO. I have to ask everyone. And frankly, a few rubies here or there are a fraction of what's going on right now. Even if you did take them, I know it would have been for a good reason, like maybe you were taking a closer look to design something special with them. I never said you stole them; just that they were missing."

Her expression softened. Was that hope in her eyes, the anger finally seeping away?

"Then why don't you act that way and let me in on your world, James? All this secrecy with Scottie. It's got to stop. If you and I are not a true team, James, we're nothing."

"Good. This is good, Stella. I can't fix something I don't even know about. Tell me what you mean."

"I feel like a spoiled child, James. I know you took me into your business, trained me, gave me Jim's best ring, welcomed me into your apartment and your life, but ..."

His heart twisted. What now?

"Why do I have to run away for you to notice me, James? Haven't you missed me as much as I've been missing you? I love you, James. I want to be with you. But lately I've just been part of the background."

"I've been busy, too, Stell. And don't you think I don't notice everything you've been doing for our business. Our custom has tripled since you joined me and keeps rising, thanks to you. Those GGT guys kept talking about your design skills. For all I know, it's you who brought them to our door."

She swallowed. It was something. He flattered her, but it wasn't enough. If they were laying their cards on the table, she had to do this, to share with him her greatest fear.

"Is that all I am to you, James? A business asset?" Her voice came out small, thin.

"Of course not, Stell. You've got it all wrong." He sighed deeply and sat, hoping she'd do the same.

She smiled, just a little. This was better, her first step up from the deepest despair, or so he hoped. Could they find one another again?

"But shouldn't we be discussing everything, together, including GGT? Sharing our ideas like we used to do, coming up with solutions." She too sat, her hands more relaxed on the table between them.

"I haven't been totally honest with you, Stell," he said. "I know I've been preoccupied with the bigger picture, like what we're doing about ownership of Huntleys and proper strategic planning options, consulting Will and Nicole and mother and Jim. Divandra's been helping me understand the global market better. Her family has some dealings with GGT International in Canada. I have to learn all about them, all about the share market. I want to make the best decisions for our future. But there's more."

"More?"

They stared at each other. The kettle on the stove began to whistle. It was James who stood and lifted it from the hob, turned off the burner, then placed it back down. The whistle died slowly as he spoke.

"The real reason I've driven all night is to apologize to you. I can't forgive myself for going to that meeting with Adam instead of going to dinner with you. I blame myself for your disappearance, Stell."

He needed to hold her. Without dropping his eyes from hers, he moved to navigate around the table towards her—but she warned him away with her eyes, and retreated further, towards the refrigerator. He stopped; maintained the distance between them; held out his hands, palms down, as if he could calm the very air they breathed—fractured with waves of Stella's shock and fury and his grief at having handled this all so badly. Had he lost her—lost his Stella?

"I would have left, too, if you'd treated me the way I've been treating you, Stell. I see that now. Believe me; driving all night, I've had time to think over everything. My motives were true, but the delivery was shoddy. I have treated you badly, Stella.

"And you're right," he said. "I am the thief. By bringing you into our business so thoroughly, without even giving you a percentage share of it, I've stolen more than your ideas and your time and your good will. I've stolen your right to vote on our future, and I regret that now, Stella. I didn't realize the implications. If you can only let me explain."

She made no move to go, so he moved behind her, laid his hands on her shoulders, gently pushed his thumbs into the tension they held, his voice low. It was easier like this, not having to see her expression.

"I never earned the right to lead Huntleys," he said. "It was given to me. I took it all for granted for years—until you turned up on our doorstep with your stall, with all your passion for making jewelry, and all your skill and energy, and your drive and dreams."

He sighed, squeezed his eyes shut and opened them, removed one hand to massage his own temples, then squatted beside her chair, seeking her eyes.

"I know now I've done the wrong thing, keeping things to myself about the business. The truth is, I'm so frustrated. I keep hoping I can change the fortunes of Huntleys so I truly have something to offer you, Stella, when you take my hand in life. I've tried to do things right. I know now I've been far too soft on Will, and for too long. I let the business support him without insisting he give back enough to keep us viable. But now he seems to be making a go of it in Nevada, I still want to give him that chance to make something of his life, for our father's sake."

He moved back to his chair and sat, his head in his hands.

"I've failed as a CEO. You've told me yourself you've seen the state of our building. I just wanted to know we were in the black and able to make the necessary repairs before we married. I've wanted to do everything I can to save the business, but I see now that was wrong of me. What will happen will happen. I've done my best. I've neglected you, the most important person in the world to me, Stella. So I've come to ask your forgiveness for shutting you out, for not sharing the full truth. I worried you wouldn't want me without Huntleys. I wanted to offer you a robust future, and the confidence to start a family, if you still want one with me."

She stood and stared at him, Flame's table still between them, the ring glinting.

"I only ever wanted to please you, Stella, to be able to bring your brilliant ideas to fruition, to retain and build on my family's legacy. I've avoided talking to you because your questions might reveal the extent of our debt. I didn't want you to know how much our business is struggling. Even your suggestion that we install a CCTV. We should have done it ages ago and then there'd be no question about those rubies. It was a great idea, another one, and I wanted to do it. All your suggestions are great. I trust you utterly, Stell. That's part of the problem. I can't tell you how much it frustrates me that I can't put all of your suggestions into place. I hate letting you down, and I keep trying to work out whether this GGT offer isn't the best thing for us after all, to free us up. I know now I've done the wrong thing. GGT has been eating away at me, taking me from you, and from what is good in life."

James curled his fingers into fists. It was all true. He'd raged at his inability to turn the family's fortunes around.

"I've been so tempted to just sell up and walk away from it all, and run away with you and start fresh. Because that's a real option for us, Stell. Always. But I thought if I kept fighting, for you and for the family, to make Huntleys strong, that's what you'd want me to do."

"You'd do that? Walk away from your business and your family? For me?"

James's phone vibrated again. He ignored it.

"If it's what you want, Stell. I should have discussed this all with you from the start. Been honest when I first proposed to you, told you the true state of Huntleys."

"I don't care about money, James. I care about you." She was there beside him before he knew it, her hands on his, their fingers intertwined, and he stood and wound his arms around her tiny frame. How he'd missed her. She belonged right here beside him. They'd work it all out. They had to.

"Stell." Now her hands were on his shoulders, her head on his chest. He lifted her; sat her on the table and held her gaze, and slowly dropped his lips to hers. He kissed her tenderly and let the heat and fire of her heal his soul. Never again could he let distrust grow between them. She must know and trust he loved her forever. He broke away.

"Stella, we'll set that wedding date. If you mean what you said about wanting me and not my company. We can marry in a month if you like, as soon as possible. I don't want to be without you. I don't want us to be apart."

He gazed into her eyes. Did she understand? Her face softened and he dropped his lips to hers again, just as the phone began to ring again, its vibrations an impossible distraction. James pulled it out of his back pocket and flung it on the table, where a message stared up at him, from Nicole.

Chapter 30

Nicole was on Cloud Nine when she turned up with Scottie for Sunday lunch with the Scotts. Her decision to sell had freed her. Even though Scottie had explained that the sale wouldn't necessarily go ahead and that Cynthia and Jim were unlikely to want to sell, maybe she could convince Will to sell, and maybe James would agree it was the best thing for them.

"It can be a fresh start for all of us," said Nicole, as they pulled into Dianne and Ron Scott's driveway. "It's the obvious way for the two of us to avoid this whole 'conflict of interest' thing, Scottie. I hate it. And even if we don't all decide to sell, I could at least sell my share to Will, mum, James or Jim. And even if none of them want it, well, I can always approach GGT myself, can't I?"

"In theory," said Scottie, reaching for the bottle of red wine.

The Scotts' pink ornamental cherry was in bloom and there was a freshness in the air that made her want to dance.

Dianne opened the front door with her apron on and picked up on Nicole's joy.

"Did you see my jonquils, too, Nicole? You must take some home with you. For me, it's the very first and best fragrance of spring. I've popped a few on our table. Not too many. The fragrance can become quite overpowering. Come on in. Drink?"

Ron Scott senior was keen to hear of developments. Like Scottie, he was adept at keeping his comments neutral.

When Nicole declared her wish to accept the GGT offer or, if not, to sell to another member of the family, Ron Scott merely smiled and nodded.

"Well, no doubt all will be decided soon," Ron said. "Next Thursday, isn't it, Scottie, your EGM?"

"Yes. James and I finalized the statement of options and sent them out a couple of nights ago. Phone calls have been running thick and fast. I have an appointment with Jim early next week to explain some of the details."

Salt and pepper was circulated, and Dianne took a careful mouthful of her slice of the roast, the signal they could all begin.

The sliver of meat felt dry in Nicole's mouth. There was a sudden ache under her chin, and a moment later she raced to the Scotts' restroom, nausea rising up in her so that even Dianne's clean and folded hand towels and the fragrance of the tiny soaps repulsed her. Her face in the mirror was white. She feared she'd pass out.

"Are you alright, dear?" Dianne's voice outside the door was gentle and welcome.

"I … I don't know. I thought I was going to faint. I've been staying up late thinking about this GGT business, and what I can do with the rest of my life if we sell. Maybe I've been overdoing it. Or is it the jonquils?"

"I'll take them off the table, Nicole, dear. Try to put your head down low. I've brought you a bowl in case you need it. Do you want to lie down, or come and sit on the lounge?"

Like a ghost, Nicole traipsed out and flopped on the lounge, her arms and legs clammy. With Dianne's guidance, she put her head down low until colors began to return to her world.

Scottie hovered.

"Should I call a doctor, Nic?"

"No. I'm feeling a bit better now. How odd."

The Scotts exchanged looks. Mrs Scott senior tried to suppress a smile.

If Nicole had an inkling, she wouldn't share it yet. If she was right, it could change everything.

…

"Mum!"

"Hello, darling," said Cynthia. "How lovely to hear from you. I'm just sorting and labeling the latest bundle of chains from the weekend markets for our Huntleys French Connection, once Jim and Stella have a chance to make a few repairs. These ones are in pretty good shape, though. How are those sales going, darling?"

"Great, Mum. We're promoting them fairly heavily. They're particularly popular in the upper north shore. My hunch was right. Please, keep them coming. How are you? How's Émile?"

191

"You're terribly good at that marketing, darling. We're well, thank you. Well, I'm very worried about the business of course. I've actually just finished thrashing it all out with Will. I do dislike this, the way we have to try to guess how everyone will vote. I agree with Jim that we should all just tell them to go away. We don't need this kind of conflict in the family, Nic. Now. Will tells me you want to sell. Is that right darling? I know you're entitled to your own opinion, Nicole, but I have to say, I don't think that's a good idea. Selling or floating it might make money in the short term, but we'd be trading away our freedoms. I had a good long chat with Camilla's husband. Do you remember Rennie Reynolds? He told me there's a reason that companies like Gucci and Aldi become household names. It's because they have the strength of generations of family behind them. And I've tried to tell you all, I've seen firsthand the damage that is caused when those multinationals move in and take away the power of individuals and families."

Cynthia lowered her voice.

"Émile's story is heartbreaking. Huntleys must dig deep to survive and thrive, independent and strong, as a resource for the next generation. I do wish you would listen to me, Nicole."

Nicole laughed. "Mum, you do realize I can't get a word in edgeways? I have no choice but to listen to you."

"No need to be rude, darling."

"Scottie and I have an announcement, Mum," said Nicole. "We're expecting!"

Silence.

"Mum?"

"Oh! That's such wonderful news! Well, that puts everything in perspective. There's nothing more wonderful! I'm going to be a grandmother! Congratulations, darling! Congratulations to Scottie, too. Imagine you becoming a mother yourself, Nicole! When? Will you still be able to come for the wedding?"

"I hope so. I'll be fairly big by then, but it's not unsafe to fly, is it? We'd love to be there."

"Oh. I'm so thrilled for you. Is Scottie pleased?"

"I've never seen him so happy, Mum. The Scotts are over the moon. Can you visit us when the baby arrives, do you think?"

"Of course, Nicole. Émile! He's polishing a piano stool. 1700s. Very ornate. There's oil all over his fingers. Oh my darling, I'm so happy for you both. Émile, we're expecting!"

Nicole laughed to hear her mother explain the situation.

"Champagne," said Cynthia. "Émile's gone to find some. Darling, does this change your mind at all? Do you have time to talk? How are you feeling? How are the mornings?"

They spoke for a while about Nicole's aversion to strong smells, and how Scottie brought her tea and vegemite toast in bed each morning, which helped to quell her sickness.

A faint "pop" alerted Nicole to Émile's return, and their toast to the child she carried.

"To you and Scottie, darling, and to your baby to be. We couldn't be more excited for you, could we, Émile?"

"Thank you, Mum. Please thank Émile, too."

"Now darling, you don't have to tell me, and I don't want to sound like a broken record, but this might just change your thinking about selling your share of Huntleys. It's a very rare thing to have a business interest to pass on to a child. Not every child has that advantage."

Nicole bit her tongue. That "advantage" hadn't been the best thing for Will, but now wasn't the time to raise the issue of his wasted years, especially since he was clearly making an effort to settle down, and Huntleys had certainly helped him do so. James and Huntleys were generous to Will and to Cynthia as they pursued their dreams under the Huntley logo, maybe too generous.

If only Huntleys wasn't in such a financial hole. James had shared with her the worst of news, that nothing short of a buyout was likely to change their fortunes, that the buyout had actually come at a great time.

Their rapid expansion costs coupled with the crumbling building had combined to create a debt they could barely trade their way out of, despite the success of all three salons and the online store.

"And Jimmy's not getting any younger, Nicole. What would happen to him if we sold? I just want you to know the value of having Huntleys in your life. It's not just about sustenance, darling. It's about meaning. It's all very well having money, but if you're not earning it, you're spending it. We've seen for ourselves what too much money did for Will early on.

He had no idea of the value of it, drifting from party to party. Thank God he's stopped now. I just hope it all works out with Lisa. He'll know soon whether she can return his love, and in the meantime, his House of Hearts is keeping him busy, keeping him stable."

"That's true, Mum."

"As I said, you might start to think of that little baby's future? I remember as if it was yesterday how Jim's wife, Eleanor, welcomed me into the business and into their lives. She made it so easy for Jimmy to marry me. Dear Eleanor. She'd wanted so many more children, but she only had the one, her Jimmy, her pride and joy. I want my children to know the value of that love, to stay involved in the business. I don't want to interfere, but you deserve the truth about how I feel about it all, especially now, now that there will be more of you. You and Scottie are starting your own family. You'll see things differently. It's amazing how often I think of Eleanor, your grandmother. She had the most beautiful smile. You know she changed old Jim's life completely. The way he tells it, he was just a drunkard, a lost soul when he returned from the Korean war. His best mate had died. He had that leg injury and nothing to show for himself. He cleaned himself up for Eleanor, and then, look what he built for her, what they built together, really—the Huntleys empire. Huntleys is special, Nicole. I'd hate to see you just throw it all away. I want to tell you more about your grandmother, darling. I haven't told anyone about this. Maybe it's the champagne and your exciting news. Eleanor always stood by me. She stood by both of us. My Jimmy had a lot to live up to. Jim's a twinkly old man now, but he was a hard taskmaster for his only son. I'll never forget the way he treated him after our honeymoon."

"Oh?" said Nicole. It was hard to imagine her mother as a young woman.

"Eleanor and Jim sent us to Paris for our honeymoon. It was Eleanor's idea. She knew how much I loved the idea of France. She may have been secretly worried I'd go there by myself, leave Huntleys and Jimmy behind forever, and she may have been right. When you're young you think everything is easy, that promises will be kept, but it doesn't always happen that way. Anyway, as part of our honeymoon, we visited the diamond markets in Antwerp, but I was incredibly unwell, pregnant with

James as it turned out, and so Jimmy went by himself to buy a whole range of diamonds for the business. He thought he was doing the right thing, but he ended up spending more money than Jim had expected, particularly on some 'specials'. Jim was furious."

"Specials, Mum?"

"The 'specials' were exquisite. Half moons and crosscuts, lilycuts, ashokas, some Royal Asschers and even some eighty eights, trielles, marigolds and fire roses. There were even some grace cuts and baronesses. I loved them all. To roll them in the palm of your hand was like watching quicksilver, or droplets of water on a fresh green leaf. They picked up the light. I grew up near the beach, and I loved to kick the spray of the waves at the edge of the beach, up into the sun. Those droplets sparkled like these diamonds. I loved their unusual nature. They were unexpected. Too unexpected for the times. Jim came down on Jimmy like a ton of bricks, accusing him of bankrupting the company with his poor choices. At the time, everyone wanted the same thing as everyone else. Even when we explained Jimmy's theory—that eventually these diamonds and their unique settings would be even more valuable than standard ones, with the same symmetrical design and the same predictable cut of diamond—Jim wouldn't relent. I never saw those diamonds again. I often wondered what happened to them, whether he'd hidden them away in one of his secret safes up in his lair. To sell a few of those diamonds would bring our financial troubles back from the brink, I'll bet."

Chapter 31

In Flame's kitchen in northern New South Wales, James's phone binged again.

"Call me, James," said Nicole's message.

"Just do it," said Stella, still nestled against him, so he did.

"I'm with Stell, Nicole. I've put it on speaker. What is it?"

"Stella!" said Nicole. "How are you? You okay?"

"Yes. Yes. Thank you."

"Stell, if you and I hadn't had that conversation about Shawn's bubble-gum we never would have known."

"What's that?" said James.

"Shawn chews gum all the time. Didn't you notice, James? Stell and I were discussing it because we weren't sure it was the right fragrance for Huntleys' brand. A bit downmarket. Anyway, Jim and I were in his lair after you left, James, trying to work out whether there might be some other way of opening the safe, and I realized. There was still this smell of bubble-gum in there, and Shawn wasn't due for another lesson until Tuesday."

"Bubble-gum!" said James. Stella nodded at him.

"So I just went and fronted him. He was on the ground floor, smooth as. It was quiet, and Lorna was there, so I asked him to come up to the tearoom with me. I knew it for sure, then. His eyes flicked to the door, as if he was going to do a runner, but I made up something about checking his roster for next week and he came up with me."

"Go on."

"Jim was already up there waiting. I wanted a witness. He came in and we locked the door, and I didn't even have to accuse him. We sat opposite Jim, and Jim just stared at him and nobody said anything for a long while. When he went to get up and leave, Jim just said he forgave him, and asked him why he'd done it. James, we need to talk about whether we're going to press charges. Jim doesn't want to."

"Hang on, Nic. I still don't understand. How did he even do it?"

"Lost wax method. Reckons he grabbed Jim's key in one of their sessions when he wasn't looking, pressed it into that rubberized wax mold stuff they use for the centrifugal casting, and went ahead and cast it out of silver at college the same day they made their signet ring molds."

"So he can make a hundred of them?" said James.

"He says he cut it up with a razor knife to get rid of the evidence."

"How would we even know whether to believe that? I don't understand why he confessed."

"He seemed relieved actually. You know what Jim's like. He looks at you with those big blue eyes and you feel like you're staring at God's representative."

James nodded and Stella smiled.

"Turns out he did it for a dare. He's still so young, James. Jim said that. Said you do anything to impress your mates when you're that age. You don't even think twice."

"Well, that's all very well, but it's a pretty calculated crime if you ask me. And where are our rubies?"

"He's given them all back, along with the emeralds he took the morning Stella disappeared. He put them on the table in front of us as if they were radioactive, as if he was glad to be rid of them. His hands were shaking. His face was so white it was just freckles."

"It's not funny, Nicole. And where did he even find the substitutes? What if this is all part of a bigger ring of crime?"

"Shawn said it was just a coincidence that Jim's gems were so similar to the glass ones he'd bought for his class projects."

"And we'd trust a thief …"

"Well, we need to see what you say about it; you and Stell. But Jim reckons we should forgive him since he's confessed and returned all our gems and the key. He laid it all out on the table, contrite as. He kept apologizing. And you know Jim. Jim gave that speech about how we all make choices every day, about whether to do good or whether to ignore that voice, ignore our conscience and follow temptation, bla bla bla. And that ultimately Shawn has to live with himself and the consequences of his actions. He asked him did he enjoy being a thief. And Shawn shook his head and kept saying 'no, sir'."

"But the police need to know. Someone has to keep a watch on this kid. We can't just let him free to do this to someone else. We might be setting him up for a life of crime if he goes scot free."

"Frankly, James, we don't need the negative publicity right now, do we? Not while GGT is offering and we might want to sell. Jim says all is right with the world again. We could write Shawn off and cancel his apprenticeship, but Jim says forgiveness is more powerful than punishment, and if he goes to jail he'll meet more criminals and we're more likely to lead him into a life of crime. He keeps saying no one was hurt, not physically, anyway."

"Could have given Jim a heart attack," said James, his fist clenched. "I'm glad the mystery is solved, but I don't want an employee I can't trust sneaking around our building. Do you?"

"We all make mistakes, James. Where would we all be without a bit of trust and forgiveness? I know what Will would say. He's flat out giving the proceeds of his skyrunning gig to unemployed young people who've taken the wrong path. All of us take a wrong turn occasionally. Look at it like this. Scottie and I wouldn't even be married if he'd never forgiven me for treating him badly in high school."

"Hmmm. Trust. Forgiveness. Nic, I've driven all night. We'll talk about this some more, Stell and I, and get back to you. Stell knows Shawn best, after all. She's been supervising him. Where is he now?"

"Jim's got him cleaning up the studio with him—maybe telling him some war stories—and he's got college again this afternoon."

'Well, thanks for calling Nic. Have you told the rest of the team, and Mum and Will?"

"Not yet. I'll do that when they're awake, hey?"

James slipped the silent phone back into his pocket and reached for Stella's hands.

"Now, where were we?" said James.

"Trust," she said.

"Forgiveness," he said.

"Stell…"

Chapter 32

In the farmhouse kitchen, Stella grabbed James's hand and pulled him out the door.

"You really don't know me, James," she said. "Jeannie and I grew up with nothing. I don't need much."

"Stell?"

"I need a notepad and pencils and a man who loves me. What do I care about a global enterprise? I don't even care about gems and gold. You've seen me create. I'm happy to arrange a few leaves, or repurpose some old toothbrushes. I care about the planet, about creativity, about being alive. I care about you, James, and I care about us."

She squeezed his fingers and led him out of the kitchen, into the garden, startling a group of lorikeets, who screeched and took to the sky, winging out across the valley in flashes of green and orange and blue. The sun was higher, shining bright green in the lush grass. James inhaled deeply, felt the sun's warmth on his shoulders, with Stella beside him. He slipped his arm around her waist and they walked as one, across to the caravan her mother had dubbed the House of Spades.

"I did go into Huntleys before I left, James," she said. "But I grabbed something far more precious than rubies."

"Yes?"

"I grabbed your gift to me—my sketchpad and pencils. Let me show you my drawings."

Inside the caravan, she showed him her designs.

"Stella! These are exquisite. They're a mix of art deco and art nouveau."

"Your mum's French bits and pieces must have inspired me. Heaven knows I've done enough repairs on them to think like a jeweler from a hundred years ago. I know I can make these in Jim's studio if I can only have more time up there."

"Twenties revivals. Everyone in the world would want these designs, Stella. Show Wolf, or Carl or Eric and they'll buy you, not Huntleys."

"Do you think so?"

"I saw how Carl and Wolf stayed close to you at the dinner. They're experts at dinner dynamics. All that seating was totally deliberate. That meeting I went to with Adam Li, he's taught me heaps about the tactics these companies employ as they snap up businesses like ours for a song and deny us the right to trade; our own birthright. I'm still worried I'll lose the business to them, Stell. We may have no choice. I emailed the options to everyone with all the details—the profit and loss statement and balance sheet, and, for each option, the costs, risks, paybacks and what we'd be likely to gain as individuals and as a company—just before I left to come up and find you. Scottie and I finally finished working them out. They're incredibly complicated. There's not just the building. We have long-term liabilities that mean we need to turn over around five million dollars a year. There are wages, stock on hand and stock in transit, insurances, customs clearance, holiday pay, sick leave, super, power, phone, advertising. Working out the mark ups and when to push specials to keep our stock turning—I didn't think you were interested in that side of the business. I didn't want to bore you with it."

"I'm not bored. I ran a business, too, James. Stellar."

"You did, and you can run it again, if you want, within Huntleys or independently. I value your insight. You're brilliant. You dazzle me, Stella."

"I'd like to see the details of the options. I want to walk right beside you in life and business."

"Of course I'll show you, Stella. I want you in our EGM, right beside me, if you want to be there, if you'll still have me, Stell. And for the record, the wedding date and venue are all in your hands. 'Yes' from me, okay?"

"Okay. Now enough about the business, James. Of course I want you. You're all I ever wanted—you and the time to create. Come with me. I want to show you the place where I drew my designs, deep in the rainforest, where we could be the only people on earth."

She grabbed James's hand and took him down the hill, down past the old dairy and the cattle crush and across the road to the wide paddock with its patches of yellow fireweed and scratchy, aromatic lantana.

They talked as they walked, swinging their arms.

"Everything grows here, James," she said. "The weeds are the worst of all. Flame explained it to me. If you look over there you'll see where they're regenerating this paddock."

"Should have brought my runners, Stell."

"You love the bush, don't you?"

"Yeah. I saw a lot of it back in my cross country running days. Smells so fresh. I wish we could stay and help your mum and Ross with some weeding or planting, but we have the meeting in the next couple of days."

"We'll come back."

"We will."

On and on they walked, down through the long grass past the piercing cries of plovers protecting their eggs, and under the tree canopy, towards the water. Along the creek they strode, over boulders and fallen logs until Stella found the fig tree where she'd cried her heart out.

She reached one hand out to the cool bark as James walked around its huge perimeter. He peered up into the branches where thousands of leaves caught the shards of sunlight. Down here it was humid and still. Up there, the tallest branches moved as if the giant tree were asleep, breathing gently.

"See this tree, James? Do you know what it is?"

"It's a fig."

"It's a strangler fig. There's another tree beneath it. It began its life as a seed in the branches of an older tree, and its roots reached down and down and into the lifeblood of the bigger tree, and it took its nutrients and grew and grew around it."

"Are you saying it killed the other tree?"

"Maybe. Maybe the other tree was going to die anyway."

"Is everything okay, Stell?"

"I sat here a long time, James. I was angry and exhausted. I'd lost myself trying to please you, trying to do everything right. I thought you no longer loved me, that everything I did you took for granted."

"No, Stell. I've been distracted, I know, but it's only because I've wanted everything to be perfect, to offer you the kind of life you deserve, a secure future."

"I don't want that, James."

"You don't want me?"

"I only want you. Before I set up Stellar, I devoted a decade to clutching at security, and it made me miserable. Only when I was doing what I loved, creating jewelry, was I truly happy."

"I overworked you. I had you looking after the building, the staff, the store, the apprentices. It was very convenient for me. You did a great job, and I just assumed you wanted all of that, but it's a waste of your gift for design. Can you ever forgive me?"

"There's nothing to forgive, James. I thought I wanted to do it all, but I know now, I only want to create."

"Well, you must create."

"But will you still want me?"

"Of course."

"But how will I know that? I'm a jealous person, James. I don't want to be, but I am. Even with your ring on my finger, I worried you were falling in love with Divandra."

James stepped closer, that wave of sun bleached hair at his forehead curving with the humidity. His eyes on hers were bluer than ever, Huntley blue, and the plane of his face just right, her James, here with her at last in the heart of the rainforest.

"I want to trust you, James, and I want you to trust me. That's all that marriage is, isn't it? A promise to love each other and maybe one day create a family together?"

"A commitment to be together no matter what happens. Yes. To have and to hold." He stepped closer still, till she saw the pulse beat in his neck, the shape of his collarbone under his shirt, strong and true as the branch of this fig tree.

"For richer or poorer," she said.

"For better or worse," said James.

"In sickness or in health," said Stella. "Till death do us part."

"Till death do us part. So this is our promise to love each other, Stell."

"This is. This is our commitment, our vow, mine to you and you to me, from this day forward."

And suddenly it lifted—that dread, the never-ending weight of expectation and worry about a wedding that may never happen. For Stella, James's focus and promise was all she'd needed, without the endless distractions of the business.

She breathed deeply moist air of the valley as the water splashed and sparkled over rocks, and birds swooped and called and flitted around them. For Stella, the promise and commitment she'd needed had now been given and received.

A bright green frog peeked out from the center of a staghorn and leaped to catch a dragonfly, which buzzed away just in time. And Stella laughed and pulled James closer, dear James, her James. And her arms reached for him as the trees reached for the sun and they kissed like lovers who would never part, as if the past, present and future belonged to them, together, inseparable.

Later, they swam in the creek, their bodies fresh and new and pale under water the color of tea, and they dried each other tenderly and laughed like children, till only the mosquitoes drove them home.

They had dinner with Flame and Ross, then curled up in the caravan all night, and left for Sydney the next morning, the EGM ahead of them like a neon sign.

Later, much later, as they drove home down the coast road together, James shared with Stella all he'd learned from Divandra.

"I did learn quite a lot from her, about doublets, about the cutting of gemstones, the different grades, about tenacity, cleavage, the mining, the faceting, the cuts, and, most of all, about the enhancements," he said. "I'd always known it happened, but it's more common than I realized. It's unscrupulous, Stell. I don't approve of it. Did you know many companies use heat to remove cloudiness in sapphires and rubies? Or they add flux to heal fractures. She told me about oiling and staining and bleaching, and about composites, where a thin, valuable gem is added to a glass base. When it's done well, and set, even an expert is hard-pressed to tell it apart from a full gem of much larger value."

"I could have told you all that, James," she said. "It's like 'gems 101.' We did an assignment on it. Even Shawn could tell you."

He reached across and grabbed her hand and they laughed. He never wanted to let her go.

Chapter 33

"**G**rab another chair, for Stella, please, Scottie," said James as he entered the Scott & Sons boardroom for the EGM. Nicole reached for the jug and poured a glass of water for her.

"Great to see you, Stell," she said. "Welcome back."

"Thanks, Nicole. James tells me you have news?"

Nicole touched her belly.

"Nothing much to see just yet, but it's sure making itself known. I feel pretty weird most of the time, to be honest."

"I'm excited for you, Nic. Congratulations." Stella smiled at Scottie as he wheeled the extra chair in behind her.

"I'm so glad you're here," Nicole whispered. "You should have been at the first meeting, too. We were scared you'd run away for good. It would serve us right. It wasn't because I was so mean to you when you first set up your stall, was it? I still feel so bad about that. I've never formally apologized to you."

"It's okay, Nic."

"So I'm forgiven?"

Stella nodded as James cleared his throat.

"Thank you all for joining me again, for this Extraordinary General Meeting," said James to his family, those present and those on the screen, in the Scott & Sons boardroom.

"It's been an action packed three weeks, and I thank each and every one of you for the care and attention you've given to the information Scottie and I shared with you a few days ago.

"You'll see there are three items on the agenda, and I propose to deal with each of them in turn.

"I want to say at the start that I know each of you has different ideas about the future of Huntleys, and I accept that. My deepest hope is that we can separate our business decisions from our personal ones, that whatever decision is taken at the end of this meeting does not spoil the respect and affection we hold for one another. I've tried to run this process as fairly as possible, and I know I've made some grave mistakes and had to ask forgiveness, but my motives have been pure. I truly want the best for all of us, and I know no other way to reach this difficult decision but to involve you all."

Silence. Under the table, Stella squeezed his thigh. At least he still had Stella, or so he hoped. How close he'd come to losing her. He closed his eyes to clear his mind, then opened them again.

"Before we begin, as I said in my email to you, I have disclosed the full finances of Huntleys, and I asked that this information remain confidential. I shared it with you so that you can truly understand the extent of the challenge we have before us. Scottie, would you please share your screen so Cynthia and Will can see what we can see?"

Scottie cast the balance sheet high on the screen and increased the size of the font.

"Scottie, can I ask you now to explain the balance sheet for those of us who may have less experience with such things?"

Scottie had tried to persuade James to keep the balance sheet fully confidential, but James argued that only full disclosure could help them make the best decision at this stage.

"You've all heard of 'in the black' and 'in the red,'" said Scottie and everyone nodded.

"Numbers can be deceptive. We have capital expenses and operating expenses; we also have liabilities in accrued leave and in repairs we need to make to our property, most notably the headquarters in Bondi Junction. Wages and taxes also need to come out of our annual turnover, as well as costs of materials, utilities like water, power and gas, insurance, marketing expenses and so on."

Scottie scrolled across the tables of numbers and onto a fresh page with more spreadsheets.

"These are the costs and expected profits from each of our salons. Of course Will's House of Hearts and Cynthia's House of Clubs are very new, so the profits are only predictions, and even for the Bondi Junction House of Diamonds store, we can only predict sales based on figures from previous years."

206

Nicole stifled a yawn. Her body was betraying her in new ways. Since when was eight o'clock time for bed? Scottie had already explained to her these details. She was interested in what would come.

"I'm a conservative accountant," said Scottie. "These predictions are on the low side, so I may be understating our predicted earnings, but there's merit in knowing 'worst case' scenarios."

"So what's the bottom line?" said Will.

"The business needs to come up with two million dollars by September."

Will whistled online while the collective inhalation in the Scott & Sons boardroom almost rattled the vertical blinds. From France, Cynthia removed her colorful glasses, peered and placed them back on her nose.

"And what's the GGT offer?" said Jim.

"Five million," said James and Scottie together.

"So if we sell up, without wanting to sound too dramatic, we lose our buildings and livelihoods and end up with three million to split between the five of us, we'll end up with $600,000 each. Adam Li is still examining the fine print. It may be that the agreement prevents us from trading in jewelry for a set time. That would be expected."

"Thank you, Scottie. Are there any questions or discussion before we move to the vote?"

"What do I want with $600,000?" said Jim. "I want to keep my studio, keep designing."

"Yeah, Jim," said Will. "You're not just thinking about your Jim's Jewel of the Month fan base? You can't disappoint those followers."

"Cheeky," said Jim, but he smiled at Will.

"What's the Bondi Junction building worth if we just sell that, and rent somewhere?" said Will.

"Hard to say," said Scottie. "Similar buildings in the area are fetching around five million, but they're in much better condition."

"I've just had an idea," said Nicole. "Why don't we develop Huntleys?"

"Baby brain, Nicole," said Will. "If we already owe two million and can't pay to even repair the place, where are we going to find three mill to cover our debts as well as all the dosh to pay for a new building?"

"Thanks for the sexism, Will," said Nicole. "We sell the space above our building. Apply for a rezoning. Fix the current facade and replace whatever needs replacing inside it. Everyone else is doing it."

There was silence.

"That could work, Nic," said James. "Brilliant idea, but Will has a point. We'd still need money for property lawyers and architects, and this would take time. The debt is now, and the buyout offer is now. Let's park that thought and discuss the next motion, that Huntleys list as a public company and raise money by selling shares on the open market. Scottie. Can you talk us through this, please?"

"By selling shares, Huntleys would raise enough funds to repay the two million dollar debt and keep trading," said Scottie. "But I have to tell you, with the current sales record and debt, this won't fly. It would cost up to another half million to list."

"And even doing that would cost money we don't have," said Jim. "And we'd risk losing control to majority shareholders."

"It would give family members the option to sell out at any time," said Will. "I suppose we can already buy each other out, though, can't we, Scottie? Except none of us has much money."

Cynthia raised her hand.

"Yes, mother," said James.

Cynthia cleared her throat.

"Émile has just had an idea. He's asked me to read it to you all. Before I read it to you I want to reiterate, to implore you, not to throw away your birthright. I can't tell you how many hours of labor and inspiration and toil and joy have been invested in Huntleys, before any of you were born, even you, Jim. Eleanor's family started that department store before you turned it into Huntleys. It has been a lasting asset in this family's fortunes, and it's our duty to protect and enhance it for future Huntleys. Nicole and Scottie, now that you are expecting, you may understand this. That said, I love you all dearly and will try not to take it personally if you vote to sell out. I hope you will still join Émile and me for our wedding at the chateau in August."

"Thank you, mother," said James.

"And, before I explain Émile's note, I want to thank Nicole for her brilliant fresh idea about developing the sky space above Huntleys. You see this is a perfect example of why we all need to stick together, of why family is so important, of how we can help each other achieve so much more together in this world than we can as separate individuals all going our own different ways. Have you put that in the minutes, Scottie?"

"Yes, thank you, Mrs Huntley."

"Good. Well then, Emile and I were talking about the missing diamonds, and Jim, please, I mean no disrespect to you. You were in tune with the times, and maybe my Jimmy did make a bad decision back then, during our honeymoon, but all that is water under the bridge as they say and the point is that right now we may be in a position to benefit hugely from my Jimmy's decision in Antwerp all those years ago to invest in the 'specials' as he called them—those diamonds of unusual shapes."

Jim stiffened and frowned.

"The point is, I need to ask you, Jim. Did you ever sell them? You made up one or two rings from them, and it's true. I remember they took a long time to sell, and only then, at very reduced prices. It wasn't a happy time for us, but I need to raise this again now."

There was silence in the room. Jim moved a hand to his face, covering his eyes.

"Those diamonds," said Jim. He exhaled. "Such trouble between me and Jimmy!" He shook his head. "In the end I gave them all to Eleanor so we didn't have to look at them. I put them out of my mind," he said, finally, and everyone breathed again.

"Thank you, Jim," said Cynthia. "I don't suppose you know what Eleanor did with them? Did she sell them, or hide them in the house? They may still be in there somewhere for all I know. Wouldn't the current owners be amazed if they ever uncovered them!"

"Eleanor never mentioned them again," said Jim, his voice deadpan. "And now I am an old man, and I'm ashamed. I gave Jimmy such a hard time about those diamonds. It was hard work, you see, to create beauty without symmetry. It was a waste of my time. I could never do it. It frustrated me, and I took that out on our Jimmy. At the time, I was worried we were going bankrupt from that purchase. He died before I could apologize. They'd be worth a fortune now, too, those diamonds. I put them right out of my mind. For the record, Jimmy was right about unique items. It's my most unusual rings which are fetching the most money at auction nowadays. Any robot or factory can put together a ring like any other. It's the one-offs, their rarity, which adds value. I never understood that then. There's greater demand for a very limited supply. I see that now. You can put that down too, Scottie, in the minutes."

"I will, sir."

"Thank you for that, Jim," said Cynthia quietly. "We all have regrets. But this meeting is about the future, our future." She shook the piece of paper and opened it up.

"Émile works with his hands all the time," she said. "Not so much with jewelry, but he can cut keys and fix old motors and engines and machinery and furniture. Most of you met my Émile at Nicole and Scottie's wedding, and it was while he was in my southern highlands home that he remembers seeing the writing chest that Eleanor gave me before she died. It's a beautiful piece, about as big as three or four shoeboxes together, depending on the size of your feet, of course, and it's just sitting in my hallway, but the important thing is that when Émile admired the box in his way—the finish and so on—he picked it up, and he remembers it being, well—exceptionally heavy."

Nicole stared at Scottie. Stella stared at James. Jim stared at Will.

Everyone spoke at once until James brought order.

"I believe Cynthia had the floor," James said.

"Thank you, James," she said. "As I was saying, Émile is very experienced with how things are made, with antiques and old wares and so on, and he says that back in the days when people made things by hand, many pieces held secrets. In fact, Émile refers to this box as 'un coffre au trésor'—a treasure box. He knows of a sewing machine cabinet in which gold sovereigns were secreted, sent from Russia to Florence with a young bride, for example. And many writing cabinets, wardrobes and desks had secret compartments, for documents, alcohol, knives, guns, poison, love letters and jewels. I am sure that when she gave it to me, Eleanor meant this box for all of us, for our future as Huntleys, and not just for me. Émile has drawn up this picture to show you how you may care to look for secret places in our cabinet."

Cynthia held up Émile's diagram, complete with arrows, to show how a secret compartment could be found and unlocked.

Nicole whipped out her phone and took a photo of the diagram on display on the screen.

"Could you send me that, please, Nic?" said James and she nodded.

Will whistled.

Jim gripped the table and stood.

"Well, well, well."

Émile's face appeared next to Cynthia's, a grin from ear to ear.

"Merci, Émile," said James. "We thank you! It's a long shot, but it's a shot worth trying. I vote we travel down together as soon as possible to test mother and Émile's theory. This evening, if you're all free. This is so important, I'm going to ask us all to adjourn this meeting. Our vote will depend on the outcome of our visit, and so we will reconvene once more later this evening."

"Drive carefully," said Cynthia.

"Go, bro!" said Will.

"Jim, would you like to travel with Stella and me?"

"I'll stay here, thank you, James," said Jim. "Could you drop me at my home at the store, please? Just phone me when you know, and I'll give you my decision. You know, if you do find those diamonds, we can put in an offer for GGT some time, after Stella and I design and manufacture to our hearts' content."

"And I'll need a larger marketing budget, Scottie and James," said Nicole. "Imagine what we could do with a story about Huntleys' hidden treasure!"

"Okay, okay," said James. "It's still a long shot. A treasure hunt. Let's not forget there may be no diamonds. We still need to make this GGT decision tonight, with or without rare diamonds. Are you riding with us, Scottie? Nicole?"

Scottie reached for Nicole's hand and squeezed it. He waited for her to make the call.

"I'd love to join you, but I'm just so tired," she said. "And I'm not sure how I'll go with the motion sickness. Scottie, would you like to go with them?"

"I'll stay with you, Nicole," said Scottie. "And Jim—We can take you home. We'll all be waiting for your call, James. I'll send another Zoom invitation to you all, once you're ready to let us know what you find."

"Only then will we call for votes," said James.

…

When their screen went black, Cynthia grasped Émile and drew him into a hug.

"Your brilliant idea, Émile! Your diagram! Imagine if it's true. The family will stay together. We can build a tower above Huntleys. Each floor will be worth at least a million dollars! We'll be able to sell them off the plan. We can ask Nathan Carmichael to design it."

Émile drew away from her.

"Émile?"

"It is nothing."

"It is. It's because I mentioned Nathan, isn't it? Émile. You're not jealous, are you?"

Émile shrugged.

"Darling, I've told you about Nathan. We're old school friends. Of course we're close, but it would never go any further. I've told you. The only person Nathan really loves is himself."

Émile's frown began to curve upwards, and she kissed him.

"Besides. You and I are marrying. Would you mind if we invite Nathan to the wedding? Maybe Nathan and Angelica will be the perfect match!"

Émile drew away again.

"Émile?"

"And if there are no diamonds, Cynthia?"

"Oh. Yes. Well, I do think Nicole is softening now she's expecting. She wouldn't have had that idea of developing the building if she truly wanted to sell it all to GGT, would she? Surely she can see the value of us all sticking together. Should I phone her? She looked a little pale, didn't you think? A little tired? Perhaps I'll go and see her. Whatever happens, we must plan a trip. Oh, Émile, it's too exciting! How can we wait two hours? Look at the time! I must go downstairs and open the shop. It's so good of Nanette to come this morning, to help, but I must do something."

"And me, I will work on the guest bathroom, yes? Coffee?"

"I'm far too excited for coffee, Émile. But thank you. You have one."

Chapter 34

In the car, as they drove south to the Southern Highlands, Stella began to talk.

"When I went up north, James, I was so lost. But I had my sketchbook and I took it with me into the rainforest."

They entered the tunnel under the airport and she continued. "The liana vine was entwined around the old strangler fig, and the fig was growing over an older tree."

"Yes?"

"Well, that's Jim and all you Huntleys. And those birds living in the holes in the trees where branches had fallen off, and the insects and the staghorn ferns with frogs in them ..."

"Yes?"

"We're all just such a tiny part of this huge ecosystem, James."

"We are. And you're a key part of us now. I've been thinking of your new designs, Stella. How did you end up designing settings for half-moons and prisms of light between the leaves, as if you already knew about Jimmy's missing diamonds? Because you know, if they're there, your designs will be perfect. The diamonds on their own may be worth a million or so, but with the 'value add' from your designs, the lost diamond collection, we'd be talking real money."

"And imagine the media coverage!" said Stella. "Jeannie and Nicole will be in heaven. This will really put Huntleys House of Jewels on the international map, James."

"If the stones are there. Even if they're not, Nicole's development idea is brilliant. Maybe that's why GGT wanted us—for the real estate value."

James's phone buzzed.

"Speak of the devil," said James. "Excuse me, Stell. I have to take this." She nodded and he flicked a switch on the steering wheel.

"Yes, Wolf," he said. "No. We haven't reached an agreement yet. I'll be back in touch when our meeting finishes. I know you're about to catch the plane. In that case, you'll have our answer when you land."

The road was almost empty at this late hour. They made the trip in record time, parked the car, and let themselves in. Cynthia's house was eerily quiet, the furniture shrouded in dust sheets, the windows and curtains shut. Last time they'd been here it had been full of friends and family celebrating Nicole and Scottie's wedding. Now it was as empty and hushed as a stage set waiting for a play to begin.

Stella identified the shape of the writing chest as it rested on an antique games table in the hall. She raised the sheet, folded it and set it aside.

James seized the box and lifted it, feeling its weight.

"Émile's right," he said. "It's far too heavy for the wood of the box, even with the brass corners and hinges. You know I've never thought to look inside it. Maybe it has glass ink bottles and old papers. They could be making it heavy."

Stella stood back and smiled.

James pulled the chest forward and lifted the lid, letting it drop back to create a wedge-shaped writing surface covered in soft leather, its edges stamped with gold leaf.

"It's a beautiful piece," he said. The cut crystal ink bottles twinkled in the hall light. Several old fashioned nib pens rested in a wooden trough.

Stella leaned forward and pressed on the end of the trough and the other end of it rose. James pinched it in his fingers and removed it, revealing a compartment beneath, but there was nothing too surprising in here—just some ink stains and spare steel nibs.

Stella removed the ink bottles on either side of the trough.

Then James pulled on a leather tab, exposing the space beneath the lower end of the writing surface. There was a small cloth bag. Stella lifted it out carefully and pulled it open, but there were no diamonds—only little pears with pointy edges."

"Oooh, James. They're teeth."

"Our baby teeth!" said James.

The papers inside were covered in copperplate writing, and a musty odor. Stella bent down and removed them carefully, conscious she was touching the past. She laid them on the folded sheet and they continued their examination in silence.

Now James pulled the tab on the upper slope of the writing surface. Here were blank pages. He handed them to Stella and gently probed the corners of the box beneath the ink bottle compartments. His face fell.

"Nothing special here, Stell. I'm sorry."

This time, Stella stepped forward again and examined the edges of the bottle compartments.

"Show me Émile's drawing again, please, James." She studied the picture, then reached over, placed her fingers on the edge of one of the compartments, and gave a short, sharp tug.

A long piece of wood shot towards them, into the empty paper compartment, revealing a series of hidden drawers.

Chapter 35

Stella jumped up and down. "James! Hidden drawers! Émile was right! And if the diamonds are inside, it was your grandmother who put them there."

James opened the first drawer. It held a folded square of paper. Stella was so excited she felt ill. Jim had similar paper in the safe in his lair, holding diamonds, preventing them from scratching and chipping each other.

James drew out the next drawer and placed it on the side table.

"Your turn, Stella." She looked into James's face, her smile contagious, spreading to his, and they beamed at each other.

Her fingers shook as she unwrapped the paper. Winking up at her from the bland surface of the paper were dozens of odd shaped diamonds.

She hugged James, who twirled her around.

"Easy does it. Let's not scatter them to the winds just yet, Stell."

There were three more drawers, the diamonds in each larger than those in the last, and the final group, so enormous, Stella gasped. James whistled.

"We have to tell the others, James."

He shook his head.

"Not yet, Stella. Now I can ask you again. Will you marry me?"

"James, as far as I'm concerned, we're already married."

"I'll be able to build you a studio, here, if you want, in the huge garage, and another in the remodeled Huntleys. This is the beginning of our time, Stella."

"Yes, but we have to tell the others! You need to phone Scottie! Get the vote. Give GGT their answer."

Hope rose up in Stella, a golden, glorious thing. As she watched the reconvened meeting on James's tiny phone screen, she was giddy with excitement.

Stella could see everyone's faces—Scottie and Nicole nestled on the lounge together, Cynthia and Émile on an ornate piece of furniture. Was it a loveseat? And there was Will, buff as ever in a white t-shirt, his face illuminated by the screen in a darkened room. Nicole stifled a yawn and Scottie placed his arm around her, squeezing her shoulder.

Jim's image was the last to appear. He seemed to be outside, up on the roof of Huntleys, the lights of Bondi Junction and Sydney Harbour behind him.

"Fancy that," said Jim, holding out the phone and giving everyone a three hundred and sixty degree view. "You know Huntleys was built up on the ridge. From here you can see in so many directions. Diamonds or no diamonds, we can make this happen. Huntleys apartments will be magnificent. I claim the penthouse for my workroom. I want it to be shaped like a diamond."

"Great idea!" said Nicole. "I love it!"

"Yo!" said Will.

James cleared his throat. "Thank you all for joining us again," he said. "I reconvene our EGM. Still for the vote are the three motions."

"Oh come on, James," said Will. "Cut the officialese. We all just want to know. Did you find the diamonds?"

James blinked.

"Will, is that appropriate?" said Nicole. "This still has to be done right. James is doing his best. He and Scottie have tried to do this the right way the whole time, no thanks to you."

Will held up his hands in apology and gave a thumbs up sign.

"Before I ask for votes, Stella and I would like to show you what we've found."

The image wobbled as James reversed his own phone and walked down the hallway to Cynthia's formal dining room, lit by an ornate chandelier. On a white cloth in the center of the glossy dark wooden table lay the treasure chest, its contents neatly stacked along the table.

James held the camera above one end of the display and slowly panned past the writing implements, the blank and inscribed papers, the open box and each of its compartments and each of its empty secret drawers. Beyond them lay the first paper package, open, its contents like sparkling afternoon sunlight on Sydney Harbour. He held the camera close to the

217

first array of odd shaped diamonds. As he pushed at them with his finger, the light shot out at the phone camera at all angles. The size of his finger against the gems in each subsequent stash revealed their numbers and size.

"Are you still there?" he asked. There was too much silence.

Then there was too much noise.

Cynthia kissed Émile. Nicole squealed and Scottie leaped up and hugged her.

"Yes!" said Will, pumping his fist.

Jim threw back his head and laughed, then asked a question.

"I can see some writing on the top of the paper," he said. "What does it say?"

James squinted. He hadn't noticed the writing until now.

"'Marcel Kowalsky,'" said James.

"No!" said Jim. "He was the best diamond cutter in the business! This is even more significant. I'd forgotten that. I'm ashamed to admit I was so angry at the amount of money Jimmy had invested without my permission. It was wrong of me to make such a big deal of it. I miss Jimmy so much. I never had a chance to apologize." Jim sunk his head into his hands.

"I understand your attitude Jim," said James. "Sinking such a huge amount of money into stock that might well have been unsellable back then could have bankrupted the business."

Jim lifted his head a little and nodded at James, but his shoulders stayed slumped.

"Eleanor took them all away from me so I didn't hit the roof every time I saw those crazy-cut diamonds," Jim said. "But now. I can't tell you how significant this is. This is extraordinary. These will be extremely valuable now—enormously rare. Collectors' items."

"So let's put all of that behind us, Jim," said Cynthia. "Let these diamonds be Jimmy's gift to us; Jimmy's and Eleanor's. Wouldn't they be pleased if they could have seen into the future and known what a boon this discovery would be for all of us, for Huntleys!"

Everyone nodded and Jim's shoulders shifted back to their usual position.

James held Stella close as he turned the camera back to themselves.

"Thank you, Jim. Now, just before we vote, I've asked Stella to show all of you her most recent designs," he said. "She actually created these a week or so ago, up in the rainforest. The fact that these designs will suit so many of these diamonds is pure coincidence. You need to see them."

As James held the camera, Stella turned the pages of her notepad, and the organic drawings leaped off the pages into their imagination.

Will whistled.

"Beautiful. This is art nouveau," said Jim. "But new. You are brilliant, Stella. I knew I was right to give you the key to my studio. Your designs surpass mine … at least in the non-symmetrical arena." He winked.

"'New nouveau for the twenty-first century, only from Huntleys,'" said Nicole. "I can market that."

Scottie cleared his throat.

"Thanks, Scottie, and just before we move onto the vote, I want to thank Scottie for his devotion to Huntleys, especially in these past few weeks. It's been a hectic time as you're all well aware. I have relied on Scottie for his steady guidance."

"Thanks, Scottie!" It was a chorus.

"Motion one," said James. "That we sell to GGT."

"No," came the chorus.

"I think that's unanimous. Motion two. That we float Huntleys to raise money to repair the building."

"No." Will held out his fist and turned his thumb downwards.

"Motion three. That we retain Huntleys as a family company and face the future together."

"Yes!"

Will gave another fist pump, but then held out both hands for attention.

"What is it, Will?"

"I'll wager I've done more gambling than the lot of you," said Will.

"And?"

"GGT don't know about the diamonds, but they'll know about the value of our building. They've only given us an opening bid so far. They're sure to raise it."

There was silence around the table.

"I don't like this uncertainty," said Cynthia.

"And there'll be other offers over the years," said Nicole.

"Well, I won't be selling my share for all the money in the world," said Jim.

"Nor I," said Cynthia.

Nicole looked at Scottie.

"How much freedom do we all have within Huntleys?" she asked. "Could I take a break from marketing jewelry and start marketing the space above our building, for example?" she said.

"That's feasible," said James.

"How do I know you mean that?"

"You can always trust James, Nic," said Will. "You saw how lenient he's been with me over the years. I hope to pay that back big time now, with the success of my US branch."

"I'm sure there are some family companies that just never sell up," said Cynthia. "Maybe they have a policy. Can we do that, please, James? What a waste of time all this has been, and with so much stress!"

"Well, I don't see it as a waste," said Jim. "A test, yes. But we've come through, together."

"You're right, Jim, and so are you, Mum," said James. "Let this be the start of a new era for Huntleys, with Stella right beside me."

There was a round of applause. Will hooted. Stella stood as tall as her height permitted, arm around James, and his around her. Her smile and eyes shone brighter than any of her creations.

"It's been a big night," said James. "Before we all go, I want to thank each of you for the contribution you bring to our family company and for your loyalty. As always, we have a lot of work ahead of us. But as our family grows, and as we prepare for the years and decades ahead, I want you to know I will be taking on a more proactive role, examining the company structure, recognising new family members more formally— Émile, Scottie and Stella—and preparing a five-year strategic plan which will see us develop the Bondi Junction site while retaining our Australian, French and American interests."

There was applause all round.

"I never want to be caught on the back foot again," said James. "I'm not saying it won't happen. Business is full of surprises, as Jim and Cynthia well know, but by including your input more often, and by actively researching our options and your own ideas more regularly, I hope that together we can grow Huntleys as a thriving, international, independent family company well into the future, for the benefit of all of us."

"Well said," said Jim.

"Thank you, darling," said Cynthia.

"Thanks to Émile, Nicole, Stella—to all of you," said James.

"See you at the wedding," said Will.

"I declare the meeting closed."

The house was suddenly silent.

"Let's raid Cynthia's freezer, stay the night and plan your new workroom tomorrow before we drive back, Stell," said James.

"Good thinking."

There in the fridge, left over from Nicole and Scottie's wedding, was a bottle of French champagne.

"To the CEO of Huntleys," said Stella.

"To the world's most brilliant jewelry designer," said James.

"To Cynthia's fiancé Émile and their wedding in the chateau," said Stella.

"To my sister, Nicole. What a plan!"

"And to loyal Scottie. You told me he's always been in love with her."

"And to their baby to be," said James.

"And to our own babies to be, James," said Stella.

And their toasts dissolved into kisses, deeper and more urgent, Stella's hands on James's shoulders, in his hair—relief and joy and excitement infecting them both, their sweet reunion an explosion of sparkles and fireworks they'd never forget.

Chapter 36

Six months later

Jim never expected to set foot in an airplane again. He'd steadfastly refused. For all that travel ads painted air travel as glamorous, he'd lost too many of his friends in Korea to conveniently forget that humans belonged on the ground.

Yet here he was, at the whole family's insistence. He buckled up next to a young couple busy pointing out the window. The seat was surprisingly comfortable.

He swallowed and reassured himself again. At least he'd get to see Will, now based in the US. If he died in transit, so be it.

He didn't die. That rush of speed, the magic of liftoff, the mesmerizing view of the ground falling away, and cars and houses like toys then maps below, the wonder of viewing clouds from above …

As the high hum of the engines became normal and the only view became a monotonous blue, he explored the interior. To his surprise, the panel on the back of the seat in front was easy to use. He found music he wanted to hear, a comedy TV series that took up hours of flight time, and there was even a good movie or two, though somehow he missed the endings. He must have gone to sleep after all.

After almost a whole day and night, things became interesting, with a bacon and egg breakfast which was perfectly edible, and below, out the window, pointy mountains covered in deep green pine trees.

His heartbeat kicked up as they descended, with Paris from above an entrancing crust of buildings of every height, and Charles de Gaulle airport an intriguing organic horseshoe shape.

James and Stella would arrive tomorrow, but Nicole and Scottie were on the same flight, and they insisted he travel with them to their hotel.

He was grateful for their care, but left them to their own devices, content to wander around Paris on his own and explore the sights.

"Well, how about that!" he said to himself more than once, surprised that so many of the famous buildings were smaller than he'd expected.

The exception was the Eiffel Tower, the base of which could straddle more than fourteen lanes of traffic.

Together, he, Nicole and Scottie caught a train to picturesque Angers in the Loire Valley, where Émile collected them in a minivan and whisked them into the countryside.

To say the wedding destination was astonishing was no exaggeration. Was Cynthia marrying royalty? No. The chateau was owned by a friend of Émile's, Angelica, an American divorcee with a penchant for parties. Émile had helped to restore her chapel. They were met by another friend of Émile's, a jolly fellow named Roddy who settled them in luxurious accommodation in the stables, which set them off on a round of horsey puns.

Cynthia and Émile were staying in the main chateau, Émile explained, and there would be a tour at five o'clock with champagne, once James, Stella and Will arrived, ahead of the main event, the wedding, the following day.

Except Will did not arrive. He did not arrive by three o'clock as planned, nor by five o'clock.

"Typical of Will to mess things up," said Nicole. "Who knows where he is! Has he forgotten? Of course he's not answering his phone. He's so selfish. We all thought he'd changed. At least he could have sent us a message; let us know what's happening."

Scottie ran his hands over her shoulders and she relaxed.

"The wedding's not till tomorrow after all," said Jim.

"Softie," said Nicole.

"I love my family, yes," he said. "Let's not worry yet, Nicole. We're here. Who would have ever thought I'd set foot in France at my age, though I quite like it here. How old is this chateau? I'm young by comparison. Let's celebrate! Let's thank Angelica for sharing her castle with a bunch of Aussies!"

As they descended the chateau steps, a tall young woman with straight blond hair stood, staring out at the grounds beyond the reflection pond.

"Lisa!" said James.

"I'm so sorry we're late," Lisa said as she turned and smiled at each of them. "Will's just parking the car."

Will bounded around the corner and up the stairs, in a white t-shirt and jeans, just as the rest of the family emerged from the ornate entrance. He glowed with good health.

"Hey! Sorry we're late. Does everyone here know Lisa?"

Émile's old friend Roddy appeared on the far side of the pond with a golf cart and pulled out two small folding tables. He placed on one of them a wide ice bucket and several bottles of champagne, and on the other, a large silver tray. He began to stack glasses in a pyramid, their edges touching.

"Désolé!" Roddy said apologetically as the family descended the steps. "*Je suis en retard avec ma fontaine à champagne*. Late, late, late with the champagne …"

"My fault," said Will. "Here, let me help you. Roddy showed Lisa and me to our quarters. Very nice, too, thank you."

"Make sure it's level," said Jim. "They're more fragile than they look, those glass towers."

"Like card houses?" said Nicole. Scottie squeezed her hand.

Will opened the first bottle with a practiced hand and began to pour the golden liquid into the top glass, letting it cascade into the ones below, as Roddy tucked the golf cart back behind the side of the chateau.

Roddy rejoined them all just as Angelica swept down the stairs in a shimmering peacock and aqua blue caftan covered in sparkles.

As the sun set slowly in the west, the lights of the chateau began to glow, reflected in the pond and in each of the glasses.

"Magnifique, Roddy," said Angelica.

"Our Nathan may be too late," said Cynthia to Émile, quietly.

"*Mais pas du tout*," said Émile. "Not at all. Roddy, he has interest in many things, but not in … the women, n'est-ce pas? Unlike me."

"Oh?" said Cynthia, as Emile's arm encircled her waist. He kissed her neck, and she giggled.

As the sky darkened and all the lights of the chateau glowed golden in the evening light, Roddy poured the contents of the final bottles into the top glass. Everyone watched and applauded as it cascaded, fizzing and bubbling, to perfectly fill the glasses below. He stood back and invited each of them to take a glass.

"No! Please wait," said Cynthia. "Roddy, would you please take a picture of us all, here at the entrance to this beautiful chateau? Do you have your mobile phone? And I want to make a speech. Shuffle up close, everyone. Jim, you go on the top step, please. Émile and I will go just below you, and I want all our children and your partners next, please."

She moved between them to the second step, to stand beside Émile, and patted her hair into place as she continued.

"Oh, my darlings, all of you. I worried so much when I came to France that I would lose you; that I would break something irreplaceable, break up our family; that you would feel abandoned. And I was alone. So alone. But then I met Émile … And then that company, GGT, barged in and tried to steal our futures … But here we are, together still, despite all the challenges, and I can't thank you enough, all of you, James, for your leadership, and Nicole and Will for your loyalty. I'm so proud of each and every one of you, and so glad to welcome Stella and Scottie and now Lisa into our family, as well as Émile. Jim, you've braved the skies again for us. And Angelica, I can't believe your generosity, sharing your chateau with us like this."

"Real glad to meet the whole family," said Angelica. "This is our first wedding, remember, a kind of trial run."

"Like crash dummies," said Will.

"Will!" said Nicole.

"*Ouistiti*," said Roddy.

"It's 'say cheese', Nicole," said Will.

"You'd know, wouldn't you, Will? The bad boy in every celebrity photo around the globe for the past decade."

"Thank you, my darlings," said Cynthia.

"*Ouistiti*," said Roddy.

"*Ouistiti.*"

Émile, tall and gallant, stepped forward. He took the top glass and another from the next row, giving the first to Cynthia, and the next to Angelica.

"To my bride, Cynthia," said Émile. "And to Angelica. We all thank you for your generosity. Your chateau, it is magnifique. My bride and I, we could not be more happy to be married here. You honor us."

"Well, let's just get this straight, everyone," said Angelica. "It's you and Roddy and all the people who've worked on this place who deserve my thanks for making it what it is today."

As Roddy and Émile handed around more glasses, Cynthia called out.

"To Angelica for lending us her chateau," she said.

"To Émile for helping restore the chapel," said Angelica. "Wait till you see it!"

"To Jim, for making it here," said James. "And to Stella, my love."

"Any mineral water for Nicole, please?" said a proud Scottie.

Stella and James exchanged a glance.

"And one for Stella, too, please Roddy," said James.

Guests arrived all next day, and gathered in the chapel.

Jeannie and her husband Dave flew in from Singapore. Little Lucy and Sienna, angelic in white dresses with gold trim, made a bee-line for the pond. It was Flame's husband, Ross, who lunged for Sienna just in time, averting a dunking. He held her hand as she balanced on the edge of it, around and around.

When the two bells began to peel, everyone made their way to the chapel.

Dianne, Ron, Scottie and Nicole took up a whole pew; Nicole was round as a piece of ripe fruit, her baby due in just over two months. Behind them sat Will and Lisa, hands clasped tight.

Ross and Flame sat with Stella and James, while Bob, the husband of Cynthia's old friend Kate, sat with their old school mate Nathan Carmichael.

On the other side of the tiny chapel sat Émile's son, Maxime, whispering to his partner, Liam, and behind them, Divandra and her fiancé who had flown in from India. Roddy and many of Émile's friends who'd worked with them to restore Angelica's chateau filed in until there was standing room only.

In the late summer afternoon, sunlight streamed through all the bright golds and reds and blues and greens of the rose window Émile had repaired, bathing them in colored shapes, as if they were in a kaleidoscope.

At the back of the church, Lucy and Sienna danced on the colored patterns on the stone floor until the organ began, a little parlor organ

Angelica had arranged from the US for just such an occasion. The triumphant strains of Handel's *Arrival of the Queen of Sheba* filled the chapel.

Émile stood in front, tall and handsome in a deep blue suit, a white rose at his lapel, Maxime beside him. As the music swelled, from the rear of the chapel, Jeannie pushed Sienna and Lucy down the aisle, each holding a tiny basket of flowers. Kate appeared after them, in an elegant cream knee-length dress. Moments later, Cynthia glided in on Jim's arm in sleek ivory satin with three-quarter sleeves, a tight waist, and a full skirt.

As she brushed past beaming guests, her red, white and blue bouquet unleashed its mix of fragrances—of roses and hyacinths and lavender, of violets and lemon blossom, of spring and summer.

Émile and Cynthia swapped their age-old vows in French and English.

"Cyntia, je te prend,

"I take you."

On the wooden pew, Stella slipped her hand inside James's.

"... pour être mon épouse," said Émile. "To be my wife, *pour avoir et tenir de ce jour vers l'avant,* to have and to hold from this day forwards."

James squeezed Stella's hand tightly.

"pour meilleur ou pour le pire," said Émile. "For better or worse, *pour la prospérité et la pauvreté,* for richer or poorer."

Scottie placed his arm around Nicole's shoulders.

"dans la maladie et dans la santé," said Émile. "In sickness and in health."

Nicole nestled her head against Scottie's shoulder.

"pour aimer et chérir, To love and to cherish," said Émile.

Will brushed the inside of Lisa's wrist with his fingers as he clasped her hand in his.

"... jusqu'à la mort nous sépare.

"Till death do us part."

Lucy wriggled again as Jeannie tried to settle her, but she could wait no longer. She rushed forwards, the ribbons bobbing in her hair. She plunged her tiny hand into the basket and threw fistfulls of red, white and blue petals at Cynthia and Émile. Lucy followed to copy her just as Dave and Jeannie swooped in to scoop the girls back to the pews and onto their laps.

"Wait! Not yet!" they whispered, but not before a photographer captured the chaos of laughter, smiles and joy as the ceremony continued.

Afterwards, they all made their way to the great hall of the chateau, where the long banquet table was laden with food, with candelabra and with red and white roses, a tower of cream-filled, puff-pastry balls, the tall, bobbly croquembouche wedding cake at the centre, leaning slightly, as if ready to be pulled apart.

When it was time for the speeches, Cynthia thanked Émile for his love, Angelica for hosting them all, and her whole family for joining them to celebrate and multiply their joy.

A small jazz band began to play, and Émile and Cynthia waltzed to whistles and cheers. Lisa and Will followed them, then Scottie and Nicole, with James and Stella inseparable. Scottie broke off to hold Sienna and dance with Lucy, while Jeannie and Dave took a turn.

Jim sidled up to Anglica and offered her his hand, and they smiled and waltzed until Nathan Carmichael cut in. Jim bowed out. Carefully, he descended the grand stone staircase outside, where stars began to stud the velvety sky.

Angelica found Jim beside the reflection pond.

"Fine project, your chateau," Jim said. "Know anything about design?"

"Oh, most of what we did was restoration," she said. "The French Government wants us to keep things authentic."

"I like the old stuff, too, but my late wife would call me stuffy. I need to design a penthouse, you see."

"Oh really? Tell me about it, Jim."

"At Huntleys House of Jewels headquarters—you Yanks call it HQ, don't you? At our old House of Diamonds, in Sydney—we have our own project—part restoration, and part brand new. Angelica, I'm a goldsmith, a jeweler. I make jewelry, things so small they fit between my fingers, but this project! We're going sky high, and I have an idea."

"Tell me."

"We'll keep the facade of our old building, but inside it, we'll go up maybe twenty or thirty floors. There'll be great views from up there, and we'll be seen. I want something different on top, Angelica. I want a diamond up there, a big one, so big you can see it from anywhere, from an airplane. Imagine that, sparkling in the sun—so big there's room inside it for my new apartment. The facets will be my windows."

"Why not?" said Anglica. Jim rubbed his hands together and chuckled.

Nathan Carmichael appeared again beside her, his round glasses a perfect match for her purple dress.

"You're letting me quote on that project, I hope, Jim."

"You're an architect?" said Angelica. "I thought you were just a fine dancer, like Jim here."

"He's an international prize winner, a judge," said Jim.

"Oooh," she said. "Know anything about mazes?"

"I do. Although I much prefer labyrinths," said Nathan.

"What's the difference?" said Jim. "Aren't they both amazing?"

"They are, but you can get lost in a maze."

"But can't you get lost in a labyrinth as well?"

"Not if you just put one foot in front of the other," said Nathan. "Eventually you come out exactly where you went in."

"Did I hear the word 'labyrinth'?" said Flame, who'd also come to enjoy the fine evening. "Hi. I'm Stella's mother. Labyrinths are restorative, Angelica. Are you planning to create one here? There's one up near Ross's farm which attracts enthusiasts from all over the world."

"I hear they're quite popular in the US as well," said Nathan. "This would be an ideal location, somewhere in these vast grounds. You could outline it with stone or plant a hedge."

"I think we've got one already, though it's awfully overgrown," said Angelica.

"Could we explore it tomorrow?" said Flame.

"Of course."

Jim stared at Flame's hand, and then took it in his, to examine her ring.

"So you're the bride of Ross!" said Jim. "Of course. He told me he was marrying a beautiful redhead. It's wonderful to see this ring on the right person."

"You made my ring? I'm so honored to meet you!"

"You married just recently?" said Angelica.

Flame nodded, just as Ross came to her side with another drink.

"Jim, can I offer you another drink, too?"

"No thank you, Ross. I was just admiring my handiwork and your taste in brides."

"Thank you," said Ross, as he slipped his arm around Flame and kissed her. "Watch out for Flame," he said to Angelica. "She tells fortunes."

"Oh, how wonderful!" said Angelica. "Me, I just own a fortune."

Everyone laughed, but Jim noted a sadness there. Could someone who'd restored a whole chateau be lonely inside it? It was certainly enormous.

"I prefer the Tarot, but I'd be glad to read your palm, Angelica, if you'd like. I can't guarantee accuracy, but sometimes I see welcome surprises."

Jim was distracted by the late arrival of more of the guests, Kevin and Raj, English expats who were friends of Cynthia and Émile and lived in the same village.

"At my age?" said Angelica to Flame, laughing at something she'd said.

"Absolutely," said Flame. "I never thought I'd be one to marry, yet here I am with Ross, and I've never been happier."

Suddenly, a beaming Cynthia appeared with tall Émile at her side. Émile clapped his hands.

"Cynthia, my bride," he said. "She tells me how she loves these flowers but that she will throw them all away. *Il faut lancer le bouquet.*"

"You sound so surprised, Émile!" said Cynthia. "You have exactly the same tradition. The florist told me. But you're right. I do love these flowers, so just before I throw them all away, I'm going to tell you more about them. Back in our village, Raj and Kevin lent me their little book on the secret language of flowers. We had such fun selecting them! I chose bluebells and blue hyacinths for constancy, bridal roses for happy love and forget-me-nots for true love, blue violets and lemon blossoms for fidelity. The white roses mean 'I am worthy of you,' and the red and white roses together mean 'unity'. Oh. And we threw in some shamrocks for our House of Clubs and its Irish heritage. Shamrocks represent lightheartedness, even though this bunch is now actually quite heavy. Thank you so much everyone! Émile makes me happy, and you make us happy. Now, regardless of who catches my bouquet, please know that we wish each and every one of you the best of fortune in love and in life."

And she turned and threw the bouquet, up, up, up into the starry night sky, high above the guests.

Jim watched it sail almost to the height of the water of the fountain before it turned and plummeted, losing a white petal or two. It fell straight into Angelica's outstretched hands.

Cynthia turned with a swish of ivory silk and lace, and her face fell, just a fraction.

She turned to Will and placed her hand on his arm.

"I'd so hoped Lisa might be next," she said to him, her second son, who reminded her so much of Jimmy.

"No need to worry, Mum," said Will. "Lisa and I married in Vegas before we got on the plane. That's why we were a bit late."

"Why didn't you say so!"

"Lisa wouldn't let me. Said she didn't want to steal your show. Said this was your event, yours and Émile's."

"Darlings," said Cynthia. "Will and Lisa have an announcement!"

Acknowledgements

At the risk of omitting the names of treasured friends, family and each of my other VIPs, it gives me great pleasure to thank the following people for helping bring Amber Jakeman's *House of Jewels* series into being.

I am grateful for my parents, Marilyn and Tim Cartmill, who introduced me to the power and beauty of the written word. My husband and partner Bruce sets the tone for all my heroes. Thank you for so many years of love and support.

I warmly acknowledge the inspirational Shauna Colnan, the irrepressible Pamela Hart and the wise Bernadette Foley for validating my quest to write fiction. To my writing buddies and critique partners Jordan Harcourt-Hughes, Dr Sal Preston, Dr Marg Rainbird, Jo Jukes, Alex Jones and Carolyn Lancaster, thank you for your careful feedback.

I thank all my beta and proof readers, whose eagle eyes and encouragement have fuelled my efforts, and those who have shared their expertise: Bruce Terry, Annie Handmer, Robyn Herklots, Heather Kirk, Jan McIntosh, Mrs Lim from Malaysia, Tom, George Raftopulos and Casey Handmer. Thanks to every reader and writer who cheers from the sidelines, including fellow writers, reviewers and publicists Emma Lombard, Cindy L Spear, Terry Collins, Pauline Reid and "Scary". To Annette Billingham, who asked me to write this fifth book and gave it the name *Full House,* and to the talented Kylie Sek who created each of the covers, thank you!

To Allison Rogers, Craig Slater and Bronte-Marie Wesson at Galaxy Bookshop, and Hannah Dooley and Emily Redknap at Harry Hartog Macquarie, thank you for being the first to introduce me and my paperbacks to your customers.

Without your generosity, Amber Jakeman's *House of Jewels* series would still be just a dream. Thank you all!

Don't miss out!

Visit www.amberjakeman.com to find out how to order other novels by Amber Jakeman. Sign up to receive occasional email updates.

Did you love *Full House*?

Then you should read each of the *House of Jewels* novels by Amber Jakeman.

House of Diamonds

Handsome James Huntley the Third faces a challenge or two at his Bondi Junction jewelry business.

Sparkles fly when newbie jeweller Stella Rhys sets up her home-made jewellery stall outside his shop.

She steals the limelight at his expensive PR stunt, and then she steals his heart.

Instant enemies, and fighting their attraction to each other, Stella and James become entangled in a social media war.

In this "enemies to lovers" romance, **will this dazzling couple ever work out what to do with an engagement ring?**

House of Diamonds is the first volume of Amber Jakeman's fast-paced, heartwarming *House of Jewels* series—with an international flavour—featuring the romantic fortunes of three generations of jewellers; the extended Huntley family. The books may be read in any order.

Praise for *House of Diamonds*

"Stella is an interesting character. Easy to read, feel good book. We need more of these kinds of books. I enjoyed it. I am looking forward to reading the rest of this series." Kris Revson

"Loving House of Diamonds… It's the perfect 'bedtime read'. I really enjoyed it. More publications, please. Please put my name down for Book 2." Annette B.

"Congratulations on a well crafted and delightful page-turner! The world of jewellery is a splendid backdrop to your romance, as are Sydney Harbour, Bowral and the south of France, with more glimpses of Boulder City perhaps in the eagerly awaited next book. Keep writing!" Sparkle-lover

House of Hearts

What does it take to be lucky in love? Opposites attract in House of Hearts, set on the edge of Las Vegas.

Gambling addiction therapist Dr Lisa Bakker never breaks rules, but her bad boy client Will Huntley, good-looking youngest heir to an Australian jewelry business, breaks them all.

The one rule neither can ignore is the two-year dating ban between clients and therapists. Will calls Lisa his "Queen of Hearts" but her hard-won career hangs in the balance.

What will it take to win her hand?

Praise for *House of Hearts*

"… a wonderful love story with a number of twists in the plot… I really enjoyed it."

"Was amazed at your extensive knowledge on counselling procedures and rules, a myriad of psychological conditions, and gambling addiction (and the triggers). Great research!" Jen

"I could not put it down."

"Many congratulations on another bestseller." Annette

"I really liked it and can't wait to pass it on to my book-reading friends." Robyn

House of Spades

House of Spades is Volume 3 in the House of Jewels series.

Can love call again later in life? He calls her a trespasser. She calls him a hermit and thief.

Free spirit and serial single Flame Rhys has sworn off love, but try convincing her reclusive neighbor Ross Archer.

Fiery redhead Flame accidentally rekindles the widower's passion for life, for his land and a wife.

But is there more to Flame than meets the eye, as Ross's daughters suspect?

Praise for *House of Spades*

"Your book inspired me to rewild parts of my property."

" ... some delightful insight into the subtropical climate and people of northern New South Wales."

"Flame is awesome."

House of Clubs

Who holds the key to her heart? When stylish Australian widow Cynthia Huntley moves to France and begins to renovate a centuries-old property, she and handsome handyman Émile tussle over a "perfect" chandelier.

Cynthia lets the mysterious yet gallant Émile into her house, but will she let him into her heart?

What is Émile fleeing? And what is worth seeking in life?

As winter closes in, will Cynthia abandon her French adventure? Or can she and Émile claim love again later in life—together?

Praise for *House of Clubs*

"Love this romance. I feel it is the best of this series. Love the ending. And I love how I seem to learn about a certain topic in each of the stories." – Gail

"This book took me to the south of France. There's more to it than meets the eye."

"From the opening paragraph I was hooked and never once during the reading was I disappointed. Well, except maybe when I came to the last page but that was because I did not want the story to end!" Cindy L Spear

Amber's contemporary love tales — on the sweeter side — may be read in any order. Enjoy "enemies to lovers" romance *House of Diamonds*, "forbidden love" romance *House of Hearts*, "friends to lovers" romance *House of Spades*, "soul mates" romance *House of Clubs* and now, *Full House*.

Also by Amber Jakeman

House of Jewels
House of Diamonds
House of Hearts
House of Spades
House of Clubs
Full House

Visit www.amberjakeman.com to find out how to order other novels by Amber Jakeman. Sign up to receive occasional email updates.

About the Author

Partial to sunsets, picnics and poetry, feel-good fiction writer Amber Jakeman was a journalist, ghost writer and editor before succumbing to her addiction to uplifting endings.

With readers in more than fifty countries, Amber writes from her tiny apartment on the edge of Sydney Harbour, creating historical and contemporary fiction with an international flavor, including romance, on the sweeter side.

When not writing, Amber enjoys time with family and friends, sailing with her husband, travel, walking and savoring other writers' creations.

Amber Jakeman acknowledges Australia's first storytellers, our First Nations People, and offers respect to their descendants.

Visit www.amberjakeman.com to find out how to order other novels by Amber Jakeman, and sign up for occasional email updates.

About the Publisher

Lorikeet Press publishes feel-good fiction for readers of all ages. If you enjoy books with uplifting endings, you're in the right place.

Visit www.lorikeetpress.com for more information.